# HOMEBOUND
## HIGHLAND MAGIC
## BOOK TWO

M000214465

# Chapter One

Old habits die hard. It wasn't entirely my fault though; if the Sidhe from the Clan Carnegie hadn't been quite so brash about flashing his wealth on the street I'd have left him alone. But when he stepped out of his chauffeur-driven, brick-red SUV, summarily pushing an elder Clan-less pixie out of the way and into a dirty puddle, then made an ostentatious show of adjusting his cuffs so we could all see his gleaming over-priced Rolex, I couldn't resist. I'd only popped out for a pint of milk but this seemed far more exciting than another conversation with the human who ran the small corner shop at the end of my road.

In the Highlands of Scotland, you were either Clan or Clan-less. The Clans were run by the Sidhe but other individuals could swear fealty and enlist. In return they received a modest wage, a degree of protection from all the ills the world had to offer, and long hours working at whatever the Clan deemed necessary. Not everyone wanted to become a Sidhe slave though. Avoid the Clans and you were left to scrub out an earning on the cold, hard streets. Neither option was perfect. I might have been the only Clan-less Sidhe in the entire country but until recently I'd always been proud to call myself Clan-less. We might be the bottom of the rung but at least we were free.

I tracked the pompous Carnegie Sidhe along Oban's main street and down towards the harbour. He strutted along like he owned the place. It didn't help his cause that he had a skinny Bauchan, a sort of Scottish hobgoblin, trailing after him with an umbrella to protect his precious Sidhe skin from the unrelenting sleet. He paused in front of a rusty boat, jerking his head imperiously at the pale-faced sailors visible on the deck. Whatever cargo he was here to inspect, it had to be valuable for him to bother making this trip.

It might have been January but spring was still a long way off. Still, even wealthy Sidhe like him couldn't order deliveries from across the Veil. For the last three hundred years, the Fomori demons had ruled the Scottish Lowlands from the other side of the magical barrier called the Veil. Unless you wanted to risk being torn apart limb by limb by a horde of murderous evil-doers, you couldn't go through the Veil and you couldn't fly over it. If you wanted something delivered from the rest of the world, you had to bring it by sea or get a plane to go the long way round.

The sailors hastily threw down the gangplank. I suspected that it wouldn't matter how quickly they opened up access for him, he would still have that lemon-sucking expression on his face. The high-born Sidhe nobles had been in their positions for too long to expect anything other than the smoothest and most immediate service. Maybe his attitude wasn't his fault; after all, he had been conditioned through generations to act that way.

He marched up, his foot catching on a patch of ice. I had to bite my tongue to stop from laughing aloud as his arms flailed dramatically and he tried to stop himself from pitching over into the dark, freezing waters below. The Bauchan, who'd remained behind on the dock, lunged upwards while the sailors darted down. The Sidhe was caught just in time, several pairs of arms steadying his body before helping him up the rest of the way. Shame.

I cast around. There was a Clan Haig tugboat nearby, its familiar blue tartan flying from the mast. I stepped back and eyed it. The distance to the Carnegie ship wasn't so great; I could bypass the waiting Bauchan by leaping from one deck to the other. The Carnegie sailors would be so distracted by the noble's visit that they probably wouldn't even notice me. I grinned to myself.

'Did you hear about what happened when the blue ship and the red ship collided?' I said to the wind. 'Both crews were marooned.'

As if in response, a stronger gust whirled round me, catching my white hair and blowing it round my head. It was usually a colour that made me stand out in a crowd but in greyer-than-grey weather like this, it was almost perfect camouflage.

Shoving my hands in my pockets and whistling, I wandered over to the Haig tugboat. It appeared deserted. With a quick look over my shoulder, I jumped up, caught hold of one of the ropes that tethered it to the dock and hoisted myself up. Keeping low, I crept along the smooth deck until I reached the starboard side. My brow furrowed. Somehow, from this angle, the distance to the Carnegie vessel looked greater.

The sailors, most of whom appeared to be mermen, were making a great show of looking busy. Keep at it, boys. I waited until most of their backs were turned then, inhaling deeply, threw myself forward, legs and arms akimbo. My fingers only just caught the edge of a porthole and my body slammed into the side of the ship a moment later. There was a heavy clunk which had my insides stiffening in alarm. I hung there for several seconds, trying to keep my grip secure. I hadn't expected the porthole to be so slimy, which in hindsight was remarkably stupid of me, and it wasn't easy to cling on. Eventually a few shouts carried over by the helpful wind reached my ears. The sailors' attention was focused on the other side of the ship. I didn't need to worry.

The ship's hull might have been slippery but it was also obviously used to far deeper waters than these. There were enough barnacles which, if I didn't allow my toes to linger on them for too long, could provide the grip I required. I craned my neck to judge my route then, knowing I wouldn't be able to hang onto the rim of the porthole for much longer, leapt up. The second I hit the deck I rolled, using the steel containers crammed along the side to conceal myself from alert eyes. The ship heaved in the water. It was no wonder I usually chose to stick to dry land; even within the safety of the harbour, the waves were enough to make my stomach rise into my throat.

I pressed myself against the container's side, not just to keep myself from being spotted but also because it was reassuringly solid. Edging along, I peered round the corner. There was an open door leading into the blackness of the ship's hold.

I was in unknown territory. Under normal circumstances I sneaked into buildings, and modern architectural design, especially when it came to interiors, tended to be much of a muchness. Even without floor plans, it didn't take much common sense to understand layouts and locations. But, beyond the fact that icebergs were to be avoided at all costs, I knew next to nothing about ships. Perhaps if I just wandered in yelling 'Ahoy me hearties!' I'd be alright.

Before I could dart inside, the Sidhe noble reappeared. He had a long thin nose, which spoke of some ancient Roman heritage, and piercing eyes. I didn't recognise him so he wasn't the Carnegie Clan Chieftain, despite his regal bearing.

'It all needs to go to the Cruaich immediately,' he said in a cultured tone, referring to the seat of Sidhe power where duplicitous Aifric Moncrieffe ruled as Steward.

One of the mermen cleared his throat. 'There's been a heavy snowfall...'

'I don't care,' the Sidhe snapped. 'We can't afford prying eyes seeing what we have.'

A tiny smile played around my mouth. So this was all supposed to be a great big secret? Even better. If his precious cargo was too large for me to spirit away, I could simply take a few photos and post them around for all to see. His big secret, whatever it was, would be exposed to the world and I'd win either way. Since I'd turned my back on the world of thievery, I had to get my kicks where I could.

The merman bowed, although it didn't take a genius to notice that he was more than slightly piqued by the command. All mermen, my friend and erstwhile colleague Brochan included, had a line of small fins running down the length of their spines. Usually this was covered by specially designed clothing which reached up to the nape. This sailor was wearing a low, crew-cut T-shirt so his first few fins were on display and, even from my hiding place, I saw them bristle and tighten. But it didn't matter how irked he was, he wasn't about to deny the Carnegie lordling. That meant the Sidhe probably possessed one of the more volatile magic Gifts – and wasn't afraid to use it against less magically inclined beings. One of the reasons that the Sidhe held the powerful position that they did was as a result of their Gifts – anything from pyrokinesis to telepathy. Most Sidhe only had one; a lucky few could boast of two or even three. My situation was a lot more complicated. I still wasn't sure what I had – or whether I even wanted it.

I waited until the Sidhe started to leave. He was more careful this time and took his time stepping onto the gangplank. While the sailors watched him, no doubt keeping their fingers crossed that he would slip and fall, I took advantage of their distraction to fly out from behind the container and duck into the doorway.

This was no pretty wooden boat like the Clan Haig tugboat. It was a working ship, not a pleasure boat, and I was surrounded by steel plates and rusting rivets. That meant I'd have to be careful to keep quiet. Metal conducted sound almost as well as it conducted heat.

Oddly, the strong tang of salt from the sea seemed stronger inside the hold than outside. I tiptoed gingerly down the corridor, ignoring the girly pin-ups from old magazines which had been fixed haphazardly to the walls. Half-naked merwomen just didn't do it for me.

I sneaked past several rooms, ranging from a galley kitchen to an officers' mess. I might not know much about ships but I was betting that the cargo the Carnegie Sidhe was so concerned about would be kept down in the bowels of the ship.

The further in I went, the more the vessel seemed to be alive. It creaked and groaned like an old man getting out of bed. I skirted to my right, avoiding the murmur of voices from the other direction, and let out a sigh of relief when I spotted some narrow stairs leading downwards. Bracing my hands on either side of the walls, I crept down, aware of every sound around me – not least the tiny, yet very audible, clank of my footsteps.

The area below was well lit with fluorescent lights hanging from the steel ceiling which gave off a harsh glow. It was also surprisingly tidy. I glanced at the first huge pallet; I couldn't tell exactly what was inside but it looked like sections of black, smoky plate glass. Certainly it contained nothing worth stealing – or nothing worth a Sidhe getting their knickers in a twist about. I shrugged and kept going, passing crate after crate filled with similar material. It was only when I heard the rattle from ahead that I paused. That was ... interesting.

More wary now, I pushed on. The rattle sounded again. I rounded another pallet, spotted a large cage and halted immediately. Was there an animal inside? Or something worse?

I strained my eyes to make out what was in there. The cage seemed empty but it was in a prominent position, with a clear space around it. That signified its importance; this was more than just an empty cage - and it was also worryingly large.

Just as I was about to take another step, there was a cough behind me. 'I wouldn't do that if I were you,' said a dry voice.

I whirled round. It was a rare day when someone managed to sneak up on me. Deciding to brazen it out, I shook out my hair and tilted up my chin. 'Why not?'

A merman stepped out from behind one of the pallets. 'She doesn't like strangers.'

Tension knotted across my spine. She? I licked my lips. 'Lord Carnegie asked me to...'

Before I could finish my sentence, the merman boomed out a laugh. It reverberated around the hold and bounced off the steel walls. 'You're no Carnegie Sidhe.'

'Maybe not,' I said softly, 'but I *am* Sidhe.' Usually that detail was enough to prevent further questions.

'I know exactly who you are.'

Uh-oh. That wasn't good. I thought quickly. The sailors above deck had been terrified of the Carnegie lord so maybe I could use that to my advantage. Right now, the merman was blocking my exit and, lithe as I was, I didn't think I'd make it back up that narrow staircase without him grabbing me. I'd have to continue down the intimidation route, distasteful as it might be.

'Then you know what I'm capable of,' I said clearly.

The merman folded his arms. 'Bad jokes and safe cracking?' He smirked. 'Because if you crack that safe, Integrity, you're not going to get out of here alive.'

I blinked, taken aback. He really did know who I was. 'How do you...?'

'I have a cousin,' he said. 'A sea-fearing idiot of a cousin. Instead of enjoying all that the ocean has to offer, he lurks around cities stealing shit.' He snorted. 'Landlubber.'

My shoulders sagged in relief. 'Brochan.'

The merman inclined his head. 'Just so.' He regarded me for a moment. 'We don't tend to talk about him. His parents aren't exactly proud that their firstborn is thalassophobic.'

Afraid of the sea. I had to admit it was certainly an unusual – and not particularly welcome - trait in a merman. But Brochan was also my friend. 'He's far more capable than most. He might have turned his back on the ocean blue but he doesn't have to kneel to a Clan and he doesn't have to worry about getting wrinkly fingers from spending too much time in the water.' I raised my eyebrows pointedly.

The merman grinned. 'Indeed. We meet up from time to time. He likes you a lot. He'll be pleased to know that you're sticking up for him.'

'He doesn't need me to stick up for him. He can fight his own battles.'

He took no offence at my sniffy comment. 'Just so. I'm Jimmy, by the way.'

I inclined my head in wary greeting and watched him for a moment. 'So what's in the cage?' I asked finally.

'Nothing you'd want to nick.'

I smiled. 'Come on, Jimmy. We're practically family.'

He laughed wheezily. 'Good one. The day I'm practically family with a Sidhe is the day my parents disown me too.'

I frowned. He already knew that I wasn't like other Sidhe. Surely he could grant me a little leeway. 'Tell me what's in the cage,' I coaxed.

He was still amused. 'If you really want to know...' He raised his head and whistled. There was another rattle, followed by a hiss. I turned to see a creature out of my worst nightmares drop down from the roof of the cage.

'We call her Debbie,' Jimmy said.

I stared at the giant spider. Her glittering eyes were fixed on me and she was the size of a horse. One long hairy leg tapped impatiently on the steel floor. I swallowed, taking in the expanse of her rounded belly. I hoped its size meant she'd just eaten because, frankly, I'd never seen anything so terrifying. 'Why the hell does the Carnegie Clan want a giant spider?' I whispered, more to myself than to Jimmy.

'Why do the Clans want anything?' He shrugged. 'All I know is we need to get this darling up to the Cruaich without anyone seeing.' He wagged a finger in my direction. 'Without any *Sidhe* seeing.'

Was the Carnegie Clan planning some kind of assault on the Cruaich? I shook my head. It didn't make sense. As far as I knew, the Carnegies were in a good position but they certainly weren't strong enough to challenge Aifric of the Moncrieffe Clan for Stewardship. He'd been the leader of the Sidhe Clans since before I was born after all. I couldn't think of any other reason why this thing was here, though.

As if sensing my thoughts, Debbie gave another rattle and scuttled towards me. I squeaked and jumped backwards.

Jimmy laughed. 'Relax. She's a sweetie really.'

My mouth was dry. 'Really.'

'You just need to get to know her.' He stepped past me and up to the bars. I watched horror-struck as he put one hand into the cage. Debbie drew up as if she were preparing to strike – until Jimmy started scratching her under her chin. She let out an unmistakable hiss of delight. Okay then.

'As I said,' Jimmy continued, 'she doesn't like strangers. But she's alright, she doesn't kill mermen.' He threw me a sidelong look. 'We're too salty.'

I took another step back, just to be on the safe side.

Jimmy grinned and pointed at the vicious-looking pincers protruding from either side of her gigantic mouth. 'Watch out for them. One shot of that poison and you'll be paralysed for a week. Debbie likes taking her time over her meals. It would be a long week.'

I tried to smile back but I only managed a grimace. 'Yeah. She's a *real* sweetie.'

The pager clipped to my belt began to buzz. Jimmy glanced at me. 'You seem to be vibrating.' He pulled his arm out of the cage. Debbie stared at him for a moment, waiting to see if this was merely a momentary lapse of concentration. When no further caresses came her way, she sprang up and twisted in the air until she was hanging from the roof of the cage once more.

I took out my phone, ready to snap a quick photo. Jimmy shook his head. 'Can't let you do that. If Carnegie finds out someone saw her, he'll stuff my gills with cotton wool.'

It took some effort to push that image out of my mind. 'So you won't tell him I was here?'

'Nah. But no photographic evidence. I don't trust technology.'

He didn't trust a mobile phone but he was happy to thrust his hand out in the direction of a giant flesh-eating spider? Brochan was obviously the only sane one in the family – and that was saying something.

'Okay,' I conceded. I still didn't understand why the Carnegies were so keen to take this hairy monstrosity to the seat of Sidhe power but I certainly wasn't going to steal her from them. My pager buzzed again. 'I have to go.'

Jimmy shrugged. 'Okay. Tell that dry-footed freak I said hi.'

I backed away, keeping my eyes on Debbie the entire time. She'd already dismissed me but I wasn't about to turn my back on her – cage or no cage. 'Will do.' As soon as I reached the stairs, I turned and ran out of there like hell itself was on my heels.

*

I made it to the mountain rescue centre with seconds to spare. Travis, the gruff leader of our rescue team, shot me a look as I jogged up.

I checked my watch. Any rescuers on call had to show up within thirty minutes of their pagers sounding otherwise the team would leave without them. 'Sorry,' I called. I was within the limit – just – but it was clear the others had been waiting for me.

Travis merely nodded. If I'd been anyone else, he'd probably have chewed them out for taking so long to appear but he was too nervous of me to say anything to my face. Much as he appreciated my skills in picking up the injured and foolish from the surrounding mountains, he still found it hard to accept that he was working alongside a Sidhe. I had the impression that he was expecting me to demand everyone's fealty at any moment. It didn't matter that I'd explained a million times that I was Clan-less. In fact, when I said I was Clan-less because my father had been the Chieftain of Clan Adair, things got worse. Considering the world believed that my father had committed genocide against his own people and destroyed Clan Adair in one single afternoon over twenty-five years ago, that wasn't hugely surprising.

I'd also believed those stories until recently. I still wasn't sure what had happened to my parents but a vision I'd received in the sacred grove at the Cruaich told me that my father wasn't the murderer everyone thought he was. And I was betting that Aifric Moncrieffe had something to do with it. After all, the Sidhe Steward had tried to kill me by handing me a bottle of water laced with poison. That'd make even a damn sheep suspicious.

'No problem,' Travis grunted.

'I'm sorry,' I said again.

He waved his hand as if it didn't matter. It'd be nice if he stopped tiptoeing round me; I wasn't anything special and I wished he understood that.

Words wouldn't help me though so I offered him a shiny smile before turning my back and hopping into the helicopter. The others – a brother and sister team of humans called Tim and Tam, and Isla, a Nicnevan witch attached to the Polwarth Clan, gave me a more enthusiastic greeting.

'Hey, Tegs. Travis giving you a hard time?'

'If only,' I said cheerfully, shrugging into my gear as the helicopter took off. Of course, it was all hot pink; I was rather passionate about that colour. As long as I could be identified against the winter snow and ice, the colours I chose to wear were up to me. Unfortunately I'd not had much success in persuading everyone else to don hot pink as well. That was a shame, it would rather suit Travis.

'So what's the deal?' I asked, shouting over the noise of the rotors.

'Husband and wife team,' Tam yelled back. 'Went out this morning to Aladdin's Mirror and were supposed to check back in after midday.'

I tied back my hair, tucking it safely out of the way, and frowned. It was already four o'clock and at this time of year, it'd be dark within the hour. Four hours might not sound like a long time to go missing but in the Scottish Highlands in the depths of winter, it could be a lifetime. Or two.

'Everyone goes to the Mirror,' Isla said, rolling her eyes.

She had a point; this would be my fourth rescue there this year. Considering the Mirror was little more than a wall of ice, I didn't understand the attraction. I reckoned it was the allure of the name as much as anything else. Names, as every Sidhe knew, had power. Aladdin's Mirror did indeed sound rather mystical. It wasn't; it was just a wall of frozen water that claimed far more broken bones and call-outs than should be allowed.

I was the newbie on the team but after four months I had a pretty good handle on how things worked. While I couldn't ever imagine this job becoming mundane, the longer I spent at it, the more confident I grew. I knew what to expect.

The helicopter couldn't fly directly to the Mirror so it put us lower down Coire an t'Sneachda. Try saying that ten times in a row; I might be getting better at these rescues but my tongue still fumbled with the different pronunciations of the locations.

Isla threw me an arch look. 'Where are we going, Integrity?'

I stuck my tongue out at her and she laughed. I tried to concentrate. I could always get the first part right but stumbled at the end when the spelling had virtually no bearing on the way the name was pronounced. 'Um, Kor In Tray...'

'Korin Tray Achk.'

I repeated it under my breath. It wouldn't matter; next time we made it up here, I'd have forgotten again. Gaelic just wasn't my thing. Whatever - I couldn't be brilliant at everything.

The sky was already darkening when we jumped out. It was the time of year when you'd miss sunset if you blinked: one minute it was day and the next it was as if someone had flipped a switch and night had descended, even though it still wasn't teatime. Travis frowned upwards, clearly unhappy at Mother Nature. The wind was picking up, sending tiny particles of ice and snow flying against our bare faces. It wasn't just in heists that balaclavas were useful. I pulled mine over my head while the others did the same. Before my eyelashes could freeze, I yanked down my goggles. Thank goodness for hardy climbing equipment.

Once we were ready, Travis held up his index finger and circled it in the air. We all nodded. We knew what to do.

Travis led the way. As the greenie, I was directly behind him carrying the first-aid equipment. Tim and Tam followed behind with the stretchers, while Isla took up the rear. It was slow going. Even with our state-of-the-art gear, there was only so fast we could move when we were laden with stuff and walking on an uphill ice-skating rink. For a long time all that could be heard were our combined breaths and the crunch of snow beneath our feet. I was as fit as anyone and I was already sweating under my layers of clothing. I kept my head down. With visibility almost at zero, there was no point in looking at anything other than my feet. That was why I spotted the tracks.

I reached out and tapped Travis on the shoulder, causing him to halt. He turned, followed my finger and glanced down. The falling snow would cover them within minutes but there was no mistaking what was there. I had never seen signs of animal life this far up the mountain; at this time of year any beast smart enough to survive was much further down the slopes. From what I could tell, this brave creature had three legs - something else which didn't make sense.

Travis frowned, crouched down and lightly touched them. They weren't large: each paw print was less than an inch in diameter. At least that was something: if a mountain beast was watching us from behind a snow-covered rock, it would be unlikely to attack five people who were a hundred times its size.

'What are the tracks from?' I asked.

Tim peered over my shoulder. 'Bird?'

'With three legs?'

He shrugged. 'Maybe its tail is broken and it's dangling down in the snow as it walks.'

We shared a glance. It was a nice theory but it was clearly wrong. This was no bird – but at least I was sure it wasn't a damned giant spider either.

Travis straightened. 'Whatever it is, we don't have time to worry about it.'

There was the sudden, unmistakable sound of a flare being set off further up. It rocketed into the dark sky, a plume of red shooting a path of pain.

'Well,' Tim murmured, 'one of them is still alive.'

We picked up our pace. Travis began jogging and the rest of us fell into line after him. As we rounded the last craggy outcrop, Aladdin's Mirror loomed in front of us. With the sky as dark as it was, it was difficult to see much of it but we weren't here for sightseeing - the whimper from the foot of the Mirror confirmed that.

Travis strode forward. He was almost as sure-footed as a fey Sidhe. He reached a shadowy lump just ahead of us and dropped to his knees. 'My name is Travis,' he said calmly, in a manner designed to put injured climbers at ease. 'Are you Maggie?'

'Y–yes. Maggie Moncrieffe.'

I stiffened. No-one had mentioned that we were here to rescue a Sidhe, let alone one from Aifric and Byron's Clan. At the thought of Byron Moncrieffe, Aifric's son, my stomach tightened. I pushed away the image of golden boy's handsome face which had popped unprompted into my head. It didn't matter who these people were; they still needed rescuing.

Tim and Tam pushed past me, already assembling the stretcher.

'You alright?' Isla asked me.

I shook myself. 'Fine,' I muttered.

Travis ran his hands over Maggie's body. 'Where does it hurt?'

'My ankle,' she gasped. 'I think it's broken.' She yelped as his fingers touched it gently.

'Okay,' Travis soothed. 'Don't worry. We're going to get you onto the stretcher and down from here. You'll be back home in no time.'

That was all very well but she was alone. I hooked my backpack off my shoulder, pulled out a splint and bandages and glanced at Isla. 'Isn't there a husband?'

She nodded. I knelt down beside Travis and started binding Maggie's ankle so that she could make the journey back down without further damage. 'Maggie,' I said softly, 'where's your husband?'

She moaned in pain. As her pupils were dilated and she was clearly drifting into unconsciousness, I had the uncomfortable feeling that she was suffering from far more than a broken bone. I reached for Travis and gripped his forearm, jerking my chin at her. He gave me a grim look of acknowledgement. We had to get her to a hospital fast.

'Maggie,' I said again. 'I need you to look at me. Where's your husband? He was here with you.'

Her pulse fluttered rapidly in her neck and her skin was hot to the touch but she was as tough as the other Moncrieffes I knew. Her eyes met mine and she managed a weak whisper. 'He went for help.'

Shite. We'd not passed any tracks other than those belonging to the strange, unidentified animal. He must have wandered off in the wrong direction. It didn't matter how often we instructed hikers and climbers to stay together when there was a problem; someone always thought they knew better.

'What's his Gift?' I asked. If he were Sidhe he might be able to call up magic which would help him survive, otherwise he might well be lost for good. Unfortunately Maggie had given us all she could; she'd already closed her eyes.

I stood up. 'You need to get her to a hospital now. She's probably bleeding internally from the fall.' I looked up at the sheer ice wall of Aladdin's Mirror. If I squinted, I could make out an ice pick buried about twenty feet up. There weren't any ropes, though. No wonder she'd landed so badly. Daft bint.

Travis nodded. While Tim and Tam carefully laid her onto the stretcher, he pressed a button on his walkie-talkie and called the helicopter to arrange the rendezvous.

'There,' Isla said, pointing to our right. 'There are footsteps.'

The continuing snow flurries were already starting to cover them. 'I'll go after him,' I said.

'You can't go on your own, it's too dangerous.'

Travis looked at the pair of us. 'You've got fifteen minutes. It'll take us longer to get back down to the landing point anyway.'

I licked my lips; they were already dry and cracked. 'And if we don't find him?'

'Then we'll take Maggie to the town and come back later.'

I nodded, although that didn't sound like a brilliant plan. Judging by the state of the weather, things weren't going to improve any time soon. I was no snow expert but I could tell that the wind was getting stronger. Dangerously so. If this got much worse, the helicopter wouldn't be able to fly, let alone drop us back here. I caught a look in Travis's eye before he turned away; he knew it too.

If we didn't find Maggie's husband and get him to the helicopter soon, we'd be forced to abandon him for the night. And he probably wouldn't make it if that happened.

'We'd better get a move on,' Isla murmured.

'Fifteen minutes,' Travis repeated. 'I mean it. This isn't the night for silly heroics.' He looked at me as he said those last words. That wasn't entirely fair; I'd followed his instructions and commands to the letter over the last four months. Still, I nodded in acknowledgment and Isla and I took off.

The footsteps were close together, suggesting that Maggie's husband had been moving slowly. That was good, it meant we had a better shot of catching up to him. I followed Isla's lead, keeping my own steps light and brisk. I counted silently in my head to keep track of the time. Realistically we couldn't follow his trail for more than eight or nine minutes before we'd have to return.

Time was not our friend and neither was the Coire an t'Sneachda. Even with the crampons I was wearing, my feet struggled to find purchase. Isla wasn't much better and we slipped and slid our way along. As more of the snow gave way to hard ice, the trail disappeared until we were surrounded by howling winds, lethal rocks and very little else.

'Which way?' I shouted to make my voice heard above the growing gale.

Isla looked around. 'I don't know. We have to go back. He could be anywhere, he could be miles anyway.'

Bugger it. Moncrieffe or not, we weren't going to leave him if I could help it. I unzipped the pocket on my thigh. There was always Bob, the genie who'd saddled himself to my side.

Before I could pull out the scimitar – or rather letter opener as it actually was – the wind abruptly changed direction. Unprepared as I was, it yanked me off my feet, flinging me to the ground. I yelled in frustration and tried to pull myself to my feet. As I did, I caught sight of the crevasse to my left.

I rolled over and peered down. There, wedged against another snow-covered rock, was a body. I couldn't tell from here whether he was alive or dead but he certainly wasn't moving.

'Isla!'

She understood immediately and joined me at the rim of the crevasse. 'Arse,' she muttered. 'He's too far down.'

'We can get him.'

'Not without going in after him.'

'Grab my feet.'

I couldn't see Isla's face because of her balaclava and goggles but I knew what her expression would be. I gave her a nudge. She muttered another curse and hunkered down as I unwound the rope I always carried on these rescues. 'How much time do we have?'

'Not enough.'

I gritted my teeth; I'd just have to work faster. Isla's hands curled round my ankles and I stretched out. At least the crevasse provided some shelter from the wind that was whipping around us. I pushed my body out as far as I could. My gloves made my fingers clumsy but I managed to snake the end of the rope round the body, tying a knot to hold it in place.

'Integrity!' I heard Isla scream. 'I can't hold on for much longer.'

'I've just about got him,' I shouted back. I checked the knot. It would hold. Hopefully. 'Okay, pull me up.'

Isla wasted no time. She heaved and pulled until, slowly, I returned to safer ground. She must have been exhausted but she still took the other end of the rope and, with both of us using all our strength, we jerked it backwards. My feet slipped on the ice but I managed not to fall. Inch by inch, we strained to bring him up. When he was almost at the lip, Isla tapped my shoulder and I nodded, darting forward to pull him up the rest of the way.

'You'd better be alive, buster,' I told him, as I rolled his body to safety and checked for vital signs. I leaned towards his face, peeling up my balaclava until I could feel warm breath on my cheek. He was still with us - for now at least.

'We're out of time, Integrity,' Isla said urgently. 'We have to go.'

'Then let's get out of here,' I told her with a dark grin.

# Chapter Two

Taylor, Lexie, Speck and Brochan, my mentor and old thief buddies who'd followed me here from Aberdeen, were far more interested in what I had to tell them about Debbie than my prowess and death-defying rescue at Aladdin's Mirror.

'A giant spider?' Lexie breathed, her eyes wide as she handed me a mug of hot tea.

'Just like in *Lord of the Rings*,' I said, taking a sip and scalding my mouth. 'But scarier.'

Brochan threw me an exasperated look. 'You're even more of a geek than Speck is.'

I punched him in the arm. 'By the way, Jimmy says hello.'

The merman's face took on a distant expression. 'I can't believe he's working for the Carnegies,' he muttered.

Speck shrugged. 'What of it? We're working for the Adairs.'

My jaw tightened. 'You're not working for me.'

'I did make you a cup of tea,' Lexie pointed out.

'Out of the goodness of your heart, I'm sure.'

'If you paid me more, I wouldn't make it so hot.'

'I don't pay you anything,' I growled.

She winked at me. 'Exactly.'

'Enough,' Taylor broke in. 'Tell us more about this spider. Would we be able to hold it here? What does it eat?'

'You mean besides tasty human flesh?' I sighed. 'Taylor, the cage wouldn't fit through the door. In fact, the spider probably wouldn't fit through the door. She's massive.'

He rubbed his chin. 'So ransom is out.'

'You think?'

He shrugged. 'It was just an idea. Pickings have been slim since we moved up here.'

I felt a ripple of guilt. My team of ex-thieves had come with me to Oban because of my Sidhe heritage. Like it or not, their lives were tied up with mine and they were vulnerable to the other Clans because of their association with me. It didn't matter that they were all Clan-less and therefore were barely worth a raised eyebrow under normal circumstances. I might have managed to live under the Sidhe Clans' radar for well over a decade since I ran away from them as a kid, but those times were long gone. And my friends were guilty by association.

Brochan was more sensitive than he let on. He tapped my arm, his fingers brushing my skin so lightly that I almost thought I'd imagined his touch. 'It's not your fault, Tegs.'

'I know,' I said with a slight lift of my shoulders. 'But it doesn't make me feel any better.'

Speck, fiddling with a circuit board at the back of the room, looked up. 'Did the spider have an aura?' he asked curiously.

Taylor frowned at me. 'You've not told them?'

Lexie tilted her head, her blue hair falling to one side across her shoulder. 'Told us what?'

I held up my fingers. 'It's been four months since I learnt how to read auras.'

She nodded. 'Since you made the Bull your bitch because he told you his true name.' She was referring to my erstwhile guardian, the Chieftain of Clan Scrymgeour.

I smiled at her. 'His Gift is aura reading,' I agreed. 'He got it along with his true name when he was thirteen years old. I didn't manage to see auras until I'd ... dealt with him.'

'Shoulda killed him when you had the chance,' Brochan rumbled.

'Oh, he's a prick,' I agreed, 'but you know I don't like violence.' Taylor beamed at me with the benevolent smile of a father. 'Anyway, a couple of weeks ago, it just kind of stopped. The aura reading, I mean.'

'You can't read auras any more?'

'Technically, I never could. I could see them but I had no idea what they meant. The ability to see them just faded away.'

Speck pursed his lips. 'Well, it would make sense. We're away from the power source of the Clan Lands. If you returned, it'd probably come back.'

I grimaced. 'I don't think it works like that. No, it feels like it's gone for good.'

'Just like the teleportation?'

I nodded. After Bob, the most annoying genie in the world, had teleported me to the Bull's after I made a wish, I was able to teleport as well. As handy a Gift as it was, it hadn't lasted. I used it all of five times before I simply ran out of magic juice. It was a bugger; mountain rescue would be a piece of piss if I could teleport up and down the Cairngorms. So would casual thievery. Nope, I really wasn't very special at all.

I'd never heard of any other Sidhe losing their Gifts. Whatever you received when you were thirteen years old was supposed to stay with you for life. I told myself it was because I was an adult when I finally got my true name and that it wasn't because I was merely defective. Most of the time I believed it.

Lexie's jaw jutted out. 'Shitty Sidhe shite.' Then she threw me a guilty look. 'Sorry.'

'Hey,' I said lightly, 'I'm with you.'

'You don't need magic anyway,' Speck said loyally. I pretended I couldn't see the disappointment in his face.

'Well, magic presents aside, what are you going to do about the spider?' Taylor asked. 'If we can't kidnap it and the Carnegies are going to use it against the other Clans, are you going to leave them to it or warn them in advance?'

I smiled. 'I'm looking for a way to twist the Moncrieffes round my little finger. Not only did I just save two of their Clan but I have knowledge which might help them avert a bloodbath.' I winked. 'You know what they say about friends and enemies.'

Brochan nodded wisely. 'Keep your friends close and your enemies closer.'

My smile broadened. 'Nah. I'm talking about what you call a fake friend.' I received four identical eye rolls. I made an imaginary drum roll. 'A faux, of course.'

\*

Bob lay belly down on my dresser, his tiny chin in his even tinier hands. 'You can't polish a turd, Uh Integrity,' he told me solemnly.

I put down the mascara wand and glared at him. 'Thanks for the vote of confidence.'

'The truth hurts.' He tapped his cheek thoughtfully. 'There is a way you could look more desirable, you know.'

I kept my mouth firmly shut. I wasn't going to give him the satisfaction.

Bob pouted. 'Aren't you going to ask me about it?'

'Nope.' I turned back to the mirror, checking my hair. It was a pain in the arse to leave it down because it was so fine. One gust of wind and it ended up plastered across my face. It would suit my purposes for now though. I'd do whatever was necessary to keep Byron Moncrieffe onside.

'Uh Integrity,' Bob whined. 'I used to belong to Marilyn Monroe. How else do you think she was discovered so suddenly? She was nothing more than the pretty girl next door before I got involved.'

I snorted. 'Yeah, and look how she ended up.'

'That wasn't my fault.'

'It never is.'

He got to his feet. 'Just make a wish and I'll turn you into the most beautiful woman in the world. Men will fall at your feet. Women too. Forget Helen of Troy. You'll be Integrity of Oban.'

I arched an eyebrow. 'It doesn't have quite the same ring, does it?'

Bob shrugged. 'It's not my fault you live here. The town with more seagulls than culture.'

'I like them,' I lied. I hated those buggers. They were the size of cats and they'd rip the food right out of your hands if you gave them half a chance.

'Come on,' he pleaded. 'One teeny, tiny wish...'

'No.'

'But...'

I pinched the tips of my thumb and index finger together, grabbed him by the scruff of his neck and held him up to my face. 'Enough of the wishes,' I growled. 'I'm not making any more.' I had two wishes left at my disposal and, frankly, would have preferred it if there were none. Capricious magical wishes were almost never a good thing.

Bob stopped wriggling and sighed. 'Fine. But there's just one thing...'

'What?'

He smiled innocently. 'Now that I'm this close to your pores, I'm shocked. I could drive a four-by-four through those babies.'

I dropped him. He howled before vanishing in mid-air. Good riddance.

Speck popped his head round the door. 'You ready?'

'Yup.' I gestured at myself. 'How do I look?'

'Um...' Speck seemed baffled. 'Like you?'

I sighed; that was probably the best I was going to get. 'Let's go.'

The plan was fairly straightforward. With Speck in tow as back up, I was going to 'escort' Maggie and her thankfully still-breathing husband back to the Clan Lands, making sure I bumped into either Byron or Aifric along the way.

When we reached the hospital, however, it was obvious that wasn't going to be the case. Standing in front of the main doors was a very familiar face.

'Jamie!' I called out, delighted to see Byron's dimple-cheeked Sidhe friend.

His cheeks went a vivid shade of red as soon as he realised who was calling his name. 'Hi,' he mumbled.

I punched him lightly on the arm. 'There's no need to be so shy.' I meant it; after all we'd had sex after a rather unpleasant encounter with a conjured stoor worm. The worm I'd prefer to forget but Jamie was kind of sweet, even if he was a Moncrieffe.

'Are you here to pick up Maggie and her man?' I asked.

He nodded. 'His name's Rory.' Then he added unnecessarily, 'Moncrieffe.'

'That's very kind of you to come all this way.'

He gave an awkward shrug. 'They're part of our Clan.' He looked at his shoes. 'We look after our own.'

No doubt he was embarrassed because I didn't have a Clan but I wasn't thin-skinned enough to take offence. Instead I glanced meaningfully at Speck and he nodded. He hadn't met Jamie before but he had a keen understanding of the situation. As nice as Jamie was, he wasn't the Moncrieffe bigwig I was looking for – but he could help me get to him. Judging from his sidelong glances, Jamie didn't know who Speck was; we could use that to our advantage.

Without any prompting, my old warlock buddy pulled back his shoulders. 'I'm Dr Speck,' he said, stepping forward and thrusting out his hand. Jamie stared at it warily before taking it and receiving a vigorous shake in return. 'I'm here to oversee the return travel of the Moncrieffe pair.'

Jamie was taken aback. 'You are? But isn't Speck the name of...'

'Maggie and Rory have both had serious accidents,' he interrupted sternly, before Jamie began to connect the dots and realised who Speck really was – a thieving warlock who had worked with me on all manner of heists. 'They need to be closely monitored.'

Jamie frowned. 'Aren't you a little young to be a doctor?' He clamped a hand over his mouth. 'Sorry. I didn't mean to be rude but...'

'I have a baby face,' Speck replied. I almost snorted. Speck's features were thin and gaunt, as befitted a typical geek warlock. The last thing anyone would describe him as would be baby-faced.

Jamie looked at me suspiciously. Unfortunately for us, he wasn't just a pretty boy; now he was getting over the shock of seeing me, his brain was starting to work again. 'The other doctor said they were both fine to travel.' What he left unsaid was obvious – that he didn't trust anything or anyone when I was in the picture. I didn't know what I'd done recently to merit such mistrust; I'd not been perfect but I'd returned the jewel I'd stolen from the Moncrieffes and helped save the damned world by freeing the Foinse, the source of all Highland magic. Surely I deserved some brownie points for that?

'What gives?' I asked softly. 'I thought we were almost friends.'

Jamie patted his pocket as if he were checking for his wallet. When he realised I'd caught him in the action, he took a guilty step back.

'Ah,' I said. 'You think I'm going to pick your pocket.'

'You did it once before.' He had a point.

'I didn't know you then. I don't steal from people I like.'

'You like me?'

I tried to look disarming. 'I do.'

'And do you like me?' interrupted a second, lazy voice.

I looked over my shoulder. Leaning against the door with his arms folded across his broad chest and burnished gold hair falling artlessly across one eye in a way that could only be artful, was Byron, the Moncrieffe heir. My stomach flipped. 'Byron,' I cooed, unable to hide my joy at his presence. 'I don't *like* you. I *love* you.'

He blinked. I realised I'd probably said the wrong thing so I slung an arm round Jamie's shoulders, ignoring his obvious flinch. 'I love Jam Jam too.'

Byron raised his eyebrows. 'Indeed.' I couldn't tell whether he was amused or annoyed. He flicked a look at Speck. 'You're the warlock.'

'Um, that's Dr Warlock to you,' Speck responded.

Byron's perfect brow furrowed. 'Pardon?'

'Never mind,' I said quickly. 'How are Maggie and Rory doing?' I spoke about the pair of them as if we were old friends.

'As well as can be expected when you've a ruptured appendix and severe hypothermia to deal with.'

'That's what happens when you wander up Scottish mountains in the middle of winter,' I said cheerfully. 'They really should have had better equipment. Maggie was attempting to climb up an ice wall without a rope.'

If I'd expected Byron to look annoyed that one of his Clanlings had thrown caution to the wind and almost been killed in the process, I was disappointed. He smiled. 'Was she really?' He shook his head. 'Good for her.'

'Good for her? Are you kidding me? She almost died! Not to mention the cost of the rescue team venturing out to find her and her fool husband. What happened to common sense?'

'You were part of the team that helped them,' he said with dawning comprehension. 'I heard there was a Sidhe involved but I assumed it was someone from the Polwarth Clan. They're usually the ones up in these mountains.'

I sniffed. 'There was a Polwarth with us but she's not Sidhe.' I wasn't annoyed that he'd not kept tabs on me. No siree. Not me. 'How's your lovely girlfriend Tipsania?' I asked snidely.

Byron's expression closed immediately. 'Fine.' He pushed himself away from the door. 'I'll tell her you were asking after her.'

'I'm sure she'll be thrilled,' I shot back.

Speck brushed against me, giving a gentle reminder about what I was really here for. Bugger. He was right. I shook out my hair and plastered a fake smile on my face. Byron Moncrieffe wouldn't be so quick to dismiss the foolish actions of others when I told him about Debbie and the fact that the Carnegies were carrying her off in secrecy to the Cruaich for their own nefarious purposes.

Byron stepped towards me. He was at least half a foot taller than me and I had to resist the urge to pull back and give myself some breathing space. I did drop my arm from Jamie, however, and he scuttled away, watching Byron and me with wide eyes.

'I've got something to tell you,' I said.

'And I've got something to tell you,' Byron returned. 'For your information, Rory and Maggie were practising for the Games. Last time the Adventure course involved some ice climbing. They were working for the glory of the Moncrieffe Clan, regardless of how lacking in common sense you think they were.'

'Games? You're kidding me? They risked their lives so they could win some pennant?'

Byron tsked. 'You really have no idea, have you?'

'Go on,' I taunted. 'Enlighten me.'

The rancour disappeared from his face and his tone dropped. 'Believe me, there's nothing I'd like more.' His gaze dropped to my mouth and lingered there; there was no doubt as to what he was really referring.

I balled up my fists. 'Oh, I'm more enlightened than you think.'

'Really.'

I flicked a look at Jamie; judging from the way his shoulders were hunched, he wanted to be a million miles away from here. Nevertheless, I pointed at him. 'Ask him,' I said. 'Your friend can tell you how enlightened I am.'

A muscle jerked in Byron's cheek. He moved away and I expelled a silent sigh of relief. 'Do you know what the Games are?' he asked.

I folded my arms. 'No.'

He smirked. 'They're held every generation. Almost every Clan participates and, while the prize for the winner is grand, they're really about the honour of beating everyone else.'

Honour? Ha! If the prize was so *grand*, then they wouldn't trouble themselves with honour. You couldn't feed a family on it, after all.

My thoughts must have been written across my face because Byron's expression lit up. 'Honour is important to the Sidhe.' His eyes glinted. 'Most of us, anyway. But I'm not lying, the prize really is worth having because the winner can ask for anything. If it's within the means of the Clans to grant it, they shall receive it.'

I hadn't been expecting that. I felt Speck shiver in delight next to me, although he managed to keep his mouth shut. 'Anything?' I asked.

'Yes,' Byron said smugly.

'Wow.' I couldn't dampen my curiosity. 'So what did the last generation's winner ask for?'

Jamie squeaked. 'Oh!' he blurted out. 'But last time...' He stopped mid-sentence.

I paused, my eyes narrowing. 'Last time what?' Suddenly Byron looked guilty, as if he wished he'd not brought up the subject. 'Spit it out, princeling.'

'The last winner asked for a black rose,' he said heavily.

My nose wrinkled. 'A black rose? What use is that?'

'They're very rare.'

Big deal. I wasn't a complete idiot though. Jamie's reaction hadn't been anything to do with the prize; his squeal had been because of the winner. Something squirmed inside me. 'Who won?'

'It was a long time ago, Integrity. Does it really matter?' I didn't say anything. Instead I just held his eyes, silently demanding the truth. Byron sighed. 'Fine. The last winner was Gale Adair.'

Both Speck and I sucked in audible breaths. My father. Supposedly the least honourable Sidhe who had ever existed - if Moncrieffes like Byron's father were to be believed. I bit down hard on the inside of my cheek.

'I'm sorry, Integrity.' Byron sounded like he meant it. 'I wasn't thinking.'

'Most people either recoil at any mention of him or pretend he never existed. You don't do that,' I said flatly. I tilted my chin. 'Any Clan can participate in these Games?'

He grimaced, sensing the direction of my thoughts. 'Almost any Clan.'

'Meaning what exactly?'

'Every generation, a different Clan is responsible for planning the Games. We take turns because it wouldn't be fair for the organisers to participate as well. It's important that the challenges are kept secret to make the playing field as even as possible.'

I felt a strange fire light up in the pit of my belly. Ohhhhhh, yes. 'And the Clan organising these Games?' I asked. 'It's obviously not the Moncrieffes because you lot are running around trying to get yourself killed before they start.'

'The Carnegies,' Byron said, confirming my suspicion. 'It's their turn. Apparently they're going all out to create a spectacle. Even though they can't participate, the organisers compete to make the Games they hold better and more exciting than everyone else's. There's a lot of kudos involved in getting them right.'

Luckily I had some experience in maintaining a poker face. I sent a quick prayer of gratitude towards Taylor for all his training. 'I see.' I shrugged. 'How interesting. Well, as you and Jamie are both here, I think Dr Speck will be happy to release Maggie and Rory into your care. Providing they stay away from any mountains, of course.'

'Thank you, Dr Speck,' Byron said drily.

Speck coughed. 'Not a problem.'

I turned, ready to go.

'Wait, you were going to tell me something,' Byron said. 'It sounded important.'

There was no way I was going to blab about Debbie now. I might not have heard about the Games before now but I was already on the inside track and I wasn't going to lose that advantage.

'Um,' I demurred, before alighting on something which would explain what I'd said. 'There were strange tracks on Coire an t'Sneachda.'

Byron looked confused - I was probably still pronouncing it wrongly. 'The mountain we rescued Maggie and Rory from.' I described the three-legged paw prints.

'What size were they?' Byron asked.

I made a shape with my fingers to indicate their girth.

'Something small, then.' I nodded. Byron patted me on the arm. 'I wouldn't worry about it. That high up, it was probably just a bird.' He grinned at me. 'Well, it was ... entertaining to see you, Integrity. No doubt our paths will cross again soon.' He leaned towards me and I caught a hint of his natural musky smell. 'The Games start in a fortnight. If participants aren't at the Cruaich and registered to enter by the fourteenth, they have to wait a generation for their next shot.'

'I do so hate killing time,' I quipped.

Byron's eyes danced. 'You should get a watch-dog.'

Speck groaned. 'You're as bad as each other.'

'Come on, doctor,' I said to him, turning on my heel. 'Let's leave the Moncrieffes to their family reunion. Byron and Jam Jam clearly don't need us. And,' I added in a muttered breath, 'we've got things to do.'

# Chapter Three

My old mentor Taylor scratched his chin while the five of us sat around my small kitchen table and pondered Byron's news. 'I've heard of the Games,' he said slowly. 'They're a really big deal.'

'You didn't think to mention them before?' I asked mildly.

He shrugged, the very picture of ambivalence. 'Only Sidhe can enter them and you didn't want anything to do with your kin, so I didn't pay much attention to Sidhe competitions. And considering how rarely they're held, it's a miracle I can even remember the last ones.'

Lexie's eyes were shining. 'You can ask for anything?'

'If you win,' I said.

She nodded distractedly. 'Yes but *anything*?'

I glanced at Speck for confirmation. He pushed up his glasses and gave a wide grin. 'Yeah,' he said. 'That's what Tegs's crush told us.'

I threw him a nasty look. He didn't even notice.

'It's a shame that only Sidhe can enter,' Brochan said, helpfully drawing attention away from me. 'Although it's probably just as well.' He gestured at Lexie and Speck. 'These two would probably get themselves killed, especially if one of the challenges involves that spider.'

Lexie shuddered. 'I hate spiders.'

'Aw, Lex, don't be like that,' Speck interjected. 'Spiders are very clever creatures who deserve respect.'

'Says the warlock who's afraid of just about every damn thing in the world,' she growled.

I held up my palm. 'Enough. Can we focus on what's important?'

Taylor smiled. 'Winning the Games and getting a pot of gold. We could be set for life.'

'No. It's not money I'm after.' His face fell. 'I'm sorry,' I apologised. 'But we can always make more money. There are some things that even the biggest treasure chest can't offer.'

'Like what?' Taylor seemed baffled that I'd even consider anything other than hard cash.

I took a deep breath. 'The Adair Lands.'

Even Brochan's jaw dropped at that. 'You'd ask for your own Clan Lands? But technically they already belong to you, don't they?'

'First of all,' I said ticking off the points on my fingers, 'the Lands were destroyed by being covered in salt and then confiscated. They've been lying empty ever since...' I didn't finish the sentence. 'If I asked for them back, every single Sidhe would have to recognise my Clan again and I'd be in a better position to find out what really happened to my parents.' And to get my revenge.

'But you're the only member of Clan Adair,' said Speck.

I grinned. 'Didn't you all say you were working for me?' The Sidhe might run the Clans but there was no law against getting others to work for them.

'I love you Tegs but I'm not swearing fealty.' Lexie flipped back her hair.

I rolled my eyes. 'You know I wouldn't ask you for that. I'm sure we could come to an alternative arrangement.'

A gleam lit Taylor's eyes. 'It would be like throwing sand in the other clans' faces.'

'Not sand,' Speck said thoughtfully. 'A whole lot of our sweet-smelling shit.'

'And we'd rub their faces in it,' grinned Taylor.

'Not to mention,' Bob's voice piped up as Brochan sneezed, 'we could leave this town and go somewhere more civilised.'

'Who says you're coming along?' I asked.

'You might need me.' I snorted but Bob looked only momentarily put out. 'If you want,' he said, warming to the topic, 'you could make a wish and win automatically. Job done.'

I didn't even deign to answer.

'Actually,' Taylor interjected, 'I'm pretty certain that there are wards in place to prevent anyone from using magic to win.'

'Participants can't use their Gifts?'

'They can use them during the individual challenges but not to control the outcome of the Games as a whole. There's some trigger system that alerts the organising Clan. Anyone caught trying to play the system is banned from competing for the next six generations.'

More of Byron's supposed honour shite. Whatever. I fixed my gaze on Taylor. 'What else do you know about the Games?'

He frowned, searching through his memory. 'There are three challenges: Artistry, Adventure and Acumen.'

Speck pursed his lips. 'Alliteration.'

'Bless you,' said Lexie. He glared at her.

Taylor ignored them and continued. 'The nature of the challenges changes every time. If memory serves me right, that ice wall thing Byron Moncrieffe was talking about came in the Adventure challenge last time around.'

Lexie clapped her hands. 'That would be a piece of cake for Tegs!'

Taylor grimaced. 'It was only part of the whole thing. The reason I heard about the competition in the first place was because of what came after the ice wall in the last Games. In the Acumen challenge.'

'Which was?'

'A Yeti.'

I blinked. 'Seriously?'

'Yeah. There were some rather brutal, er, deaths.'

I swallowed. 'Wow. So we can make a reasonable guess about which part of the competition Debbie is going to be in. Do you know anything else?'

Taylor shook his head. 'No. I could find out. If I asked around, I'm sure someone would have some information.'

I thought about it. 'Nah, best not. We don't want to seem like we're cheating. And I'm betting the Clan Chieftains will do whatever they can to stop me participating. We don't want to give them a reason to cancel my entry.' A smile played around my lips as I imagined their reaction if I won. 'Besides, if the challenges aren't repeated from one set of Games to the next, information about the last ones won't help - although it wouldn't hurt to keep our ears to the ground. We know the Carnegies are the organisers so maybe something will drift our way. Debbie did.'

'So you're definitely going to compete?' Taylor asked.

My smile spread until I was grinning so hard it was possible my carefully applied make-up would crack. 'You can count on it.' Aifric's face hovered in my mind for a moment before I added, 'And I'm going to win.'

*** 

Travis was only too happy to give me time off from mountain rescue. He was so quick to agree that I almost opened my mouth to argue with him but in the end I decided it was easier not to look a gift horse in the face. It was a close-run thing though. I really had to stop letting my emotions get the better of me.

Once that small matter was taken care of, my posse set about making the necessary preparations. That meant locating supplies – not to mention finding the cash to buy them.

'We could just nick everything we need,' Lexie said pragmatically when we pooled our money and realised how little we had.

It was tempting but I couldn't take the risk. 'We don't steal from our own. And if we steal anything from the Sidhe who turn up at the Cruaich...'

'Yeah, yeah. But buying all that food will be expensive.'

I grimaced. After Aifric Moncrieffe tried to poison me we couldn't take any chances: no food or drink could pass our lips at the Cruaich so we had to buy in. It was necessary – but costly.

'We also need to get hold of your Clan tartan,' Lexie continued, 'and weaponry for when...'

'Whoa. No weapons.'

She looked exasperated. 'I know you don't like fighting but I don't think you'll be able to avoid it.'

'I'm not going to give those bastards another reason to slag off my name. If I win through force then that's not a win. Weapons won't be necessary.'

'Hello?' She knocked the side of her head. 'Gigantic spider to beat off? Not to mention what else they've found or what they'll ask you to do. This is a weakness of yours, Integrity. If the other Clans are determined to stop you from winning, they'll exploit your unwillingness to fight.'

I shrugged. 'They don't know about it so they can't exploit it.'

'I think they'll realise it quickly enough,' Lexie grumbled.

'If they do,' I responded calmly, 'we'll deal with it.'

'Fine,' she said, with a toss of her blue hair. 'You still need your tartan, though. In fact, if we're going to be your entourage, we need to wear it too.' She pursed her lips and indicated a mark on her thigh just below her arse. 'I'm thinking mini skirt. Or hot pants.'

Unfortunately for Speck, he chose that moment to wander into the room.

'Hey Speckster!' Lexie called. 'Do you think I should wear hot pants?' She twirled round. 'Or a mini skirt?'

His face immediately went flame red. 'What?'

Mischief glinted in her eyes. 'In the Adair colours. It's to support Tegs. I could always run up a tartan bikini as well.'

'It'll be February, Lex,' I said. 'In Scotland.'

She grinned. 'That's okay. The Cruaich is bound to have a hot tub, right? Although,' she added, her face taking on a thoughtful cast, 'we'll save money if I just go in the nude.'

Speck didn't know where to look. Feeling sorry for him, I came to his rescue. 'What have you got, Speck?' I asked.

He coughed. 'First of all,' he said, looking pointedly at Lexie, 'you can't use the Adair tartan. It's verboten.'

I screwed up my face. 'Those pricks. No wonder it wasn't present in the Cruaich main hall.' Every single one of the other twenty-four Clans' tartans was proudly displayed there for all to see – except the one for Clan Adair. 'Can't we resurrect it?'

'No – but you can use a variation of it as long as it's not the original thing.'

I shook my head. I shouldn't have felt disgusted because I'd never been an Adair by name; when I ran away from the Sidhe and their damned Clans, I took Taylor's name as my own. But banning my own Clan's tartan seemed like spitting in my face. 'They're really going all out to wipe any trace of the Adairs off the planet.'

Speck gave an uncomfortable smile. 'Sorry.'

'It's hardly your fault.' I sighed. 'Is that all?'

This time his grin was wider. 'No. I managed to hack into the Cruaich's system.' He held up his palms. 'Before you say anything, I didn't go near any of the secrets - I think the Carnegies are keeping those to themselves. But I did access all the information which the other Clans have already received and which the Carnegies neglected to send to you.'

'I don't think they're expecting me to turn up and resurrect the Adairs. In fact, they're probably hoping that I'll crawl back beneath the rock they found me under so they can pretend I don't exist. They certainly won't want me at the Games.'

'Byron Moncrieffe seemed to expect you to attend.'

I ignored the slight flutter I felt and focused on what was important. 'What did you find out?'

'The opening ceremony will take place on the tenth. It's the second new moon after the Winter Solstice. It's also...'

'Chinese New Year,' I finished. 'Is there a link to the Zupu?' I asked, referring to the Chinese version of our Clans.

'Not as far as I can tell. I think the ceremony's always been then. With a new challenge starting every two days and time allowed for the opening ceremony and the prize giving, the Games last for a week. You receive points for how highly you're placed in each challenge. There's a sort of league table displayed at the Cruaich's main door which keeps the tally. Each Clan can field up to five Sidhe but each challenge is a competition for individuals so only one person can win.'

'No prizes for the runner-up then,' I said drily. 'And the challenges themselves?'

'Taylor was right: Artistry, Adventure and Acumen. You're allowed to bring one object into the arena for each one. Details of the Artistry challenge have already been sent out so the competitors can prepare.'

He lapsed into silence. Lexie and I stared at him.

'Well?' she demanded.

'Well what?'

'What is the Artistry challenge?' I asked. 'If the others are preparing for it then I need to get ready too.'

Speck dropped his head. 'You understand that if you do poorly in one challenge you can still make up points in the others. You don't have to come first in everything. No one ever does.'

'Speck,' I said, using my best warning tone, 'what is the challenge?'

Taylor appeared in the doorway and watched us with interest. Speck looked at him for help but he'd already been rescued once today; it wasn't going to happen again.

Speck sighed. 'The Artistry challenge will involve music.' He crossed his arms defensively. 'Don't shoot the messenger.'

I paled. 'Music? Oh, shite.'

Lexie gazed at me in dismay. 'You're screwed.'

'With time to prepare, I might manage it. Taylor can sing, he could teach me.' I turned to him.

His eyes were wide with alarm. 'No, no, no, no, no. We've been down that road before. My ears are still bleeding.'

I frowned at him. 'That was eight years ago, Taylor. I was only a teenager.' He gestured to his ears, wincing as if in terrible pain. 'You're a crappy actor,' I told him.

'And you're tone deaf. A block of wood has more rhythm than you.'

Brochan wandered into the kitchen, oblivious to our glares, and slumped shoulders. He filled a glass with water before realising anything was wrong. 'What's up?'

'Artistry,' Speck said glumly. 'It's the first challenge. Tegs is supposed to prepare something musical.'

Brochan went pale too. 'Ah.' He put the glass down carefully. 'The Adair lands aren't really that important to you, are they, Tegs? I mean, they're covered in salt and they're right next to the Veil. They'll be more trouble than they're worth. I vote we all stay here and have a party instead.'

Lexie nodded vigorously. 'Drinking games, not Sidhe Games.'

I cleared my throat. 'We have almost two weeks. That's more than enough time to practise.'

Speck shook his head. 'We're doomed. This is going to be the longest two weeks of my life.'

*** 

Speck may have learned that the Artistry challenge involved music but we didn't know much beyond that. Taylor sat me down with a triangle, wary reluctance all over his face.

I held it up. 'A triangle? Really? I'm not going to win any prizes with this.'

'It's to get you started. Take the small pointy stick and hit it against the side.'

I gave him a long look. 'I understand how a triangle works, Taylor.' He muttered something under his breath. It wasn't very complimentary. 'What was that?' I asked.

'Nothing.' He sighed. 'I'm going to play you a piece of music. All you have to do is hit the triangle every eighth beat.'

'Every eighth beat. Got it.' I paused. 'Do I hit it hard or softly? Does it matter where I strike it?'

'Let's just focus on the beat for now,' he said firmly. He pressed play. 'Let's hear you then.'

I concentrated hard, I swear I did. I heard the first chimes of some classical piece which I was sure I recognised and began to count. One. Two. Three. Four. Five. Six. Seven. Beat.

'Integrity!'

'What?'

'I said every eight beats.'

'That's what I did.'

He ran a hand through his hair. 'Are you even listening to the music?'

'Of course!'

He gazed at me, exasperated. 'So why aren't you hitting the beat?'

I flicked my hair and pouted while he started plucking the stuffing out of my favourite cushion. Shreds of synthetic wool dropped onto the floor, creating an arc around him as if he could shield himself by dint of polyester. Unfortunately, from that point things went downhill. Three hours later, I was ready to jam the triangle up his nostrils. Preferably the left one – it was hairier.

'Singing,' Brochan suggested, appearing when Taylor let out such a howl of frustration that the entire flat shook.

'You try,' Taylor snapped. 'I've had enough.'

I watched him leave. 'I don't know why he's so upset. I was trying. We all know music's not really my forte.' I smirked. 'Geddit?'

Brochan was not amused. 'Let's try some scales, shall we?'

I only got halfway through the first octave before Bob appeared in a blinding flash of light. 'Please, Uh Integrity, I can't take this any longer. I have Amnesty on speed dial and if you continue with this, I shall have no choice but to report you for torture.' I'd have argued with him if Brochan hadn't looked so relieved.

I sighed. 'This isn't going to work, is it? How bad is it if I place last in the first challenge?'

'Speck estimates your chances of winning the entire Games at around 0.5 percent,' Brochan said quietly.

I sank down into the nearest chair. 'Shite.'

From nowhere, Bob drew out a miniature violin and launched into an impressive rendition of Barber's 'Adagio for Strings'. I couldn't tell if he was any good but Brochan seemed impressed. 'It's a shame the wee one's not Sidhe.'

Bob halted mid-note and glared. 'Who are you calling wee?'

'I've known taller leprechauns,' I told him. I rubbed my eyes. 'There has to be something I can do.'

The genie snapped his fingers. 'There is!'

'I am *not* going to make a wish.'

He nodded solemnly. 'You can't. But...'

A kernel of suspicion formed in my belly. 'But what?'

Bob put his hands behind his back and acted bashful, his foot tracing a pattern on top of the table. 'Leprechauns,' he said.

I was puzzled. 'What about them? Because even if they are musical, we'll never track one down in time.'

'Leprechauns are Irish.' He beamed at Brochan and me as if he'd just discovered the secret of alchemy.

'Bob,' I said, 'you must be all of – what? A thousand years old?'

He patted his cheeks. 'I look young for my age. It's closer to two.'

'Fabulous,' I replied drily. 'You're two thousand years old and you've only just discovered that leprechauns are Irish. Impressive.'

'You can tease me all you like, Uh Integrity. It's not going to change the fact that I can save your Sidhe bacon.' He flew onto my shoulder and picked up a lock of my hair. 'I told you you'd need me.'

'Do you have short-term memory loss? I can't make any wishes. It'll nullify any chances I have of winning the Games.'

He yanked so hard on the curl that I yelped in pain. I reached up to brush him off but he danced out of my grasp and settled on the top of my head. Two tiny feet began to stamp into my skull in a continuous, drumming beat. It didn't hurt but it wasn't improving my mood.

'What's he doing?' I asked Brochan.

The merman's face had taken on the most peculiar expression. It wasn't helped by his eyes starting to stream because of his proximity to Bob. Poor Brochan was allergic. 'Riverdance, I think.' He wiped his eyes.

Bob swung over my forehead, hanging upside down and waving. 'Ireland is the answer!'

I growled and tried to grab him again. He disappeared in a puff of bright green smoke, reappearing on the tip of Brochan's ear. The merman sneezed three times in quick succession but Bob didn't react; he just crossed his legs and smiled. 'I will do what I have never done.'

Resigned to the situation, I blew air out through my pursed lips and glared. 'What?'

'I will accept an IOU.'

'Huh?'

'IOU. I realise you are not the most intelligent Sidhe, Uh Integrity.' He leaned down, whispering loudly to Brochan, 'Sharp as a sack of wet mice. An IOU is...'

'I know what an IOU is.'

'Then what's the problem?' He blinked innocently.

'You'll help Integrity out if she promises to make another wish,' Brochan said.

'A pot of leprechaun gold to the man with the runny nose!' Bob applauded noisily. He lifted an eyebrow in my direction. 'Well?'

'I promise to ask for a wish in the future and you'll help me become musical?'

'I won't make you musical but I'll tell you where to get the equipment you need to pass the test.' His brow furrowed. 'Or win the challenge. Or whatever.'

'Equipment?'

'Magical equipment which even you could play.'

I met Brochan's eyes. 'That doesn't sound so bad.' The 'future' could be an eternity.

'Just one caveat,' Bob chirped. 'You have to make the wish within the next six months.'

Bugger. 'Can I think about it?' Although it sounded like a brilliant idea, everyone knew that asking a genie for wishes would only end in disaster. I'd already made one and it had almost led to me having my head lopped off by the Bull when I'd been transported into his quarters on the back of a poorly conceived desire.

Bob shrugged. 'Okay.' Ten seconds later, he pulled up his cuff and gazed at his watch. 'Time's up!'

'Do you have a better idea?' Brochan asked me. 'Because however bad you sound to yourself, Tegs, you sound a million times worse to an audience.'

I muttered a curse under my breath. 'Fine.'

Bob beamed. 'Say the words.'

'I'm probably going to regret this.' I looked at him. 'If I win the Artistry challenge, I promise to make my second wish. Alright?'

Bob made a face. 'No, this is not contingent on success. I'm not having my life's goals disrupted because you're an idiot. You either promise or you don't. There's nothing in between.'

I gritted my teeth in defeat. 'I promise.'

There was a tiny clap of thunder. Bob jumped up in the air, hovering for a second with his arms stretched upwards. 'Hurray!' He executed a perfect somersault. 'Best decision you've ever made.'

Somehow I doubted that. 'Go on. What information do you have?'

'Dagda.'

'What the hell? That doesn't mean anything!'

'Man.' He shook his head. 'You really are the poster child for contraception, aren't you? Dagda? The ancient Irish hero?'

I folded my arms. 'Never heard of her.'

'Him.' Bob rolled his eyes. 'Women aren't heroes.'

'That's it! I'm going to melt down your damn letter opener at the nearest smithy.'

'Women are heroines, Uh Integrity.' He wagged his finger at me like a disapproving teacher. 'Get your grammar right.'

If the genie lived to the end of the day, it would be a miracle. 'Who was Dagda?'

'Ugly guy. Great long beard which used to get in his way all the time. There was food stuck in there for...'

'Bob,' I warned.

He threw up his arms. 'Fine, fine. Anyway, it's not really Dagda you want - he's been dead for five hundred years. What you seek is his harp, Uaithne.'

'If I can't play the triangle, I'm hardly going to be able to play a harp.'

Bob shook his head. 'This is a special harp. Play Dagda's harp – even just one note – and you're almost guaranteed to win the challenge. I can't account for the Sidhe, mind, but I know the harp.'

'One note?'

'Yep.'

'And this harp is in Ireland?' I tried to calculate. We could take the nearest ferry and be there the next day. It was definitely doable. And surely even I would be able to play a single note.

'Ah, well, to be sure, to be sure, it's an Irish harp which belongs in Ireland,' Bob said with an affected Irish lilt.

'But?'

He shrugged nonchalantly and flicked Brochan's ear. The merman growled and tried to throw him off. 'But the Fomori stole it a while back. They're not interested in it these days though, so it's shoved in a cellar in a back street in Glasgow.'

My jaw dropped open. 'In Glasgow. In the Lowlands? Beyond the Veil?'

Bob nodded. 'Yes!'

'Where the Fomori demons are and no other living person has set foot for three hundred years because if they do they'll be slaughtered into a bloody mess of bones and sinew and torn flesh?'

'That's not strictly true...' Bob's voice trailed away when he saw my expression. 'Yeah, okay. Pretty much.'

Well crapadoodle.

# Chapter Four

'Isn't this taking things a little too far?' Taylor asked as we stood in front of the Veil, staring at its dark cloudy expanse. It stretched the entire length of the country, from the North Sea on one side to the Atlantic Ocean on the other, blocking off the Lowlands from anyone who wasn't a demon. It had been this way since the Fissure in 1745 so goodness only knew what was on the other side. Unsurprisingly, there wasn't another soul in sight. Few people ventured this close to the Veil on purpose.

My stomach was churning and I worried that I was going to heave up my guts right onto Taylor's feet. Bolts of lightning lit up the darkness from time to time, just in case anyone wasn't already fully aware of the dangers of the Veil.

'Look on the bright side,' I said. 'The Fomori won't be expecting me.'

'That's not very comforting. Whoever your father was, I doubt he'd be impressed at you dying to win back the Adair Lands.'

I was silent for a moment. The truth was, none of us had any idea what would have impressed my father. Since the day I'd seen a vision of him in the grove at the Cruaich, however, the thought of him had been gnawing away at me. I set foot upon this course months ago; I wasn't going to back down just because it was a little bit scary. Or a lot scary.

'You know,' I said softly, 'those lands are very close to here. My father probably saw the Veil on a regular basis. He might even have stood on this very spot.'

'Your father is dead,' Taylor said.

I turned to him. 'He died because of the Sidhe, not the Fomori. I can do this.'

'You don't even know if the bloody genie is right about the harp.'

Actually, I had the feeling that despite Bob's posturing he really wanted me to succeed. I shrugged.

'You should take him in there with you. At least then if you need to make a wish to save yourself...'

I shook my head. 'No. I've already committed myself to one wish. I'm not going to bring him along and be tempted to say the words while I'm under pressure. What if it went wrong and I wished myself out and the wish made the Veil disappear? I could be responsible for the Fomori taking over all of Scotland, not just the Lowlands.'

'If they wanted to do that,' Taylor said, 'they probably would have done it already.'

I sighed. 'You know what I'm saying.'

He squeezed my shoulder. 'I do. And I see that you're committed to this course.' He heaved a breath. 'To be honest, I almost did this when I was younger. Crossed the Veil, I mean. It wasn't for a good reason like yours, though.' He looked rueful. 'I'm no honourable Sidhe.'

'Really?'

He nodded. 'There are tales of a lot of riches on the other side. And I wanted to be a hero.'

'What stopped you?'

He gave a crooked smile. 'In the end, I was too frightened.'

I smiled back. 'I'm pretty damn terrified myself.'

'Yeah. But you're Integrity Adair. You'll be fine.'

I pursed my lips. I'd been Integrity Taylor for so long that hearing him call me something else jarred. 'I'll always be a Taylor too,' I told him.

His expression grew serious. 'I know.'

I wrapped my arms tightly round his thickening waist. 'I might be doing this for my biological father,' I whispered, 'but you've been my real father.'

Taylor jerked back. 'Don't you dare.'

'What?'

'This is not a suicide mission. You are not going to die and you are not saying goodbye. Don't you dare talk as if you are.'

'Okay.'

He glared at me. 'I mean it.'

'Sure.' I nodded. 'I'm just going for a stroll and a bit of shopping and I'll be back before you know it.' I tried not to notice the way his eyes glistened.

Taylor raised a hand. 'Happy travels. I'll be right here when you get back.'

I filled my lungs, breathing in the fresh Scottish Highland air. The faint scent of heather clung to the back of my throat. This was my home and I'd be back soon.

'See you,' I said quietly. And I pivoted and plunged in.

My skin prickled with a thousand shots of pain. Individually, each one felt like nothing more than a light pinch but, combined, they made my whole body judder. It felt as if my very bones were crackling. Holding my breath, and keeping my head down, I forced my way forward. I was already starting to regret trying this. I squeezed my eyes shut. Come on, Integrity. Come on. I pushed ahead, one foot after the other.

The relief when I passed through the barrier of the Veil was over-whelming. I rubbed my hands up and down my arms, trying to rid myself of the last of the painful tingling, and looked around. I wasn't sure what I'd been expecting but if I'd thought about it, it would have been pretty much like this. The sky was dark grey and the ground un-derfoot didn't contain any evidence of plant life. In fact, there wasn't evidence of life anywhere. The earth was hard and compacted and, while I could still see evidence of the Scotland I knew with its dark hills and mountains, this was a scarred and troubled landscape.

The one good thing was that I knew exactly where I was going. I'd chosen my entry point carefully as the nearest point from the Veil to what had once been Glasgow. I had less than fifteen miles to cross before I reached the fringes of the city. If I kept up a good pace and didn't have to hide to avoid any Fomori, I'd be there in less than three hours. I adjusted my watch and set the stopwatch to keep track of time – who knew how things worked in this part of the world – and set off.

There wasn't a trail as such but it didn't matter. The ground was so hard that I could have been running on concrete. There weren't any roots or holes to avoid and though the air was both clammier and staler than that which I'd left behind, it didn't hamper my progress.

I kept going in a straight line, looking for anything which suggested life - or danger. There were no lights, no creatures and no demons. Perhaps all the Fomori eschewed a rural life and were city dwellers; if so, they were city dwellers who enjoyed the dark. Before too long I could make out the shapes of the buildings in Glasgow but there wasn't a single light to illuminate them.

Unlike Aberdeen – or even Oban – the structures were low-lying. The Fomori hadn't spent the last three hundred years matching the rest of the world's bid to create cloud-reaching skyscrapers. When I reached the edges of the city, it was even clearer that this was a place caught in a time warp. I half expected William Wallace himself to come charging out from the ramshackle stone houses, kilt flying up around him and swinging a vast broadsword in my direction. There was nothing. The city was as silent as the countryside had been.

Warier now, I slowed to a walk. I'd memorised Bob's directions so I knew exactly where to go. He'd assured me that his information was accurate as of 1923. Considering that was close to a century ago, it wasn't the most comforting thing to hear. Bob had been with an English lord who wanted to woo his new bride and whose wish had thrown up Dagda's harp to help him. Needless to say, things hadn't turned out very happily for the lord and the harp ended up staying exactly where it was. When I'd pressed Bob for more details, he'd given an enigmatic shrug and suggested I could wish for the information if I really wanted to know. Genies. Honestly.

My slower pace meant that I noticed more of what was around me. The buildings, which were growing in number and density, might have been simple and covered in a sticky dark mould which I was far too sensible to touch, but their craftsmanship was obvious. Abandoned or not, they were built to last. It was difficult to avoid the sense of history which imbued the atmosphere; the tragic fate of all those who'd lived here prior to the Fissure left me feeling empty.

It felt as if I'd been walking for hours. I was starting to wonder whether the entire race of Fomori demons had died out and no one had noticed because no one ever came here, when something from the interior of one of the buildings caught my eye. I didn't want to make a detour – I didn't want to spend more time here than was absolutely necessary – but my curiosity was too strong. For all I knew, I was the only non-horned being to have been here in centuries. The least I could do was to get a proper idea of what the Lowlands were really like. I owed all those lost souls that much.

Stepping over a broken oak door which had fallen off its hinges and was lying across the threshold, I tiptoed carefully inside. I didn't have to go far to see what had attracted my attention. Etched into the wall was a name. I squinted at it through the half-light: Matthew MacBain.

I hadn't felt cold before but I certainly did now. I had no idea who Matthew MacBain was but the MacBains were one of the remaining twenty-four Clans. Did the graffiti mean that he had wandered through here from the Highlands like I had? And if he had, what had happened to him?

The letters were crude, as if carved out of the stone with a blunt instrument. I reached out with my finger and traced them. 'Who were you?' I whispered.

I turned my head and looked further into the gloom of the house. If I went much further from the door, the dim light would vanish. Outside remained as silent as before. I was completely alone and, because I was inside, completely concealed from any dark demon eyes. I pulled out my phone and turned it on so I could use its light to look around properly. Not surprisingly, there was no signal. No matter: I wasn't about to chat to anyone or update my Facebook page with my current location.

Now that I could see better, I noticed a dark patch trailing down from Matthew MacBain's name. Frowning, I leaned forward and sniffed. All I could smell was damp but the patch looked suspiciously like old, dried blood. I sidestepped to examine it from a different angle – and tripped over something on the floor. My feet flew out from underneath me and I landed with a heavy thud, expelling the air from my lungs.

When I looked at what I'd stumbled on, I threw myself backwards, my heart racing.

It was a skeleton. Scraps of flesh and a few rags still clung to the bones but it had obviously been here for a long time. I reminded myself to breathe, my hand rising to my chest until my pulse began to calm. Then I went back to look more closely.

Physiologically, humans and Sidhe were almost the same and my knowledge of biology wasn't extensive enough to tell the difference between them. Even so, I bet that this was poor Matthew. When I spotted the signet ring on his third finger, I knew for sure: it was engraved with the MacBain crest.

Holding my breath, I bent down to pull it off. 'It's only a skeleton, Integrity,' I muttered. 'You can do this.' It came off easily – after all, there was little more than bone for it to cling to.

I examined it. Even covered in dust, dirt and goodness knows what else, its rich, buttery gold shone through. By the looks of things, Matthew MacBain had been highly placed in his Clan.

'I'm sorry for what happened to you,' I said to his body, aware how pathetic my words were.

I shoved the ring deep into my back pocket and glanced to my left. There was something else written on the wall. When I got close enough to read it, my bones turned to ice. This was worse than Matthew MacBain's body.

There were only two words. They weren't cut into the stone but drawn on it with what again looked like blood. With my heart in my throat, I backed away. I didn't want to be here; I had to get the damned harp and get out of here.

I left quickly, returning to the makeshift road and picking up speed. It was probably my imagination but it felt like it was getting hotter and it was becoming harder to breathe. The dark sky felt oppressive. I started to run again. There was no one here; I could afford to be less careful.

Fortunately, it didn't take long to reach a crossroads. On the far corner there was an old church. The steeple had long since fallen but there were five pillars in front, which Bob had described to me in painstaking detail. I was to turn right and count down twelve buildings. From there I would see a thin bridge leading across the Clyde River and then the house I was looking for would be twenty-seven steps east.

I whispered the numbers as I passed. 'Ten, eleven, twelve.' I looked over and saw the bridge. It looked precarious; there were no handholds, just a long strip of cracked stone starting from the bank and stretching over the river. I peered down. The oily black waters of the Clyde were far below.

The rivers in the Highlands were of every imaginable colour. Up in the mountains, they tended towards a deep crystal blue. In Oban, the smaller rivers included tinges of green, while in Aberdeen they were a murkier brown – though they still contained fish. Many of the Clan-less who couldn't find gainful employment or couldn't afford seaworthy vessels regularly fished there before selling their catch cheaply in the streets. Somehow, I didn't think the Clyde here had any life in it. A rank odour rose up from it, reminiscent of sewage and rotting rubbish. I guessed the Fomori hadn't yet cottoned on to recycling.

I left the river to count my steps and find the house where the harp was hidden. Disturbingly, it was exactly the same as Bob had described, an unremarkable structure of weathered sandstone with the faint etching of a four-leafed clover over the entrance, like an X marking the spot. Someone wanted Dagda's harp to be found.

Taking a deep breath, I pushed open the rusting door and stepped inside. This was far grander than the place where Matthew MacBain had breathed his last. It was also far, far darker. Using my phone to light the way, I picked my way across a floor filled with rubble and unidentifiable detritus. Towards the back, where a large stone fireplace indicated that this room had once been a kitchen, was the gaping maw of the entrance to the cellar.

Despite the fact that it seemed to be my lot to venture down into the depths, I wasn't a bloody troll. I much preferred airy heights. I decided that from now on, I was going to avoid anything below sea level.

The cellar was small and dry with several rotting old barrels standing at one side. On top of one stood a bottle. I blew off a thick layer of dust and examined the label: Auchentoshan whisky. I shrugged. I'd never heard of it but that was hardly surprising as I wasn't much of a connoisseur. Taylor, however, would enjoy it. I grinned for the first time since I'd come through the Veil, amused by the idea of bringing back a souvenir. This beat a fridge magnet. I shoved the bottle inside my jacket, zipping up so it would stay safe, then I looked round some more. The harp was supposed to be here.

I was starting to think that Bob had sent me on a fool's errand when I spotted it, hiding in the shadows of the far corner.

'Yahtzee,' I whispered.

I'd worried that I wouldn't be able to carry a harp – they are hardly the most portable of musical instruments. Bob had assured me it would be fine and, yet again, he was right. Maybe Dagda was a particularly petite hero because his harp was little more than the size of a lute.

Still, after Matthew MacBain's skeleton, I was glad not to fall across the bones of the last lord who'd come seeking the harp. I tried not to think about what might have happened to him and picked up the instrument. Unlike the bottle of whisky, there wasn't a speck of dust on it. It was a pale wood, with taut strings which looked virtually new. I almost plucked one of them before hastily drawing back my hand. If Dagda's harp had the sort of powers which Bob had alluded to, playing it here in the Lowlands wasn't a wise idea, even if there wasn't a demon to be seen or heard.

I tied the instrument to my back using a small length of knotted rope which I'd brought with me. When I was sure it was secure, I shrugged. 'Well, this harp certainly isn't in any treble.' I looked round the cellar one last time. 'Time to go.'

I was halfway between the house and the bridge and humming tunelessly with a lightness of spirit that I should have known better than to feel, when the clanging of a loud bell nearly gave me a heart attack. I froze in my tracks. What the hell was that? It didn't stop, clanking and shrieking in a way that would have had Taylor eating his words about my musical abilities. Dread poured through me and I checked my watch: it was exactly midday. That couldn't be a coincidence.

From all around me harsh, guttural sounds started to fill the air, drowning out the clanging bell. I couldn't work out where they were coming from until I looked upwards. On top of every building along the street, dark shapes were rising up and moving. I saw a vast set of wings stretch out on one corner and a spitting, snarling fight start up on another. I glanced fearfully back at the house but it was too far away to offer a refuge. I couldn't stay out here in the open, though. As the bell stopped and the shrieks and caws from the demons took over, I did the only thing I could to hide myself: I pitched to my right and dived into the evil-looking Clyde.

The shock of the cold, almost viscous water came close to being my undoing. It coated every part of me until I was like a bird caught in an oil slick. I kicked as hard as I could, reached the side of the river and pressed myself against it, praying that it would hide me. The last thing I wanted was to duck my head underneath the water.

It was a struggle to stay afloat, not just because my clothes were saturated and pulling me under but because it felt like the river itself was beckoning me down into its depths. I flattened myself against the bank, my fingers clawing into the wet dirt, and held my breath. The demon shrieks were giving way to keening cries as hundreds of warped, twisted things rose up into the dark sky. Not all of the creatures were winged; some pounded down the street above my head like an unsynchronised army on a march to the depths of hell. At least a dozen of them turned onto the narrow bridge ahead. I wanted to look away but I couldn't help myself. Hieronymus Bosch eat your heart out.

They were, to a demon, ugly bastards. Every one that I could see was naked, the male Fomori with grotesque large penises which hung down between their legs, slapping against their balls as they ran. The females proudly displayed wrinkled breasts with puckered nipples which seemed to catch the weak light. Most were completely hairless, their gaunt, sinewy bodies shaped for the most arduous of physical activities, although I spotted a few with hair sprouting in patches from their skulls and chests. Every so often, a head turned and I caught a glimpse of searing red eyes and sharp yellow teeth. I began to shiver and it wasn't just because of the cold water. If one of them saw me, I'd be ripped to shreds before I could tell them my best demon joke.

By now, the skies were heavy with the flying Fomori. This wasn't a flock of birds and there didn't appear to be any order to the way they moved. The winged, wheeling shapes collided frequently, sending each other spinning off in different directions. There was a lot of jostling and snapping of teeth; seemingly the demons didn't even like each other.

One high-pitched shriek sounded louder than the others and suddenly heavy wings began to beat in my direction. I'd been spotted. I prepared to do whatever I could to defend myself. In the Cruaich grove, my parents had given me my true name of Layoch, Gaelic for warrior. I hated violence but I wasn't going to lie down and let the demons take me. I'd go down at least attempting to fulfil that name.

But it wasn't me that the winged demon had seen. It swooped upwards and away from the Clyde's oily surface at the last second then flung itself towards the demons that were still crossing the bridge. Most of them scattered but one pulled itself up and gestured arrogantly. Almost forgetting the danger, I watched as the pair launched into a vicious, bloody brawl.

The bridge demon landed one or two swift punches, making its opponent hiss and pull back. He wasn't going to give up that easily though. He sank sharp claws into the other demon's back and flapped as he rose into the air. There was a screech and they pulled away from each other. I expected the non-winged one to crash down into the river below with a tremendous splash but it hung there, suspended in the air.

I blinked. That meant the Fomori demon was Gifted, just like the Sidhe. I should have realised: how else would they have managed to over-run half of the country if they didn't have the same powers as the Sidhe? This one could obviously levitate. Damn, that would be a handy Gift to have and for a moment, I wished I could do it too - it might have made escaping a bit easier.

A breath later I felt a wave of dizziness and my stomach was assailed with nausea. Shite. The cold was getting to me more than I'd realised.

Just then, the floating demon squawked and flapped his arms in alarm. A heartbeat later he plummeted downwards, crashing into the river and creating a mini tsunami in my direction. Panicked that he would notice me, I took a gulp of air and plunged underwater. I couldn't see a thing; I just hoped that I could hold my breath long enough to keep out of sight.

I stayed under until my lungs were burning with a fire I'd never felt before. I had a choice: either drown or break the surface to get more air. I kicked, fighting against the pull of the water. My legs felt heavy and sluggish and it was only because I was next to the bank and could dig my hands into the mud that I managed to heave my head back up.

I gasped loudly but the noise of the demons covered my involuntary wheeze. The demon who had fallen in the river was already at the opposite bank, being helped out by a friend. I wiped the clinging, dark liquid from my eyes and peered across. He was gesturing into the air, confused; he obviously hadn't expected his Gift to fail like that. Despite my shivers, I felt a flicker of curiosity – and suspicion.

His friend laughed and patted his shoulder then the pair of them turned their backs and walked away. My gaze flitted back to the bridge. There were only one or two Fomori on it now, still jogging across to catch up with the others. The skies were emptying. I had no idea where all the demons were off to; I was just thankful that they were leaving.

Five minutes later, everything was silent again. My heart was drumming against my ribcage, my fear still not entirely gone. If it hadn't been for the water, I probably would have lingered for longer until I was sure it was safe to clamber out, but it was too cold. The chill was penetrating my bones and I realised that I would soon be in danger of severe hypothermia, despite the hot clammy air.

I moved along the bank, looking for a spot where it would be easier to pull myself out. There was a good metre of mud bank between where I was and the street further up where I wanted to be. No spot appeared better than any other so I reached up, thrust my fingers into the sticky mud and dug in my toes. Mustering up all my strength, I flung myself upwards. It was time to get out of here.

I made about five inches before the drag of the thick water was too much. I was still wearing my shoes and carrying the harp on my back but even without them the mud would have been too slimy for me to get sufficient purchase. I tried again but this time was even worse and I fell back into the water with a loud splash. Forcing myself to lie still, I waited in case something had heard me. Fortunately, I seemed to be in the clear - but I still couldn't get out of the Clyde.

'Shite, Integrity,' I muttered. 'Think. How can you do this?'

The answer popped into my head: levitate. I snorted. Yeah, right - then my skin tingled and suddenly I was doing it. My body was pushing upwards of its own accord. The water level moved down to my chest, then my stomach, then my waist and still I continued to float upwards. I waved my arms around, sending drips of dark water flying in all directions. How was this happening? First teleportation, causing the Bull and I to end up tumbling through the sky at the Cruaich. Then aura reading after I took the Bull's true name from him. Now I was capable of levitation. I had learnt to levitate just by watching that demon. It didn't seem possible. I'd certainly never heard of anyone else tripping from Gift to Gift like this. I thought of the expression on the demon's face. Something had happened to him. Had that something been me? Fear and worry flickered at me. It wasn't normal. *I* wasn't normal. I shook my head and tried to push away my thoughts and focus on getting the hell out of there.

Finally free of the water, I wobbled in mid-air. My clothes felt heavy and their weight was sapping my energy. I bit my tongue as hard as I could and tried to concentrate. All I had to do was reach dry ground. I wobbled again before righting myself and turning to face the street.

'Come on,' I whispered. Thankfully my body obeyed and slowly drifted over.

Less than a foot across the street I let go, crashing to the ground with a thud. What I wanted to do was roll over, kiss the hard Fomori earth and then sleep for a few hours. What I did was jump to my feet and run. I couldn't stay out in the open.

The only positive aspect of my situation, other than still being alive and unharmed, was that I appeared to be taking half the Clyde with me. I was covered from head to toe in a black oily film. It made movement difficult and I was leaving a visible trail of footprints but it did help to camouflage me. I was now a shade darker than the sky and my white hair was a sticky black. All the same, I clung to the side of the buildings and used what cover they offered. There was neither sight nor sound of the hundreds of demons but I could no longer afford to take any chances.

I reached the bridge again and veered round to the main street along which I'd arrived. It was as clear and empty as it had been an hour ago and I breathed a sigh of relief. Thank goodness; I could be back home and dry before teatime. All I had to do was run. I shook my body like a dog, trying to get rid of some of the strange water. And that was when I heard a sudden hiss and looked up to see a demon right in front of me.

# Chapter Five

She was smaller than the others I'd seen but she possessed the same glowing red eyes and sharp teeth. Her breasts were criss-crossed with scars; disturbingly, there was what looked like an old bite mark where her right nipple should have been. She cocked her head at me for a moment as if puzzled. Then she lunged.

I couldn't move fast enough and the demon's teeth ripped into my forearm, making short work of my jacket before piercing my flesh. I yelped in pain. It seemed that she didn't appreciate the taste of the Clyde any more than I did, however, because she withdrew quickly, spat on the ground and glared at me as if the bitterness on her tongue was my fault.

I held up my palms, trying to ignore the lancing pain in my arm. 'Let's talk about this,' I said, ignoring the tremor in my voice and trying to stay calm. 'I don't want to hurt you. I'm *not* going to hurt you. I just want to leave quietly and go home.'

The demon was confused. She'd probably expected me to fight, not try and talk my way out of danger. I didn't even know whether she understood me. I tapped the centre of my chest. 'I'm Integrity,' I said helpfully. 'Integrity.' I pointed towards her. 'What's your name?'

She didn't like that and she threw herself at me once more. I didn't even think; I simply rose upwards and levitated away from her grasp. Her fingers were long with cracked, dirty nails; whoever this demon was, she certainly wasn't living the good life.

Her mouth dropped and she gaped at me. She had no tongue; I couldn't see whether it had been removed or whether it was some kind of naturally occurring phenomenon but it made my flesh crawl. Her eyes were wild with an edge of vicious insanity. Clearly, she hadn't expected me to use a Gift. To be fair, I probably looked as far removed from a Sidhe as it was possible to get – if this demon even knew what a Sidhe was or what one looked like.

She swiped upwards but I remained out of reach, wary that she'd use her own Gift against me. Instead she flung back her head and howled, an ear-shattering sound that could probably be heard miles away. Bugger. Dealing with one Fomori demon was one thing; dealing with a thousand would be a different matter.

Unsure about how high I could ago, I kept pushing up through the air. The trouble with levitation was that it was only a distant kin to flying and it felt as if I were moving at a snail's pace. I rose higher while the demon below grew more frustrated. She jumped up and down, lunging for me even though I was out of reach. A minute later there were some guttural shouts in a language I didn't recognise, followed by the sound of running feet. I threw myself towards the roof of the pillared church and lay flat on my back, scanning the sky for more of the winged bastards. Fortunately none appeared.

There was an anguished scream from below and I flipped onto my belly and peered over the parapet. Two other demons had joined the female. One had grabbed her by the scruff of the neck and was holding her so that her feet dangled in mid-air. The other spat indistinguishable words in her face, no doubt demanding to know why she'd made all that noise. She pointed upwards, her jaw working uselessly and nothing more than moans coming from her mouth. I pulled back as both Fomori males looked up and then there was another pained scream.

I sneaked another look. The demon in front of her launched a sharp kick to her stomach and she doubled over. The one behind stretched out his claw-like fingers and swiped at her neck; dark blood gushed from the wound, splattering onto the black earth. The first one spat something at her and stalked away in disgust. The second kicked her again and then did the same. She whimpered, curling into a foetal position. I rolled onto my back again, stared up at the clouds and breathed once more.

When I was sure the two demons had gone, I floated back down and started running down the street. I had to get out of the city – and fast. I'd barely gone fifty metres, however, when something tugged deep inside me. I sighed, slowed to a halt and turned around.

The female demon was still lying where the two pricks had left her. The wound she'd received to her neck looked pretty nasty – I didn't know how much blood a Fomori demon had but unless her Gift was healing, she probably wouldn't make it until nightfall. I sighed, then gritted my teeth and jogged back to her.

She didn't even twitch as I approached. 'I'm not going to hurt you,' I said softly.

She still didn't respond so I moved a bit closer and crouched down. Taking a deep breath, I reached out and touched her shoulder to let her know I was there and I wasn't dangerous. She flinched, cowering on the ground like the beaten thing she was.

I peered at her neck. That demon had bloody sharp claws; blood was still pulsating out and, even with the mess of ripped flesh, I could tell the wound was deep. She was lucky it hadn't slashed into her jugular. I bit my lip and tried to work out what to do.

Moving back to give myself room – and because an injured animal is the most dangerous of all – I untied the harp and laid it carefully on the ground. Next I unzipped my jacket and took out the bottle of whisky. 'Sorry, Taylor,' I murmured.

I pulled off the top and edged back to the demon. She smelt really bad, a combination of wet dog and rotting flesh. Or maybe that was me. Ignoring her trembling recoil, I knelt down and motioned with the bottle. She stared at me with wide red eyes. I moved the bottle towards her and she flinched away.

'It's alright,' I told her. 'It'll help.'

To show her, I put the bottle to my own lips and took a quick swig. It was surprisingly mellow. I swallowed and held the bottle out to her again. Her expression seemed resigned to whatever fate I was about to deal her and she tilted back her head. I tipped a small amount of whisky in her mouth; her face screwed up at the taste but she let it slide down her throat. Her lack of tongue didn't seem to make any difference so I gave her some more. By the second swig, she seemed to be warming to the taste.

I took my jacket off and pulled my T-shirt over my head. Despite her fear, the Fomori demon goggled at me. Given that she was naked, she'd probably assumed my clothes were part of my skin. My T-shirt had protected my torso from the worst of the Clyde and I was aware of how strange I looked – black hair, black face, black neck, white middle and black legs.

I poured a tiny amount of whisky onto the T-shirt's sleeve where the water hadn't seeped through so much and used the underside of the material. I kept adding more, making the spot as sterile as I could, then held it towards her wound.

'This is going to hurt,' I told her. I grabbed hold of her hand and she stiffened, clearly waiting for a blow. When it didn't come and I squeezed her fingers in reassurance, she relaxed slightly. Then I pressed the whisky-sodden material to her neck.

She yelped but cut off the noise herself by clamping her free hand over her mouth. She wasn't stupid; she knew what would happen if more demons heard her and came running. I wiped away as much of the blood as I could, hoping the alcohol would prevent any infection.

There was a faint mark on her shoulder, a tattoo. A tattoo of a small Scottish lion on its hind legs with its front paws splayed out into the air. Shaking my head in confusion, I pressed the material against the demon's wound and moved her hand up to hold it. 'You need to keep it like that until the bleeding stops.'

She blinked at me and I sighed. I pushed down on her hand once more, trying to make her understand. When I finally stepped away, she kept her hand in place. I nodded, satisfied. 'I have to go,' I told her. 'I can't stay here.' My eyes drifted down the street. If those others demons came back... 'I'm sorry.'

She jerked suddenly and I leapt back, alarmed. She pointed at her chest and made a strange sound. I frowned, suddenly realising what she was doing.

'Ay? That's your name?' She shook her head and tried again. 'Bay? Hay?' Damn it. 'May?' The demon nodded vigorously. 'May. Your name is May.' I met her eyes. 'It's nice to meet you, May.'

Her face twisted into a strange semblance of a smile. I smiled back until she moved her hand away from her chest and pointed behind me. I turned round but the long street was still empty.

'Yes. I have to go.' I took a deep breath. 'Look after yourself, May.' I picked up my jacket, put it on and zipped it up, then I returned the harp to my back and gave her a wave. I really did have to skedaddle.

I looked at myself ruefully. Even standing next to May, I looked like a half-dead zombie. Maybe demons really were a ghoul's best friend.

*

I made better time than I expected getting back to the Veil and I located the same spot that I'd emerged from with relief. Nothing followed me and I saw nothing else. Wherever those demons had marched off to, it wasn't here. Thank heavens for small mercies.

I shook myself. The strange water from the Clyde had dried on my clothes and skin and black flakes fell off when I moved, like the world's worst case of dandruff.

I gave the dark, unforgiving landscape one last look; I never wanted to come back here again. It seemed that there were worse places than the Cruaich after all. Even Aifric Moncrieffe and his wily, manipulative, murdering ways seemed a piece of cake compared to this nightmare. I took a deep breath and stepped back through the Veil.

The sensation as I passed through was as agonising as before and the noise as I came out onto home turf immediately put me on edge. My eyes darted round. Something was wrong; maybe one of the demons had invisibility as a Gift and had followed me here.

When I realised what was making the noise, I simultaneously relaxed and grimaced. I nudged Taylor with my toe. 'Wake up!'

He mumbled something and rolled over. 'Taylor!' I crouched down and shook him. 'You're snoring loud enough to bring a horde of Fomori stampeding through the Veil. Wake up!'

He grunted and opened his eyes blearily. 'Huh?' He fixed his gaze on me. 'Integrity! You're back!' He sat up and pulled me towards him, enveloping me in a tight hug – then immediately let go. 'You smell worse than a badger's arse. And what on earth are you covered in?'

'Long story,' I told him. I glanced back at the Veil. 'Let's get home to the others and then I'll tell you.'

\*

I'd never before had such a rapt audience. All four of them were on tenterhooks, listening to my every word.

'You helped a Fomori demon?' Brochan appeared thunderstruck.

I shrugged. 'It seemed like the right thing to do.'

Lexie goggled at me. 'She wanted to kill you!'

'Out of instinct rather than anything else, I think.' I gestured at myself. 'I do look like the creature from the black lagoon. Besides, being a pacifist isn't about apathy and turning your back. It actually involves taking action too.'

'I'll have to take samples,' Speck muttered, still focused on my appearance. 'It's like no water I've ever seen.'

Lexie rolled her eyes. 'Ever the scientist.' She leaned forward. 'And you levitated. Like hovered-in-the-air levitated?' I nodded. 'Can you do it now?'

I furrowed my brow and concentrated. I managed to rise half a foot before the effort was too great and I sank back down again. 'I think the power is fading just like with the other Gifts.'

Brochan stared at me with unwavering intensity. 'What were you thinking? When you saw the demon levitate?'

I paused. 'That I'd really like to be able to do that,' I admitted. 'I also suddenly felt dizzy and sick.'

The merman scratched his chin. 'And do you remember what you thought when you learnt the Bull could read auras? Did you feel dizzy then as well?'

'It was the same,' I said slowly. 'I thought it was a cool Gift and I felt a bit sick.' I paused. 'You don't think...'

Taylor jumped to his feet. 'It would be perfect. We thought that you were *learning* Gifts from others but it's more than that. You see something you want and you can take it. You see a Gift you want and somehow you leech it into yourself. That's why the Gifts don't last. That's why the demon lost his. You stole it from him.'

I pursed my lips. 'That doesn't explain the teleportation. I never met another Sidhe who could do that. Not that I know of anyway.'

Taylor snapped his fingers. 'But the genie can teleport.'

My mouth dropped open. 'You're right.' I looked round. 'Where *is* Bob?'

Brochan gave a long-suffering sigh. 'I locked him in your bedroom. I just couldn't listen to him prattle on any longer. And he's still making me sneeze.'

I pushed back my chair and flung open the door. Bob was standing on my dresser, wearing what looked like a long cocktail dress and a pink feather boa. He was turning this way and that, admiring himself in the mirror. 'Bob!' I said sharply.

He froze before slowly moving his head to look at me in comical astonishment. 'Um, hi, Uh Integrity. I was just, um ... never mind.'

'You look beautiful.'

He curtsied. 'You don't. You're covered in some strange icky black stuff.'

'Never mind that now.' The others were crowding round at my back. 'Bob, you remember yonks ago when I made that first wish and you teleported me to the Bull's rooms at the Cruaich?'

'Technically, I didn't do that. The wish did that.'

'Whatever. After that happened, I could teleport. Did you...' I wrinkled my nose. 'Did you feel any different afterwards?'

He twirled the end of the boa in the air. 'You mean did I notice that you'd stolen some of my power from me? Sure. Why do you think I spent so long falling through the air with you when you teleported out of the window? It certainly wasn't through choice.' He shrugged amicably. 'There's no need to worry though. I'm a genie. I have limitless powers which you can only dream of. My teleportation returned quickly enough.'

I folded my arms and stared at him. 'You didn't think to mention this before?' I asked through gritted teeth.

'You didn't ask.' He gave an innocent smile. 'I thought you already knew.'

Brochan growled. 'I'm going to take that damn letter opener you live in and...'

Bob wagged his finger. 'It's a scimitar.'

'Bob,' I said, 'this is important. After I visited the grove, someone attacked me with fireballs. I saw Byron use pyrokinesis. I couldn't do that though even though I tried.'

He tsked. 'Because you didn't want to. You're a natural thief. Your subconscious only takes the Gifts that you want.'

'For a limited time.'

He shrugged. 'Yup. Depends on the Gift though. You took aura reading and it lasted for ages, probably because you made the Bull your slave first so it was easier to draw more of it from him.'

'He's not my slave,' I snapped.

'He kind of is,' Lexie whispered. I glared at her over my shoulder.

'He didn't say anything about losing his Gift.'

'Again,' Bob said with a weary air, 'you didn't ask him. You need to learn the right questions, Uh Integrity.'

'He was probably afraid of showing you how weak he was,' Brochan agreed.

'Or,' Speck added, 'he was shitting his pants that he'd lost it completely and he was terrified of you and what you're capable of.'

'Either way,' I mused, 'no-one else knows I can do this.' My brow furrowed and I looked at Bob. 'Right?'

'Right!' he responded cheerily. 'Now do you mind? I want to try something sparkly.' He gestured at his outfit.

'Fine.' I turned to go.

'Oh, Uh Integrity,' he called out.

'What?'

'I'm really glad you didn't die in the Lowlands. The harp will help.' His tone was both honest and earnest.

I blinked. 'Uh, thanks.'

'You're welcome.' He twirled the boa. 'It's probably a good idea if you don't try to play it before the actual challenge.'

I was instantly suspicious. 'Why not?'

'You'll see.'

'Bob...'

'Trust me, I'm a genie.' He waved at me. 'Now, shoo.'

Taylor, Brochan, Speck, Lexie and I sat down again in the kitchen. For a long time nobody said a word.

'You realise what this means?' Taylor said finally. We all looked at him. 'You have the potential to be the most powerful Sidhe in the country. The most powerful being in the country.'

I shivered. I wasn't sure I liked that idea. 'It's nuts,' I said, shaking my head.

Everyone nodded solemnly. 'It truly is,' Brochan rumbled, scratching at his gills.

I picked a flake of dried Clyde off my arm. 'I should go and get cleaned up,' I said. The shower was calling out to me, like heroin to an addict.

'Sounds good,' Speck said, with perhaps a little too much fervour. I guessed I really did smell bad. 'We should probably try and get this harp cleaned up too. Goodness knows if it'll work after the dip it's taken.'

I grimaced, glancing at the dirty instrument. 'All we can do is try.' Bob's warning not to play the thing niggled at me. I hoped I wasn't going to regret going to so much trouble to retrieve it.

'Tegs,' Taylor said when I was at the door. 'What were the words?'

'Hm?'

'The words you found written in blood inside that house. Next to Matthew MacBain's body. What did they say?'

My reply was quiet. 'Save us.'

# Chapter Six

Despite my vociferous protestations, Lexie sold off some jewellery she'd held back from an old heist and paid for our transportation to the Cruaich. Last time I walked up the long winding driveway, I had to deal with a hundred gawking eyes. This time we still had onlookers but for a different reason. Lexie had hired a horse-drawn carriage and flirted with its owner to persuade him to drape it in the new, improved Adair Clan tartan – the old version shot through with lines of hot pink. It certainly wasn't a tartan for the shy and retiring. I felt a little dismayed for my descendants, should I have any, who would have to endure it for generations to come. I did, however, really, really like it.

Brochan and Taylor sat up front, essentially acting as my guards. It suited me; it meant I could lounge in the back like the Sidhe noble I was supposed to be and, more importantly, stay well away from the horses. If I thought about it long enough, I could still feel the ache in my arse from the journey on horseback to the Foinse last year.

Even Speck was in on the action. He'd rigged up the carriage with some kind of overly boisterous speaker system. As we passed through the magical border and into the land surrounding the Cruaich, it cranked up with 'I Love a Lassie'.

When I threw him a look, he merely shrugged. 'We want to make a grand entrance. There can't be any sneaking in and pretending you're not really here. The bigger the noise, the harder it will be for the other Clans to turf you out.'

He had a point. Although technically speaking I was within my rights as a Sidhe to enter the Games, I wouldn't put it past the Clans to find some way of stopping me from taking part. I had to do whatever was necessary to avoid that. In any case, thanks to the music we had an impressive audience by the time the carriage pulled up outside the Cruaich's entrance.

Aifric Moncrieffe strode out as if he'd been expecting us all along. He beamed happily as I examined his face for signs of dissemblance. He'd fooled me before when I'd believed he was on my side. The Steward, however, was a far better actor than even Taylor. It didn't matter how closely I stared at him, I saw nothing but warmth. I wasn't likely to forget that he'd tried to poison me, though – and killed poor Lily MacQuarrie in the process. She'd known my parents as a child and had only wanted to help me out. Unfortunately it hadn't done her any good in the end.

Lexie muttered a curse under her breath and I squeezed her arm. 'Appearances, remember? We don't want him to think that we suspect him of anything.' She remained tense. 'I mean it, Lex. It could save our lives.' We had to be alert to further attempts on my life; there was no point in asking for more trouble at the same time.

It took the blue-haired pixie some effort but she managed to calm down and relax. I forced my mouth into a dainty smile and waited while Taylor, clad head to toe in a suit made out of the new Adair tartan, came and helped me down.

'Integrity,' Aifric boomed. 'What a pleasure. It's so good of you to come and support the Games.'

I leaned forward, kissing him effusively on both cheeks and looking for all the world as if I'd missed his presence terribly. 'It's lovely to see you again,' I said. Then I raised my voice to make sure no-one missed my words. 'But I'm not here to support the Games.'

Aifric's smile wavered slightly. 'You're not?'

'Goodness no!' Careful, Integrity, I warned myself. That was dangerously close to a simper. I had to be sure not to overdo it. 'I'm here to compete.'

His mouth dropped open before he remembered himself. 'Er, were you invited to participate?'

Ha! He knew very well I wasn't. I looked concerned. 'Oh, I thought that any Sidhe could take part. Isn't that what it says in the rules?'

'Well, yes, I suppose so. It's usually for the honour of your Clan though - and with their full backing. I'm sorry. I'm sure you understand...'

'Of course! Of course! I don't have a Clan. It's just as well really. Knowing what I do about the Adairs, I think it's best that they're consigned to the history books.' They weren't even allowed that; the history books at the Cruaich had virtually wiped out any mention of them. My smile widened and I leaned forward to whisper, 'Can I trust you?'

'To death and beyond, my dear.'

I smiled at him like I'd expected nothing else. 'The thing is,' I told him, 'it's very lonely being Clan-less. I'm the only Sidhe without a clan and my friends are ... well, they're not Sidhe, if you know what I mean. I want to win so that I can ask to be accepted into a Clan as one of their own. Return to the fold, so to speak. The Scrymgeours looked after me before. Maybe I could prevail upon their goodwill and...'

Aifric looked delighted. No surprise there: if I swore fealty to a Clan like the Scrymgeours – hell, if I did that to any Clan – then the Adairs would be laid to rest once and for all. There would be no one left to take up their cause.

'I think that's a wonderful idea. Simply wonderful.'

I managed to blush. Go, girl! 'I probably won't win because I don't have any Gifts like the others. But if I can use this opportunity to get to know everyone better, who knows what might happen?'

'You're so right.' Aifric gazed at me like a proud father. As much as I abhorred violence, my fists itched. 'But it will depend on the other Clans agreeing to your participation. Naturally you have my full support but you'll need two supporters to secure your place. It's a formality for most competitors but we do like our traditions. You'll need their agreement before the opening ceremony if you're going to compete.'

Damn it, that's what I'd been worried about. Aifric was happy to lend me his support because he wanted me to think he was on my side – and right now he didn't see me as a threat. Getting two other Clans to throw their hats in the ring for me would be tough.

'Also,' he continued, 'we didn't expect you, so we've not prepared any quarters. The competitors stay in a specially converted village. We find things work better that way. I'm sure we can find you some space though.'

'You're very kind, my liege,' I murmured.

Aifric laughed heartily. 'Oh, I'm only the Steward. It's nothing like a liege lord, I assure you.' Yeah, yeah. I laughed back; Aifric didn't seem to notice how false it sounded. 'You must be tired after your journey,' he continued. 'Let me arrange for some refreshments while someone sorts out your accommodation.'

I dipped a curtsey. The light in his eyes still glimmered. Good; Aifric Moncrieffe thought I'd fallen hook, line and sinker for his lies. All I had to do to succeed was keep it that way.

*

Six hours later, we still hadn't been shown to our rooms. The plates of food and goblets of wine, water and some indefinable liquid lay untouched in front of us. Even Brochan's patience was being tested. For the last hour he'd been pacing up and down the flagstones, his arms crossed and his glower dangerous. Speck was glued to his phone. Lexie, Taylor and I were taking a different approach: every time someone passed by, no matter who they we were, we did our best to charm them into conversation. Operation Smarm was well under way.

Despite not having an ounce of Sidhe blood, Lexie did a sterling job of flirting with the older nobles. It was difficult for anyone to resist her impish smile and I saw more than one flushed cheek when she inadvertently brushed her body against her targets. Taylor was almost her equal; he oozed charm, gently complimenting the ladies without appearing overly familiar and using his down-to-earth attitude to remain unthreatening to the men.

It was markedly different for me. Every time I tried to engage someone in conversation, they shied away. More than one of them clutched their jewels, their bags or their pockets, as if I were going to spirit away their wealth from beneath their noses. It didn't matter how I approached each Clanling, nothing worked. I'd never been as skilled at verbal dexterity as Taylor but I'd been pulling street cons before I hit puberty. I knew how to talk to people – and these people were having none of it.

The various non-Sidhe flitting around would probably have been friendlier - I spotted a few warm glances from the servants and errand boys - but they were in a rush and it wasn't their approval I needed. Winning the Games would be one thing; I'd still need some Sidhe on my side to have any real measure of success afterwards –and I still needed to secure two votes to let me participate.

Despite the cold shoulders, I persisted. Sooner or later, someone would soften up.

'I never took you for a social butterfly,' drawled a familiar voice as my attempt to get close to a Clan Orrock woman failed miserably and she all but sprinted away.

I turned. 'You can't really be sociable when people act as if you've got the plague.'

Byron shrugged languidly. 'They'll come around.'

'You mean when they realise I've not nicked their family heirlooms? Someone's obviously been telling tales.'

His look of discomfort was answer enough. 'There have been ... stories,' he admitted. 'What happened with the Foinse doesn't help.'

'What do you mean?'

'No-one's seen it. It's the source of all magic, Integrity. You were the last person to hold it and you possess a clever sleight of hand.'

'You think I palmed it when no-one was looking? You saw the damn thing fly away just like I did, Byron.'

'I know,' he replied equably. 'But people don't trust you.'

'Gee,' I said sarcastically, 'blow me down with a feather. I never realised.'

'You *are* a thief, Integrity.'

'Reformed.' Sort of. 'Besides, I've never stolen from any of the Clans.' Actually, that was a lie; I'd spotted at least one noble who I'd relieved of a rather ugly-looking emerald ring. But that was years earlier and he'd have no reason to suspect me of the crime.

Byron tilted his head and gave me a long look. 'You stole from me.'

'That's where you're wrong. I stole from Jamie.' I smirked. 'Call it foreplay, if you will.' Byron's eyes suddenly darkened. 'And I returned your silly jewel.' I said, referring to the stunning Lia Saifire.

A muscle jerked in his cheek. 'Are you expecting my gratitude?'

'No.' I nibbled on my bottom lip. 'Why didn't you tell your father that I was going to compete in the Games?'

'I had no idea you were going to do such a thing.'

'Yes, you did.' I eyed him speculatively. 'In fact, I think you told me about the Games because you wanted me to compete. Were you missing me?'

His face took on a look of mock sorrow. 'Yes. I couldn't sleep at night without knowing where you were. Food tasted like ash in my mouth. I couldn't find joy in anything. When the sun shone, it was as if the very heavens were laughing at me.'

'Yeah? And when was the last time the sun shone?'

Byron grinned suddenly with such a flash of pure enjoyment that I wished I'd done more to see it earlier. 'Probably October.'

I smiled back. 'Holding these Games in February seems a deliberate action to freeze my tits off.'

I thought maybe I'd been too crude and wished I could back take the words but Byron responded with his own spark. He leaned forward and whispered in my ear, 'My balls are blue. I can't imagine what they'll be like tomorrow when I have to wear a kilt.' He winked and my mouth went dry. I didn't normally have fantasies about those particular body parts but I had a very vivid image now. 'Nice tartan, by the way. I'm guessing the hot pink is your personal addition?'

Before I could answer, I spotted Tipsania in the doorway. Her eyes landed on us and she wasted no time in making her way towards us. 'Your girlfriend's here,' I murmured. I gave her my most professional smile.

She sniffed and stopped inches from us. 'Integrity.'

I tried not to look surprised that she'd remembered my name.

'That tartan wouldn't look out of place in a mock Highland stripper show in Vegas.' She bared her teeth. 'You know, in one of those smaller venues where a shot of vodka costs about a dollar. A real ... classy joint.'

'I wouldn't know,' I returned coolly. 'I've never been to one.'

'Haven't you?' She moved alongside Byron and hooked her arm through his, laying claim to her man and marking her territory. I was surprised she didn't hike up her skirts, squat down and urinate on his shoe. 'We went last year, didn't we, By? It was just the two of us. It's more romantic than you'd think.' She giggled. 'There was a wedding chapel I really liked. You weren't so keen, were you, Byron?' She glanced at me. 'I think he'd rather have a large traditional ceremony.'

I raised my eyebrows. 'You're engaged?'

Tipsania preened. 'Not yet.' She cast a sidelong look at Byron. 'But who knows what might happen when the Games are over?'

Byron cleared his throat; he was obviously uncomfortable and I had a sudden flash of insight. He was going to compete and if he won, he'd ask for a monetary reward to help bring his Clan out of their dire financial straits. If he lost, he'd probably end up having to wed good old Tipsy. The Scyrmgeours were loaded. I felt a flicker of unexpected sympathy for her. It didn't last.

'You don't really think that you can win the Games, do you?' she asked me. 'It'll be so embarrassing when you come last. And you do understand the terms of participation? That each participating – and losing - Clan has to help provide the prize for the winner. That'll be rather difficult for you when you have no Clan.' She pasted on an expression of mock concern. 'You don't want to find yourself heavily in debt for the next twenty years.' She touched my arm. 'I'm just thinking of you.'

'Your kindness knows no bounds,' I managed through clenched teeth. 'But my mind is made up.' And then, because I could think of nothing better than seeing the expression on her face when I outdid her in every single challenge, I asked, 'And you? Will you be competing?'

She tittered. 'Of course. But we all know who's going to win.'

'Do we?'

Her grip on Byron tightened. 'Of course. He's the most powerful Sidhe we've seen in decades, aren't you, darling?'

'It takes more than brute strength to win the Games,' he said, his eyes on me. His focus – especially while Tipsania was hanging off him like a limpet – was making me uncomfortable.

'May the best Sidhe win,' I murmured. 'I'll look forward to holding the same title my father did.'

Tipsania was taken aback that I'd chosen to invoke my father's ghost but Byron smiled.

Seeking the fastest route out of the conversation, I searched for anyone who might provide an escape route. Brochan gave me a meaningful glance – he was ready to step in if necessary – but I'd spotted someone else.

'Chieftain MacBain!' I called.

The woman, draped in her Clan tartan and holding herself stiffly upright as she swept through the hallway with numerous Sidhe trotting behind her, turned at the sound of her name. When she saw me, she blanched.

I wasn't going to let her get away. 'Excuse me,' I said to Tipsania and Byron and darted away before the Chieftain could make a run for it.

'I was hoping we might get a chance to catch up,' I said, sweeping a wholly unnecessary curtsey.

She looked down her nose. 'How nice but I'm in an incredible hurry.' She tried to push past me but I held my ground, ignoring the vicious looks I was receiving from her hangers-on.

'I have something you might be interested in,' I told her.

She sniffed. 'I doubt that.'

'When did Matthew MacBain go missing?'

Her body stilled. 'Pardon?'

You heard me, you old bint. 'Matthew MacBain,' I repeated. 'One of your ancestors. When did he disappear?'

She looked speculative. 'A long time before you were born.'

'Do you know what happened to him?'

I could see that she desperately wanted to get away from me but curiosity was getting the better of her. 'There are ... stories,' she said stiffly.

'He went to the Veil, right? Passed into the Lowlands?'

She had a good poker face but she couldn't control the faint flush around her neck. It drew attention to the ugly silver and pearl necklace which hung there. There was no accounting for taste.

'How did you know that?'

I looked round. There were too many people eavesdropping on our conversation. 'Perhaps we can meet in private later,' I said. 'I really do think I can shed some light on what happened to him.'

She stared at me. She had dark hair shot through with threads of grey which was pulled back tightly in an elaborate bun. Her mouth was pursed and tight. I had the impression that this was someone who wouldn't suffer fools gladly. All the same, I'd piqued her interest.

'Very well,' she said finally. 'I am otherwise engaged tonight but after tomorrow's opening ceremony, I will grant you an audience.'

The MacBain leader had delusions of grandeur – grant me an audience indeed. Out of the corner of my eye, I spotted Taylor shake his head at me. He was right. She might well prove to be my ticket in. 'How about before the ceremony?' I hedged.

Chieftain MacBain's eyes turned cold at my presumptuousness. I thought she'd deny me but she wanted to know what information I had. In fact, I'd say she was desperate. 'Was Matthew your grandfather?' I asked, before she could answer.

'Uncle,' she said shortly. She glared at me for a moment as if it were my fault he was no longer with us. 'Very well. My quarters at 11 a.m.' Then, in case I tried to change the time again, she marched away.

I watched her go. If I played this correctly, I'd have her vote to get me into the Games. Perfect. I looked at Tipsania and Byron who were both still watching me. 'Tipsy,' I called out cheerfully, 'where is your father right now? I'd love to catch up with him.'

She turned away, pretending not to hear me.

'He's at the main tent out the front,' Byron told me. There was a question in his eyes: why would I seek out the Bull when I'd run away from his so-called guardianship when I was a child? There was clearly no love lost between us. But Byron didn't know everything.

I called my thanks and beckoned to my posse. 'I need you to stay here. Sooner or later someone will show us where we can sleep. They won't want to lose face by having us bed down here.'

'They should have taken us there the moment we arrived,' Brochan growled.

'Let them play their petty games,' I said. 'We'll keep our big guns for the important stuff.'

Lexie fiddled with her hair. 'I've been trying to get the Sidhe on-side. They're all being very friendly but as soon as I mention your name...'

'I know. Someone's been spreading nasty rumours about me.' I shrugged. 'It's no big deal. Much as it galls me to accept it, Aifric has promised to give me his support and if I go and talk to the Bull now, I can force him to do it too. It looks like Chieftain MacBain might just be our third supporter.'

Taylor's chest puffed out. 'That's my girl.'

I grinned.

# Chapter Seven

Byron was correct: the moment I stepped into the vast tent designed to keep the Games' attendees pampered and refreshed, I spotted the Bull leaning heavily against the bar. At least it was still early, so the tent was virtually empty. No doubt it would be a different scenario tomorrow when the Games began.

Weaving my way through the empty tables and chairs – and avoiding the harassed-looking servants of every ethnicity and race who were under pressure to make everything ready – I made a bee-line for him. I didn't think he had registered my approach but he didn't look surprised when I made my presence known.

'Chieftain Scrymgeour,' I said, with a hint of amusement. 'Buy me a drink?'

The sour turn to his mouth proved how unhappy he was to see me but he couldn't refuse. In order to save his life, he'd given me his true name and now he was mine. He couldn't say no to me – no matter what I asked of him. He did, however, have some wiggle room.

'I'll have a Buckie Delight for the lady,' he said, crooking a finger at the barman.

'Water will...'

He held up a palm. 'No. I think you'll enjoy this.' I could tell from his tone that a Buckie Delight was probably the most disgusting drink known to man. I shrugged. I could make him order me something else or brazen it out; for some stupid reason, I chose the latter.

While the barman turned away to make my drink, I focused on the Bull. If anything, he looked heavier than the last time we'd met. For someone with his wealth and position, he didn't lead the healthiest of lifestyles.

'You should take better care of yourself,' I told him. 'You look like Jabba the Hutt with a bad case of stomach flu.'

'Who?'

I sighed. The least I could have done was find myself an unwilling slave who knew something about popular science fiction. 'Never mind.' I propped an elbow onto the bar and rested my chin on my hand. 'How's your Gift doing these days?' I asked.

Suddenly his face was wide and fearful. 'I don't want to talk about it,' he growled. I'd asked the question though, so he couldn't evade it that easily. 'It is ... diminished,' he said through gritted teeth.

I sucked in a breath. So it was true. My subconscious was stealing Gifts, whether I wanted it to or not. I absorbed the information, my mind whirring through the possibilities.

Malevolence glittered from his dark eyes. 'It's because you stole my name from me.'

No, it wasn't but he didn't need to know that. 'So it's been like that since our escapade through the air?' I prodded. 'Your Gift lost its power and it's not returned?'

He glared at me. 'No. It's not. I can still see auras but they're weaker than before.'

Interesting. I wished he'd thought to mention that to me before. I could only conclude that I'd unconsciously stolen part of his Gift and, while whatever magical pizzazz it imbued me with had gone from my system, it had not returned to him. The idea that I could strip all those proud Sidhe of their Gifts was exciting. I tried – and failed – not to appear too happy.

He put down his drink. 'What do you want? Are you just here to gloat?'

'No,' I said cheerily. 'I got hold of some anti-gloating cream to stop me doing that.' I paused. 'Although it is very tempting to rub it in.' The Bull stared at me. 'Oh, come on, you have to admit that was at least a little bit funny.'

The barman placed a long glass with a thick purple liquid inside it. I gazed at the glass then pushed it towards the Bull. 'Drink,' I ordered.

'Don't you trust it?' he sneered.

'No, funnily enough I don't.'

He rolled his eyes and took the glass, took one large gulp and licked his lips. Then he placed it back down and slid it towards me. Without thinking I picked it up and took a sip, then choked and spluttered as it hit my tongue. I pulled away from the bar and doubled over. I was pretty sure my liver screamed.

The Bull smiled for the first time. 'But that's funny.'

I wiped my mouth. 'What is in that thing? It's strong enough to fell a damn troll.'

'The Wild Men like it.'

'That's hardly a ringing endorsement,' I grunted, eyeing the glass as if it were about to leap out and attack me.

'It's Buckfast, tequila and beer. You have to use the right beer though or it just tastes rotten.'

'Really.' I wiped my mouth once more. Buckfast was a fortified wine brewed in England which had gained a loyal following up here. It tasted like cough syrup and packed a punch powerful enough to make even Brochan dance on tables. Lexie would probably love it.

'So,' the Bull said, 'what do you really want? I don't imagine you're really concerned about my health.'

'You're right. I need you to sponsor me as a competitor for the Games. I need three Clan Chieftains to okay my entry.'

He threw back his head and laughed, a ringing guffaw that made even the bustling servants stop and stare. 'You? You're entering the Games?'

I put my hands on my hips. 'What of it?'

He laughed again. 'You'll be eaten alive. There's a reason only Sidhe are allowed to compete. It's too difficult for anyone else.'

'Hello? In case you've forgotten, I'm as Sidhe as you are.'

His lip curled. 'In name only. You've not been brought up like everyone else. You don't really know what it means to be like us.'

I narrowed my eyes. 'You were my guardian,' I pointed out. 'Any gaps in my knowledge are your fault.'

'I didn't bring you up. I gave you a roof and nothing more.'

I drew myself up. 'You gave me a shitty childhood, a servant's apron and regular beatings.'

'I didn't lay a hand on you.'

'No,' I shot back, my anger growing. 'You couldn't even take that responsibility, could you? You got others to do that part.'

'Your father was a homicidal maniac. The apple doesn't fall far from the tree.'

'My father won the last Games,' I spat. 'And you'd better watch yourself, Cul-Chain,' I added, using his true name.

The Bull froze before darting a nervous look around him in case anyone had heard. He was fortunate that the barman was engaged in conversation at the other end of the bar and no one else was nearby. With slightly less vigour than before, he spoke again. 'Even with your Gift, you'll be no match for the others.'

He still thought all I could do was teleportation. Fool. 'All the same.' My voice hardened. 'You will openly support me in this.'

'You might have my vote,' he sneered, 'but you won't get anyone else's.'

'Aifric has already given me his support.' At least the Steward had done it publicly so he couldn't withdraw it, no matter how much he might want to.

'That's still not enough.'

I leaned in towards him, enjoying his flinch. 'Watch this space.'

*

By the time I got back to the main hall, my smile had returned. I wasn't going to let the Bull keep me on edge and in a foul mood. Unfortunately, the expression on Brochan's face suggested something far, far different.

'What's wrong?' I asked.

His brow had settled into deep, lined furrows, the creases displaying an even darker shade of green than I was used to. 'The Steward,' he said, refusing to use Aifric's actual name, 'has finally deigned to show us where we'll be staying.'

'Ah. I guess it's not up to your standards.'

He glowered further. 'It's not up to the standards of a bedevilled newt. You are a Chieftain in all but name. To expect you to stay somewhere like that is an affront.'

I was touched that he was so angry on my behalf. Truth be told, as long as there was a bed and a lack of rats – which was pretty much a given at this time of year as it was far too cold for even their furry hides – I didn't much care. 'We'll manage,' I told him. 'It's not going to be for long.'

His irritation didn't subside. 'Wait until you see it,' he said.

He led me through a side door and down a winding path. The competitors' village looked rather pleasant with twinkly lights which were just coming on as dusk settled. The path was lined with trees and free from frost. Someone had been using pyrokinesis to make sure no one slipped and broke their ankle before the Games began. I wondered idly if it was Byron and then pushed the thought away.

There was a hubbub of noise from the largest of the buildings. The different Clans might be in competition with each other but there was obviously a sense of camaraderie. It would probably disappear once the competition began – and I doubted that this fellowship would be extended to me. Nonetheless, the laughter was pleasant to hear; usually the Clans were at each other's throats, vying for a foothold in their invisible hierarchy and forming and breaking alliances here, there and everywhere. The Games happened so infrequently that maybe this was an opportunity to put aside petty expressions of one-upmanship, even if only for a night or two.

Brochan marched ahead, his clunky shoes that were designed to hide his huge webbed feet slapping against the ground. We passed building after building until most of the lights were behind us and I felt my first trickle of foreboding. Aifric was certainly making sure we were well out of the way – and that could only be for a reason.

It was another five minutes before we reached the small cabin. There was a glimmer of light from inside and I could see that the exterior was flimsy. The last time I was at the Cruaich, when I'd agreed to help save the Foinse, I'd been granted luxurious rooms. Part of me preferred this set-up – it was more honest.

Brochan rapped four times on the door, a staccato beat which we'd used for years as a code to indicate safety, and then entered with me on his heels. That was when I realised just how bad things were.

The light was cast by candles dotted around on the floor at strategic points although they still only gave off a weak glow. There were four scabby-looking sleeping bags – annoying considering there were five of us – and I could swear it was colder inside than it was out. My gaze swept round, taking in the glum faces. Speck's teeth were chattering.

'Wow. Where's the en suite?' I asked.

'For our ablutions,' Speck said, his words vibrating, 'we are expected to walk for another ten minutes down that way to an ancient stone house with an outside loo.'

Charming. 'Well,' I said, trying to make light of the situation, 'I'm sure things could be worse.'

Taylor's shoulders slumped. 'You had to say it, didn't you?'

Lexie shook her head and shivered. 'Now you've done it, Tegs.'

I pointed at Speck. 'He's meant to be the superstitious one. Don't be silly.'

Just then, a loud patter came from the corrugated iron roof. Rain: and it took Mother Nature all of five seconds to find a suitable gap. One drop landed directly on the bridge of my nose and rolled down, hanging off the end until I shook it away.

'That's your fault,' Lexie said, barely audible above the racket.

'What they're failing to say,' Brochan rumbled, 'is how dangerous this is.' He gestured at the door. 'No lock. Even if there was one, the walls are so flimsy that anyone could break them down. We can't afford to take chances like this. It's not safe.'

The merman had a point. Between us, we could probably make the place more comfortable but making it secure from potential assassins was another matter entirely.

'A Sidhe, a pixie, a warlock, a human and a merman all walked into a hut,' I began.

Speck groaned.

'Don't forget a genie,' Taylor said, with raised eyebrows.

I grinned at him and snapped my fingers. 'You're right.' I took out Bob's letter opener as Brochan hurriedly sought a handkerchief in preparation. 'Oh, Bob?' I sang out, in my best casual tone. 'Are you there?'

There was a pause. That was good, it meant he'd not been paying attention to the outside world. I called again and the blade shimmered. We covered our eyes just in time to avoid being blinded by the flash of light as he appeared. 'What is it, Uh Integrity?' he asked eagerly. 'Do you want to use up that wish? Make it a good one, darling!'

Brochan sneezed violently as I shook my head. 'The Games haven't started yet. I promised I'd do it afterwards, remember?'

Bob's shoulders slumped. 'Oh yeah. What is it then?'

'I don't want to drag you away from whatever TV box set you're currently enjoying but we thought this would be a great time to have a pre-Games party. Just us as a team.' I gave him my best smile. 'And you're part of that team, Bobster!'

A slow smile spread across his tiny face. 'Am I? Am I really?' He bit his bottom lip and held his hands up to his chest. 'That means so much. Usually I'm left out of things like that. People forget that I'm a person and that I have needs too. I'm a social animal really. But it's *soooo* hard to socialise when you're stuck inside a scimitar all day long. And when you're the size of a sparrow.' He bobbed his head from side to side. 'You lot are considerably below my normal standard and it's difficult for my superior intellect to maintain polite conversation when your brain capacities are so small but I can cope for now. Where are the jelly shots? Do we have strawberry?'

I smiled as he looked around. The further his head swivelled, the more his jaw dropped. 'Uh Integrity,' he whispered. 'Where are we? Is this hell?'

I laughed. 'Don't be so silly! We're at the Cruaich. We decided we'd bond together before the opening ceremony tomorrow and stay here instead of somewhere nicer. You know,' I told him with a conspiratorial wink, 'sleeping on the floor is very good for your back.'

Another drop of rain slid from the roof and splattered down next to him. He leapt out of the way with a shriek. 'No! I will not do it! You cannot make me stay here!'

I shook my head in dismay. 'Bob, what on earth is wrong? This place is great. Rustic living is so fashionable these days.'

Brochan sneezed again. Bob drew himself up and pointed in his direction. 'Even the merman is feeling the cold.'

'His sneezing has nothing to do with that and you know it.'

Lexie got in on the action. 'Yeah,' she agreed, although her lips were twitching. 'Brochan loves this place. Being close to nature like this makes you feel as if you're at one with the planet. I thought we might do some yoga later on and then some early morning mediation before the sun rises.'

Bob's face screwed up like a squashed tomato. 'No!'

'Does it matter, Bob?' Speck asked, shrugging. 'You've got your letter op— I mean, scimitar to hang out in. If you don't like communing with the earth, you can stay there.'

The genie jabbed his thumb at Speck. 'But I'll still know what is out here. I'm almost two thousand years old!' he howled. 'I deserve better than this!'

'Well,' I said, 'we're staying. If you want to leave, that's fine. We can catch up with you after the Games.'

'Oh no.' He shook his head. 'I know what you're doing and I'm not going to let you fool me like that. You can't rid of me that easily, sister!' He glared. 'Don't go anywhere,' he hissed. 'I'll be right back.' And with that, he snapped his fingers and disappeared.

We looked at each other. I felt a little guilty for pulling the wool over Bob's eyes yet again but it wouldn't do any harm to see what solution he came up with. What was the point in having an all-powerful genie if you couldn't manipulate him into giving you what wanted from time to time?

Brochan wiped his nose. 'Should have brought antihistamines,' he grumbled. 'Damn genie.'

'Where do you think he's gone?' Taylor asked.

'Hopefully to magic us up a five-star hotel,' Lexie replied. 'In the Caribbean.'

I gestured around the room. 'And miss out on all this?' She stuck out her tongue. 'We're in Sidhe lands, Lex. If the wind changes...'

Her features quickly smoothed. 'Bloody magical bastards ruining everything.'

There was a crackle and Bob reappeared. He gave a smug smile and waved his arms. 'Mamamamamama,' he chanted.

Brochan frowned. 'What...?'

'Shh.'

The air shimmered as molecules snapped and re-formed. I blinked in astonishment and looked around: everything glinted and gleamed with a rich opulence. Whatever I'd been expecting, it wasn't this.

'I have re-modelled based on what the Sultan of Brunei is currently enjoying in his palace,' Bob announced with considerable flourish.

No wonder there was so much gold. The cabin was the same size but now there were shiny walls and large mirrors, creating the illusion of something far larger. Plush cushions and five red brocade-covered beds took the place of the sleeping bags.

I whistled. 'Pretty impressive, Bob.'

His smile widened. 'I know.'

Brochan was still frowning. He opened the door, stepped outside, look around and then came in again. 'It looks exactly the same as it did on the outside but in here … good work, genie,' he said grudgingly. Then he sneezed again.

'Well,' I said, 'that's the comfort part taken care of. Now we just need to worry about security.'

Bob's eyebrows snapped together. 'Hold on a minute,' he said. 'Are you telling me that…?'

I interrupted him before he could get worked up. 'We should take turns to stay on guard,' I said. 'We need to be prepared for anything.'

'Do you expect Aifric to attack?'

'I think that where he's concerned, we need to expect anything,' I said grimly.

'I'll take the first watch,' Taylor said.

'Great.' I yawned and jumped on the nearest bed, stretched out and closed my eyes. Judging by the last few hours, I was going to need all the rest I could get.

'Good idea,' Lexie said approvingly. 'I think I'll bed down my-self.'

There were murmurs of agreement from Brochan and Speck, followed by faint creaks as they also lay down. Taylor grunted and headed outside to take up position.

'You're all having me on, aren't you?' Bob said gleefully. 'Very funny, guys. Pretending to sleep instead of partying? Hahahahaha!'

There was a loud snore which only Speck could make. I pressed my lips together and tried not to smile.

'It's barely evening!' Bob yelled. 'What about that party? The team-building? The jelly shots?'

Nobody answered.

'Guys?'

Silence.

'I hate you all.'

# Chapter Eight

I slept for a good five hours before doing my stint outside, then returned to bed for a further snooze. When I woke up, Bob was obviously over his sulk because he was curled up next to me in a pair of silk pyjamas and snoring louder than Speck.

I yawned, stretched and got up. Then I frowned; it was already morning but the outside world was remarkably quiet. Something felt wrong.

There were five sudden taps in quick succession on the door, the code for danger. I woke the others, putting my finger to my lips to encourage silence. Bob refused to open his eyes but everyone else was alert within seconds.

I stepped to the door and pressed my ear against it. Lexie was outside on guard duty. 'What's going on?' I said, hoping my voice would travel enough for her to hear.

The door creaked open and she rushed inside, her face pale. 'Something's out there in the woods. Something big.'

Brochan tensed. 'Friend or foe?'

'As far as the Cruaich is concerned,' I grunted, 'everyone is a foe.'

Taylor glanced at me. 'You're the expert here, Tegs. What do we do?'

Some expert. I felt the weight and pressure of their expectation. Drawing a deep breath, I kept my voice low. 'We need to know what we're facing. If it's a Sidhe and they're close by – and I see them using their Gift – then maybe we'll get lucky and I can steal it from them. If that's not the case, we need to know what we're dealing with so we can defend ourselves properly. Lexie, wander back out. Don't look around, just head out the back as if you're ... um...'

'Going for a pee?'

I snapped my fingers. 'Perfect. I'll take the front. The rest of you wait for my signal.'

I propelled Lexie forward without waiting for their agreement. She swallowed, masking her fear with a blank expression as she strolled out. I counted to five in my head and followed.

When I realised Brochan was at my heels, I scowled. 'You're supposed to stay inside!' I hissed.

'Yeah, yeah. If you think I'm going to let that blue-haired cretin face the action out here while I cower inside, you've got another thing coming, Integrity Adair.'

'I bet the other Clan Chieftains don't have this problem,' I grumbled, my eyes scanning the landscape for any sight of the monster that might be about to rush us.

'What problem?' Brochan asked innocently.

I was saved from answering by a flicker of bright green, such an unusual colour for this time of year that it stood out against the dark trees and layer of white frost. Brochan stiffened. I nodded and directed him to the right while I went left. We hugged the walls of the cabin. Whatever it was, it would make a move soon. Lexie had definitely been right about one thing – it was huge.

I might have bowed out of group heists but it wasn't that long since Brochan and I worked together. We both possessed a sort of sixth sense about what the other was going to do, the kind that only develops after years of working closely together. Like symbiotic twins, we glanced at each other and began moving stealthily towards the trees on the other side of the path. I ducked behind a fir, struggling to peer round its bushy foliage; Brochan sensibly concealed himself behind a pine tree so it was easier for him to get a bead on what was ahead. While I shifted and craned my neck to get the best vantage point, out of my peripheral vision I spotted him do a double take. I turned towards him as he held up his hands and sketched a shapely female figure in the air. That didn't make any sense. Then I heard the voice.

'Hello? Candy? Are you there?'

I stiffened. Tipsania. What the hell was she doing here? While her antagonism towards me was no secret, she'd always been open about her hatred and I wouldn't have put it past her to attack me in public. Skulking around in Scottish trees didn't seem like her style. And who the hell was Candy? That name was worrying familiar.

I edged round the fir, adjusting my position so that I could see her and remain hidden. Peering through a gap in the needles, I understood why we'd assumed she was some enormous beast. The dress she was wearing looked like a full-blown ball gown; it was a ridiculous, with a Cinderella-type, meringue-shaped skirt that had to be five feet wide. I liked a pretty dress myself but her get-up wouldn't be any good for covert action. This wasn't about us at all. Something else was going on.

There was a loud wheeze, followed by the crunch of heavy footsteps. Brochan plastered himself against the tree trunk as the unmistakable form of a Wild Man appeared from beyond a dense copse of trees. I suddenly realised where I'd heard the name Candy before: he'd been working for Byron when we first met in Aberdeen. He'd also knocked me unconscious.

Like most of his kind, he was barefoot and built like a rhinoceros. When he spoke, however, his gentle tone completely belied his size. 'Tip?'

Tipsania let out a girlish squeal and ran towards him, ignoring the fact that her skirt was catching on twigs and dead leaves. She flung herself at him while Brochan and I both gaped. Candy grabbed her waist and spun her round, lifting her up so he could kiss her. It was a passionate clinch. She'd been all over Byron yesterday; what on earth was going on?

'I can't stay long,' she breathed, when he finally let her go. 'I'm supposed to be at the competitors' breakfast in twenty minutes.'

My stomach growled. A hot breakfast sounded really good. I shouldn't have been surprised that Aifric – or anyone else – had 'forgotten' to tell me about it. Neither should I have been pissed off because it wasn't like I could eat anything for fear of it being poisoned. The invitation would have been nice though.

'I've missed you. Can't you skip breakfast?'

'Everyone else will be there and my absence would be noted.' She sighed and leaned her head against his chest. Compared to the Wild Man, Tipsania looked tiny, even in that massive wedding cake of a dress.

'It's not too late to back out of the Games,' he rumbled. 'You know the later challenges are going to be dangerous and I don't want you to get hurt.'

'I can look after myself. And you know it's the only way.'

'The chances of you winning...'

'Hush.' She tilted her head up and gazed into his eyes. 'I'm very motivated.'

He breathed in. 'Tipsania Scrymgeour, I love you.'

She smiled, her expression reflecting a softness I hadn't thought she was capable of. 'I love you too, Candy Man.'

They kissed again while I cringed. He started fumbling with her dress, his large fingers surprisingly nimble, as if he was in the mood to shag her right here. I motioned to Brochan. We *really* didn't need to see this. He nodded enthusiastically and we tiptoed back to the cabin. It was just as well it was the merman who ventured out with me; if it had been Taylor or Speck, they'd have wanted to stay and watch.

When we got back inside, Bob was awake and flitting from bed to bed. 'I wanna kiss you,' he sang. 'I wanna fu...'

'Enough.'

He faltered. 'You're no fun, Uh Integrity.' He arched an eyebrow in my direction. 'Is it because you're too cold-hearted to understand the language of *l'amour*?'

I threw him a dirty look. He just grinned.

'The genie's right?' Taylor asked.

I sat down heavily on the nearest bed and nodded. I still couldn't believe it; the Tipsania I knew would never stoop to a dalliance with a non-Sidhe especially when she had Byron, the Steward's son, in her sights. Was this some kind of ruse? Did she know more about the Games than she was supposed to and was she using the Wild Man so she could earn an advantage?

'The look in her eyes,' I mumbled.

Brochan nodded. 'She's head over heels in love. It sounds like she's entering the Games so that if she wins she can ask for the Clans' approval for her relationship with the Wild Man as her prize.'

He was probably right and I felt affronted on Byron's behalf. Sure, I knew he was using her because of his Clan's financial situation but she didn't know that. What if he was also in love with her? She was waltzing around behind his back, canoodling with a Wild Man ... and a Wild Man who worked for Byron, at that.

'Uh Integrity,' Bob piped up. 'Your face has gone a most curious shade of purple.'

There was a sharp knock from the far side of the cabin. 'Lexie is still out there,' I said, glad of the diversion.

'I'll go and get her,' Speck said.

I gave him a tight smile of acknowledgment. Unbelievable. I couldn't even muster an appropriate joke.

*

A couple of hours later, still reeling from the revelation that Tipsania was tiptoeing around behind Byron's back, I met with Chieftain MacBain. She still maintained the taut pout of disapproval but curiosity no longer lingered behind those sharp eyes. I felt a faint trickle of foreboding down my spine which was confirmed when her first words had nothing to do with her missing uncle.

'Was it you?' she demanded. 'Because if there is any evidence that it was, you will be thrown out of here before you can so much as say Clan Adair.'

I blinked. 'Excuse me?'

'You know exactly what I'm talking about.'

I took a step back and folded my arms. 'No,' I said coolly. 'I don't.'

She pointed to her neck. She was dripping in finery in much the same manner as Tipsania. Clearly this opening ceremony called for grander clothes than I possessed.

I shook my head. 'I'm not very good at charades. How many syllables?'

'My necklace,' she sneered. 'I took it off last night before I went to bed. Now it's nowhere to be found - and there's only one thief here, Ms Adair. What have you done with it?'

Actually there were five thieves hanging around the Cruaich but I didn't think she'd appreciate me pointing it out. I immediately wondered if one of the others had taken a midnight jaunt to line their pockets but I knew none of them was daft enough. They wouldn't risk this entire escapade for the sake of some silver and pearls. Nah: forget five thieves – there were at least six.

'I didn't take your necklace,' I told her. And then, because I wanted to be honest, 'I only take pretty things.'

Her mouth twisted angrily. 'You...' She seemed unable to get the words out.

'Bitch?' I shrugged. 'I've been called worse.'

'You're almost as bad as your father,' she spat.

'Really? Because I understand he was really something of a good man.'

'Apart from the time he murdered over a thousand of his own Clan.'

'Did he really, Chieftain MacBain?' I asked. 'Did he really do that?'

She didn't answer. 'Just give it back.'

'I didn't take it.' Understanding was beginning to dawn, however. Apparently Aifric Moncrieffe had decided that killing me at the Cruaich was too dangerous, even for him. Why assassinate someone and leave a bloody mess to clean up when all you have to do is discredit them by stealing a few choice items and letting others point the finger at your victim?

'I don't believe you,' Chieftain MacBain sneered.

'Until you've got proof I took it, your accusation is demeaning,' I told her, using the Sidhes' own warped sense of honour against her. I'd have offered to let her search the cabin if I didn't think that the necklace had probably already been planted there. At least Bob had returned the place to its original squalid state before we left that morning. It paid to be careful; unfortunately, we'd not been careful enough.

The calm demeanour which MacBain had shown yesterday had vanished and turmoil was written all over her face. This necklace must be important to her. She wanted to clap me in irons but, without evidence to back up her claims, she didn't dare.

'Look,' I said patiently. 'I didn't take your necklace and I'm not here because of it.' I dug into my pocket and pulled out Matthew MacBain's signet ring. She didn't give me the chance to show it to her.

'Until you return my necklace, I have nothing to say to you. Get out.'

'But...'

She raised a trembling hand and gestured towards the door. Damn it; obviously she wasn't going to listen to a single thing I had to say. I'd probably have to run back to the cabin to find the damn necklace and dispose of it before she sent out troops to ransack the place. So much for getting her on side for the votes I needed to participate in the Games.

I looked at my watch. If I hurried, I could still check out the cabin.

I ran out of the MacBain suite of rooms, yelling to Taylor, Lexie, Brochan and Speck who were waiting outside with hopeful expressions, and sprinted down the castle stairs, taking them three at a time. Narrowly avoiding crashing into a nervous-looking pixie laden down with a tray of canapés, I ran out of the castle towards the competitors' village, damning the fact that our cabin was located so far away.

I was too late. By the time I reached the cabin, the door was already wide open and there were shouts from within – and two burly Sidhe guys on guard outside. No doubt there would be questions about the amount of food we'd brought with us and I hated the thought of some Cruaich guard rummaging through my underwear. It wasn't the potential discovery of the necklace which worried me the most, though – it was what might happen to Dagda's harp, sitting quietly in the corner.

I stormed over, demanding to be allowed in and to know what right they had to invade our private space, just as Lexie showed up behind me. No doubt the others were close behind.

'What the hell is going on, Tegs?'

'Necklace. Stolen.'

I didn't need to go into detail. Lexie immediately understood and tossed back her blue hair defiantly. 'And they think we took it,' she said flatly.

'Actually, they think I did.'

'One and the same,' she grunted as Brochan arrived. He didn't ask questions – he took one look at the cluster of bodies ransacking the cabin and barrelled forward. 'Get the fuck out!' he yelled.

The guards exchanged glances then moved to intercept him. 'Sir,' one said with undisguised loathing, 'you need to wait outside.'

'No chance,' he snarled. He made to push past them but the second one raised his hand.

'Brochan!' I shouted in warning but it was too late; the guard, whose Gift seemed to involve some kind of electrical lightning strike, had already made his move. Brochan was thrown back, his body rising several feet into the air then landing some distance away with a heavy thump. Sickeningly, his limbs were still twitching.

'You wankers!' Lexie screamed, ready to follow in Brochan's wake. Fortunately Speck appeared and grabbed hold of her. She struggled against him. 'Let me go!'

'You're going to pay for what you've just done,' I said calmly to the guard.

His lip curled as he looked me up and down. 'I'm quaking in my boots,' he sneered. I glared at him with the most hate-filled look I could muster up and his face paled. 'Shit.'

'Yeah,' I told him. 'I might not look much and I might hate violence but that doesn't mean I'm not capable of doing whatever is necessary to protect me and mine, buster.'

'Could someone,' said Byron from behind me, 'explain what's going on here?'

Realisation dawned and I looked at the guard. 'You're afraid of him, not me.' I nodded. 'Right.' Then I shrugged and tried to look fierce. 'You'll learn.'

The guard bowed to Byron while Goon Number One began babbling. 'Integrity Taylor stands accused of theft. Chieftain MacBain's necklace was stolen in the middle of the night while she slept. It's worth thousands of pounds and...'

'Enough.'

Taylor appeared, breathing heavily and with sweat on his brow. He caught sight of Brochan, still lying inert on the ground and ran over. 'Is he...?'

'He's fine,' Speck said, peering over Lexie's shoulder. 'Just a bit winded.'

Just as fucking well. I looked at Byron. 'They have no evidence and no right to barge in to our room and rake through our stuff. We were all here all night. He,' I jabbed my thumb in Goon Two's direction, 'assaulted a member of my entourage for no good reason. I demand reparation.'

Byron, his jaw set, gave me a grim look then strode past the guards and stared into the hut. Whoever was in there had stopped searching when they heard him arrive. 'Out,' he ordered.

He looked round for a long moment before turning back to us. 'Who gave you this cabin?'

'A servant brought us here,' Speck said, loosening his grip on Lexie. She wrenched herself away with a glare that said he was in serious trouble later on and rubbed her wrists.

Byron looked even madder. 'Does my father know this is where you are staying?'

That's pretty much a given, I thought. 'I have no idea,' I said aloud. 'Why? Is something wrong?'

Angry as he was, Byron still had time to look at me suspiciously. I tried to flutter my eyelashes but it probably looked like a fly had flown into my eyeballs. Thankfully, he switched his attention to the wankers who'd just left our cabin.

'Did you find anything?' he demanded. 'Any necklace or stolen property?'

The guards wouldn't meet his eyes. 'Well, there's a harp which looks pretty expensive.'

I balled up my fists. 'If you've damaged it...'

Byron held up his index finger and I quietened. I'd made my point. 'Anything else?'

'No.'

I gave a silent sigh of relief. Was that because they'd not had time to find the necklace? It had to be planted somewhere.

'Get out of here.'

I thought for a moment that Byron was referring to me but I relaxed when I realised he meant the Cruaich guards. 'Yeah,' I added. 'And for your information it's Integrity Taylor Adair. A. D. A. I. R. Adair. Got that?'

'Integrity,' Byron said.

'Yep?'

'You can shut up now.'

'Everyone's a hater,' I mumbled. 'Just because who Adairs wins.'

He didn't smile. I rolled my eyes and stepped up beside him to peek inside. When I saw the harp uncovered but seemingly unharmed, I stood up straighter. Thank goodness for small mercies.

'I apologise,' Byron said stiffly, 'that you were given accommodation like this. You should be in the village with everyone else. I'll arrange for you to be moved there immediately.'

I looked quickly at the others, noting the glint in their eyes. 'It's not so bad here. The peace and quiet is nice and we like rustic living.'

Lexie nodded. 'Communing with earth.'

'At one with nature,' Speck threw in.

Byron frowned but didn't pursue it. 'If you wish.'

I smiled. 'We do. Although if you could install a permanent guard then we can avoid any future misunderstandings of this sort.'

His frown slowly evaporated and he scratched his chin; he knew where I was going with this. 'You understand why you'd be a suspect, Integrity. You *are* a thief.'

I met his eyes. 'I *was* a thief. Maybe you're right and I still am that person but I'm not going to jeopardise my chance to compete in the Games. This wasn't us.' Brochan groaned and sat up, rubbing his forehead. My voice hardened. 'Any of us.'

'I believe you,' Byron said quietly.

I nodded. 'Thank you.' Then, because I could afford to, I widened my smile. 'I don't suppose you could help us clean up?'

He bowed. 'It would be my pleasure. Stand back.'

I raised my eyebrows and did as he requested. He smirked slightly and the green in his eyes deepened. I jumped about an inch into the air as there was a clatter from the cabin.

'Have you ever seen *Mary Poppins*?' Byron asked. 'Or *Fantasia*?'

'It's been a while.'

He leaned in towards me and lowered his voice. 'Then watch this.'

More clatters sounded. As the rest of us gaped, all manner of objects rose up and righted themselves. A pair of off-white Y-fronts floated in the air. Taylor coughed. 'They're mine. Black suitcase.' They danced away and folded themselves neatly inside it.

A teddy bear waved at us. Byron crooked an eyebrow towards me but Speck raised his hand. 'Into the backpack, please.'

The sleeping bags – which were unused, of course – rolled themselves up. The cartons of juice, bottles of water and pot noodles stacked themselves on the counter. A hot pink bra edged with lace dangled in the air.

'I know who this belongs to,' Byron murmured. I swallowed.

'Neat trick,' Speck whispered as everything slotted back into place.

'You're right,' I agreed. 'I wish I...'

Oh shite. I swayed slightly, feeling both dizzy and sick. 'Byron, I didn't mean it.'

He looked at me confused. Brochan got to his feet, albeit rather slowly, and threw me a warning glare. I grimaced and fell quiet, passing my hand across my forehead.

'Lord Byron,' Taylor asked, 'do you feel okay?'

'It's just Byron. And yes, I'm fine.' He was still puzzled but at least his attention was elsewhere. 'Why do you ask?'

'Er ... I just wondered if using your Gift took much energy,' Taylor replied hastily. 'That's all.'

Byron smiled. 'Not unless it's for protracted periods of time. And that rarely happens with telekinesis.' He tapped the side of his nose. 'It was definitely handy when I was a teenager and had to tidy my room in a hurry though.'

We all laughed, although the sound was forced.

Byron checked his watch and swore. 'I have to go. The opening ceremony is starting soon and I promised Tipsy I'd help her with her dress.'

'Go,' I urged, wincing inside with every word. 'You don't want to let her down.'

He leaned towards me again and for a second I thought he was going to kiss me on the cheek. His face hovered near mine and his musky, male scent tickled my nostrils. I stared into the depths of his emerald-green eyes and licked my lips. 'I'm sorry about the false accusations,' he said. 'And the ... sleeping bags.'

'Like I said,' I told him, 'we're fine.'

He grinned, his gold hair flopping over his forehead, then he pulled back leaving me ridiculously disappointed. As I watched, he turned and jogged away.

I covered my eyes with my hand. 'Oh no,' I moaned.

'Did you do it?' Lexie asked. 'Did you steal his Gift?'

My shoulders slumped. 'I'm afraid to check.'

Brochan walked over and held out a leaf. He let it go and it fluttered to the ground. 'Try.'

'How are you feeling, Brochan? That Sidhe hit you with a hell of a wallop...'

'I'm fine. Try to lift the leaf, Tegs.'

I sighed, looked down and concentrated. It didn't take long: three or four heartbeats of focus and the leaf moved upwards.

'Can you levitate at the same time?'

I tried. Sweat popped out across my brow but it was no use. 'I think the levitation has gone.'

'We'll have to experiment with multi-tasking next time,' Taylor said.

I drew in a sharp breath. 'Don't you get it? I just stole from Byron! I told him I wasn't a thief and I wasn't going to steal from anyone and he believed me! And then I did just that! Not only that, but I took his buggering Gift. What if he needs it? What if he notices?' My shoulders slumped. 'This is shite.'

'You didn't mean to take it,' Lexie pointed out.

'And,' Speck added, 'it's a pretty cool Gift.'

Lexie glared at him. 'I'm still not done with you yet.'

He threw up his arms. 'That's not fair! I saved you from being zapped like Brochan.'

'At least I was trying to help Brochan, you geeky warlock. What were you doing?'

The merman interrupted them both. 'Stop it. Aren't we forgetting something? If that necklace isn't in here, where is it and who took it?'

There was a rustle of leaves from across the path and the Wild Man appeared. Seeing our shocked faces, he grinned. 'Really? Did you *really* think I wouldn't notice you spying on me this morning?'

Uh oh. I tried to stay calm. 'Why didn't you say anything at the time?'

He gave an amiable shrug. 'Tip would only get flustered. It's easier this way.' He reached into a pocket and pulled out Chieftain MacBain's silver and pearl necklace.

'Where did you get that from?' I asked.

The Wild Man jerked his head towards the cabin. 'In there. In a backpack.'

'I didn't steal it!' Speck babbled. 'I promise! Sir...'

The Wild Man continued to smile. 'Call me Candy.' He nodded at me. 'Nice to see you again.'

Speck drew back. 'Tegs? You know this monster - I mean, Wild Man?' He dropped his chin. 'Fuck. Sorry.'

Candy didn't appear to have taken offence. Considering his size, that could only be a good thing. He raised the necklace a little higher. 'One of the Moncrieffe servants dropped by earlier and left it for you as a little present.'

Taylor lunged for it but the Wild Man was too quick and held it out of reach. 'I'll hold it for safekeeping. I won't tell anyone about it if you keep your mouths shut about me and Tip. Say anything, though, and it might end up back in one of your bags.' His smile widened. 'And we know what that will mean.'

I let out the breath I'd been holding. 'We can do that. We can keep a secret.'

'You can't tell anyone,' Candy warned. 'Not even your own mothers.'

My mother was long gone. 'No problem.'

'Tegs, are you sure we can trust him?' Lexie eyed him with an expression that suggested she'd have no qualms about hitting him over the head with her handbag and then chopping him up into tiny pieces to dispose of the evidence.

I looked at Candy. He'd certainly been gentlemanly towards me before and I reckoned he was alright. 'Yes.' Anyway, what choice did we have?

The Wild Man gave a happy nod. 'Excellent.' He turned and lumbered away.

'Tegs,' Taylor whispered, as the Candy vanished. 'Do you think he heard us talking about you stealing Byron's Gift?'

'I have no idea.' I shook my head. 'What a freaking mess.'

'If it was a Moncrieffe servant who planted the necklace, does that mean your Byron is a double agent?'

'Fucked if I know,' I muttered. 'But it definitely makes me more shaken than stirred. Come on. We need to get to that ceremony.'

'What about Chieftain MacBain?'

I sighed. 'I think we might be too late. Let's go and get ourselves thrown out of the Games. At least the masses will be entertained.'

# Chapter Nine

The opening ceremony was taking place at an open field near the main tent where I'd found the Bull the previous day. The field was surrounded by a grandstand and the sounds of the thronging crowds proved what a big deal these Games were. Considering the prize, it wasn't surprising they were held so infrequently but it was a shame this seemed to be the only time that Clan differences were set aside. Then I spotted a Fairlie Sidhe being deliberately jostled by a small group of Dundas Clanlings. Whatever camaraderie existed yesterday had already vanished; the serious business of winning was in the air.

The competitors were crowded into a small area, waiting for their grand entrance to the showground and making a great show of admiring each other's costumes. As I walked up with my team behind me, there were nudges and hushed whispers. Obviously the news about my 'crime' had spread quickly and I wondered if news of my exoneration had been transmitted with the same speed. Judging by the dirty looks, it didn't appear so.

I glanced down at my jeans and warm jumper, wishing I'd had time to change into something more appropriate. I might not have a gown to match Tipsania's but I looked like I'd not made any effort at all. Not everyone was wearing evening wear, of course; I spotted all-in-one jumpsuits made of Clan tartans, traditional kilts and even a top hat and tails.

I couldn't stop my eyes drifting towards Byron, who was lingering at the front of the crowd with Tipsania. Thanks to her massive skirts, there was quite a gap around them. He looked damn good in his kilt.

He didn't even glance in my direction. I wondered whether he was too embarrassed to claim a friendship – of sorts – with a dirty rotten thief like me. The thought stung more than I would have liked.

Fortunately, Lexie had a scarf in the new Adair tartan which she pulled off her shoulders and looped round my neck. It was better than nothing. I untied my hair, shaking it out and letting it fall down my back. Yes, it was white, just like my father's had been; I wasn't going to hide my heritage.

'That's it,' Taylor nodded. 'Don't let these bastards make you feel anything less than you are.'

'Was I being that obvious?'

He squeezed my arm. 'I know you pretty well.'

I tried to smile as an elderly Sidhe official in Carnegie colours cleared his throat and began to speak. 'Competitors will enter with their individual Clans, parade past the grandstand and halt in front of the royal box where their participation will be verified. Remember, it takes three Clans to validate entry.'

I felt sure he was saying that for my benefit. It didn't help that several of the other competitors turned in my direction, mocking amusement glinting in their eyes.

'Clans will enter not in alphabetical order, as was previously stated, but in order of importance.'

I shared a look of disgust with Taylor. Since I'd taken on the Adair name, I'd moved to the top of the pack as far as ABC was concerned but this wasn't Sesame Street. I had no doubt that despite the tradition attached to the Adairs, and the fact that my blood had been keyed into the Foinse as the sole member of one of the older, supposedly important Clans, I'd be in last place. I shrugged. If nothing else, I'd give this lot something to remember.

Brochan eyed me. 'You're planning something,' he accused.

My mouth twitched. 'When they throw me out for not being good enough or strong enough or whatever enough, I want to make sure they all realise what a mistake they're making.'

'Tegs...'

I grinned, although there wasn't much humour in it. 'My new trick is telekinesis. Let them see what I can do when I choose to use it.'

'Is that a good idea?'

'The witch in *Sleeping Beauty* is always painted as the villain,' I murmured. 'But she was left out in the cold. Depending on which version you read, her invitation was either forgotten or she was deliberately left off the list. She took her revenge - and then some. I'm not going to curse any Sidhe damsels but I'm not going to let them humiliate me without saying something about it.'

'Tegs,' Speck said, looking troubled, 'the witch in *Sleeping Beauty* was vanquished.'

'Well,' I growled, 'it's good that we're not living in a fairy tale.'

Unsurprisingly, the Moncrieffes were called first. There were five of them in total: Byron, Jamie and three others whom I vaguely recognised. Unsurprisingly, neither Maggie nor Roy made an appearance; their attempt to practise in the mountains, which Byron had so admired, had put paid to that. The crowd of competitors fell silent as music sounded.

'It's the Moncrieffe anthem,' Taylor murmured.

'It's bloody awful is what it is,' I replied. I was having a hard time discerning a tune. It was a screeching wail, played on bagpipes to make it sound even worse. 'I don't suppose they'll have the Adair anthem to hand.'

'It's disallowed.'

I grunted. Big surprise.

Speck smirked. 'Don't worry, Tegs. I've got it covered.'

I shot him a grateful look. Screw the Sidhe. I didn't need them when I had this lot by my side.

The last notes faded away and an imperious voice sounded over a microphone. I recognised it immediately; it belonged to the Carnegie lordling whom I'd seen on the ship where Debbie the Spider was being held. Knowing who he was - and what a prick he was - would it make it easier to sneer in his face when he ejected me.

'Clan Moncrieffe. Who will stand for you?'

'Clan Scrymgeour,' boomed the Bull.

'Clan Calder,' added another voice.

'Clan Orrock.'

'Clan Moncrieffe has the requisite three votes and is permitted to compete.'

My fingers jerked and I bunched my hands into fists to avoid giving a slow, sarcastic round of applause.

'Scrymgeour,' the official grunted. 'You're next.'

I folded my arms. No doubt that was because of Tipsania's relationship with Byron. I tried to keep the sour grimace off my face as she trooped out with four others from her Clan. The same pattern was followed: loud, tuneless music, the voices of three other Clans stating their support, and then acceptance into the Games. I plonked myself down, sitting cross-legged on the ground. If this was going to take a while then I was going to conserve my energy.

The others joined me as the Kincaids were called. 'Tell us a joke, Tegs,' Speck urged.

I raised my eyebrows. 'I thought you all hated my jokes.'

'We do,' he responded cheerfully.

I smiled. 'What do you call a faerie who hasn't taken a bath?'

'I don't know, Tegs,' Lexie said in a loud voice, ensuring that as many of the other competitors as possible heard her. 'What *do* you call a faerie that hasn't taken a bath?'

'Stinkerbell.'

She collapsed in laughter and Speck and Taylor followed her lead. Even Brochan managed a guffaw. They might be faking their amusement but the irritated glances we received from those around us were well worth it.

One by one the Clans were called and each was quickly granted entrance to the Games. It seemed like a long wait but suddenly we were the only people remaining and I had to stride out there alone because my friends weren't Sidhe and couldn't participate. It suddenly felt like the last hour had flown by.

There was a final bellowing roar from the crowd as the MacQuarries passed muster. Taylor straightened. 'You'd better go.' He threw me a look. 'We'll be watching, Tegs. You're not on your own in this.'

I smiled at him but we all knew that when it came to rejection – especially rejection on such a wholescale level – you were always on your own. It was always personal. I stood up and dusted myself off.

'How do I look?' I asked.

'Gorgeous.' Lexie paused. 'Apart from that big smudge of dirt on your cheek.'

I lifted my hand to my face and started rubbing. 'What smudge?' Lexie had already turned her back. 'Wait!' I yelled. 'Is it still there?'

She didn't answer. I wetted the edge of my cuff with saliva and rubbed some more. It was one thing to be a genuine orphan returning to the Sidhe fold, but the last thing I wanted to look like was a grubby urchin. Bugger it.

The Carnegie official peered at me. 'It is time,' he said with a sniff.

'Do I have mud on my face?' I asked.

He looked away just as the opening to 'We Are the Champions' started up. I closed my eyes. Speck. Of all the bloody songs to choose...

The official appeared even more unimpressed. I wasn't surprised. While the Sidhe tended towards obvious and unpleasant side of arrogance, that wasn't what I'd been aiming for. Then again, I supposed it didn't really matter.

I walked past him and into the tunnel that led out to the grounds. Was it my imagination or was the crowd considerably more subdued now?

Light flashed, making me falter. 'Bob!' I complained. 'This really isn't the time.'

'It's the perfect time,' he purred. 'If they're not going to let you compete, this is exactly when you should make that wish. You could wish for every Sidhe to have their head on backwards. I had a client once who did that at a concert. It went down a treat.'

'Would you piss off?'

'Of course,' he continued blithely as I continued towards the light at the end of the tunnel – and the metaphorical darkness of pariah land, 'if that doesn't take your fancy, you could wish for their children to be struck down by madness. Or give them bubonic plague.'

'Jeez, Bob. I had no idea you were so bloodthirsty.'

'Come on, Uh Integrity. Wishes were made for revenge.'

'I'm not here for revenge,' I said. As soon as I said it, I realised it was true. I'd toyed with the idea of it before but really I just wanted answers – and I didn't need to compete in the Games for those. I could find another way. 'Thanks,' I grinned as the tunnel gave way to the field. 'I needed that.'

'What did I do?' Bob asked, his voice growing muffled as he wriggled into the folds of my scarf to hide.

I didn't answer. Instead I held up my hand and waved enthusiastically as the grandstand blurred into a mass of colours and shapes. At least a few people cheered and some more clapped; thank goodness non-Sidhe were permitted in the audience.

I flipped my hair and tilted up my chin. As long as I didn't trip, I could do this. I could do anything. Growth mind-set. Easy-peasy.

An official beckoned me towards the royal box. I stopped, eyeing Aifric and the twenty-three other Chieftains who were sitting there. Come on, I thought, do your worst.

'Clan...' There was a pause. It seemed like the twenty-thousand-strong crowd were holding their breath. '... Adair,' the Carnegie lordling finished.

I smiled broadly. 'See?' I said to him. 'You said the word aloud and you didn't spontaneously combust!'

He ignored me. 'Who will stand for you?'

Silence rippled across the crowd like a Mexican wave.

The Bull reluctantly got to his feet. 'Clan Scrymgeour.'

Several of the other Chieftains did double takes and there were a few nudges. The Bull shrugged. From where I was standing I heard him mutter a vague explanation: 'She was my ward. What else am I supposed to do?'

I almost snorted. If I didn't have his true name and hadn't forced him to speak up, he'd have spat on me before supporting me. And his support didn't even matter.

I turned to Aifric, waiting for him to throw in his hat. The voice which followed, however, wasn't his.

'Clan MacQuarrie.'

I took a half-step backwards. The MacQuarrie Chieftain twinkled down at me. 'For Lily,' he mouthed.

I was taken aback; I thought they'd blamed me for Lily's death. After all, I did show up at their gates with her corpse in my arms. I was going to gain admission to the Games after all. A tiny smile tugged at the corner of my mouth. No. Way.

Aifric looked at me. He remained sitting, but there was no mistaking the overdone sorrow in his expression. My eyes narrowed. I knew he was a murdering bastard but he'd promised publicly to support me. It appeared, however, that I couldn't count on honour from him. I drew in a shaky breath. To have come this close and have the opportunity snatched away at the last moment ... talk about a roller-coaster.

'Clan Polwarth.'

There was a flash of darkness from Aifric. I was dumbfounded – I wasn't even sure who the Polwarth Chieftain was. I searched the stand, finally alighting on the rake-thin figure of the Sidhe who was standing up. Of everyone, he was dressed appropriately for the weather with an animal skin draped round his shoulders. I spotted the glint of an old carabineer at his belt and understood. Isla, my mate from mountain rescue: she wasn't a Sidhe, but clearly her role in mountain rescue meant something. The man who'd given his support flashed me a smile and sat down again.

'Clan Adair has the requisite three votes and is permitted to compete.'

I lifted my eyes and looked at Aifric. He was probably as surprised as I was. The sorrow on his face had been replaced by a beaming grin and he clapped loudly. I curtsied and wished him dead, before remembering that I was a pacifist and I shouldn't ever wish for someone to die. Not with Bob clinging to my neck or this weird Gift knocking around in my blood.

The Carnegie lordling moved towards me and gestured irritably. I ignored him, scanned the crowd and looked for my friends. When I finally caught sight of them at the back, jumping up and down, I relaxed. I waved at them and received a ragged cheer from several others in return.

'Hurry up!' the lordling hissed.

Of course, I didn't do that at all. I took my time, treating the audience as if they were my biggest fans. Fake it till you make it. The many blank faces only made my curtseys, waves and bows more energetic. I was tempted to make good on my threat of telekinesis but I thought better of it and moved across to the other competitors with a buoyant hop, skip and jump. Byron raised his eyebrows. I grinned at him, wondering if he was as good an actor as his father. Then I turned and took my seat.

Tipsania, positioned in the back row which was reserved for the top seeds, leaned forward. 'Anyone would think you'd already won with the way you're carrying on. You poor child.'

Considering she was about five months older than me, that was some endearment. I smirked at her. 'You don't understand, do you? For me, that was the hardest part. From here on in, you won't even see my dust.'

She let out a tinkling, derisive laugh. 'Oh my dear, you're so entertaining sometimes.'

My eyes gleamed. 'I suppose I am somewhat on the...' I paused, '*wild* side.'

Her jaw tightened a fraction. If I hadn't been looking for it, I wouldn't have spotted it. Buggering hell. Did all these Sidhe spend years learning how to act? I thought I was pretty skilled, and manipulation and con artistry were tools for my trade, but I was starting to think I had nothing on this lot.

# Chapter Ten

As organisers of the Games, the Carnegies put on quite a show. Once the formalities were over, the field exploded into a riot of colour. Young women danced on with streaming ribbons billowing out behind them. In perfect formation, they arranged themselves into different shapes, ranging from a bank of thistles to two battling figures. The lone piper, who'd been responsible for the ear-bleeding Clan anthems, was joined by a large band. I was amused to see that the bass drummer was a tiny Seonaidh, a water sprite who was dwarfed by the gigantic drum he held in front of his belly. He was out of his depth in more ways than one.

As the dancers and pipers marched off, a tall Carnegie Sidhe woman strode out. The competitors around me, most of whom had pasted on expressions of utter boredom, leaned forward and there was a buzz in the audience. I had no idea who she was or what she was about to do, but I bet it would be impressive.

'Morna Carnegie. She calls nature,' the MacQuarrie competitor next to me said, registering my curiosity. He stuck out his hand and grinned. 'Nice to meet you. I'm Angus.'

I smiled back and shook his hand. 'Integrity,' I murmured.

'I know. I don't think there's anyone here who isn't aware of who you are.'

'I'm not convinced that's a good thing.'

'Are you kidding? The other Clans have been at the top for so long, they've forgotten what it's like to have some real competition on their hands. I'm expecting good things from you, Integrity Adair.' My unspoken question must have been reflected in my face. 'Lily was my cousin,' Angus MacQuarrie told me. 'She was a good person.'

A wash of sadness overtook me. 'I'm sorry,' I said, inadequately. 'She helped me a lot.' I sucked in a breath. 'She deserved a better end.'

He touched my arm. 'You brought her to us so we could lay her to rest in the MacQuarrie grove. A lot of others wouldn't have bothered, not least because we're considered the weakest and most unimportant of all the Clans.' He grimaced. 'The madness we experience has a lot to do with that.'

I felt a prickle along the back of my neck and turned to see Byron glaring at me. What was his problem? I looked back at Angus, wanting to ask him more about the infamous MacQuarrie insanity, but the boom of a cannon drew my attention.

'Watch this,' Angus whispered. 'Morna's amazing.'

The Carnegie woman reached the centre of field and raised her arms to the heavens, her head tilted back as if she were talking to the clouds. A heartbeat later, the ground beneath my feet began to vibrate. I jerked up my feet, alarmed. Angus laughed although I noticed that a few others had reacted the same way as me.

The air crackled as if coalescing into something heavier and more oppressive. I didn't like this at all and I sat up straight, ready to bolt at a moment's notice. There was no need, though – it was all part of the show. As I watched, gobsmacked, Morna Carnegie snapped her fingers and a row of purple heather sprang out from her left. I gaped. She clicked again and the same thing happened from her right hand. She spun, moving faster and faster. Now more and more lines of different coloured heather appeared in an intricate and predesigned pattern. I shook my head in amazement. 'How...?'

'Impressive, right? When it comes to flora, there's very little that she can't call up.'

This was a Gift that I wanted. I sat on my hands, willing myself not to unconsciously steal it. I couldn't just go around ripping magic from everyone I met. It was too late, though: whatever made my blood sing when I saw Morna Carnegie's Gift was already working.

My senses swam with the now-familiar head rush and stomach-churning nausea. I closed my eyes to steady myself while next to me Angus stiffened.

'I've never seen her falter before.'

Shite. I opened one eye, worried about what I'd see. This was an elderly woman; who knew what would happen if I stole part of her Sidhe nature? I bit my lip while Morna Carnegie paused, confusion clouding her face. All around her the banks of multi-coloured heather swayed, their tips leaning towards her as if they were concerned about her. She blinked once, twice, shook herself and continued. I breathed out. She'd obviously felt something happen but she still had some of her Gift left.

I had to find a way to control my new power. I couldn't be responsible for sending Sidhe, who were no more of a danger than professional flower arrangers, into an early grave.

'What happened there?' I asked, wishing my heart would stop racing.

Angus looked puzzled. 'I don't know. Maybe she skipped breakfast or something.'

I leaned back, sitting on my hands to stop them trembling, and watched her finish. She certainly had amazing control. As her arms continued to flick out around her and her fingers snapped with increasing speed, the design of the flowers around her started to take shape. A Celtic knot entirely made out of heather - damn, that was clever. Everyone else obviously agreed with me, leaping to their feet with thunderous applause.

Morna curtsied, although there was no denying she still looked shaken. She walked off, the flowers parting to allow her to leave without trampling on a single bloom. Then a man of similar age strode out to take her place.

'Who's that?' I asked.

Angus scowled. 'Morna's opposite.'

His actions were similar to hers: he raised his arms, swung them out with a flourish and clicked his fingers. The first row of blooming heather withered and died. An involuntary cry escaped me, followed by a snicker from several of the other competitors. At least Angus didn't laugh this time and he squeezed my hand reassuringly.

The man spun round, snapping away. One by one, each row of flowers died. What a shitty Gift. Where Morna had provided life – natural life filled with beauty and optimism – this Sidhe was completely different. I glared at him as he killed off the intricate design, leaving behind little more than blackened roots. Needless to say, I felt no dizziness; I wanted no part of this Gift, subconsciously or otherwise.

He bowed. The response from the crowd this time was less enthusiastic. As he strode off arrogantly, there was a whine from the microphone and the Carnegie lordling spoke up once more.

'I am sure the symbolism is not lost on this esteemed crowd,' he intoned. 'With one breath, you can be riding high and winning. But these are the Games; one false step and your success will wither and die before your very eyes. As might you. We have done what we can to assure competitors that their safety is uppermost in our minds, but accidents do happen. There may be severe consequences for those who fail in the two more risky challenges.'

I didn't think I was imagining the bloodthirsty glint in his eyes, or that he flicked a look at me. I straightened my shoulders. They could underestimate me all they wished; it would only serve to make my win sweeter.

'The Artistry challenge will begin at dawn tomorrow. We don't expect any life-threatening wounds in that one.' He paused while the crowd dutifully chuckled. 'Until then, we beg you to enjoy the refreshments we have arranged. These Games will go down in history as the best ever. The Carnegie Clan will see to that.' He stepped down from the dais.

'Yeah, right,' Angus whispered in my ear. 'Last time around, when Gale Adair - your father - won, the Jardine Clan were the organisers. They had twelve Gifted illusionists. Apparently the show they put on was so spectacular it will never be beaten. The Carnegies hate the Jardines but it doesn't matter what they do, they can't surpass that kind of spectacle.'

I raised my eyebrows. 'Were you even born when the last Games took place?'

'No, but I've heard a lot about them.'

I ignored the Sidhe around me who were getting up and preparing to leave the field. 'My father?' I asked. 'What did you hear about him?'

Angus smiled. 'He was a hero. According to Lily, anyway. He could have asked for anything but all he wanted was a black rose.'

I was fascinated – and very, very eager to know more. 'Why?' I asked. 'Why a black rose?'

'Lily told me that it was because he wanted to prove that it wasn't about the prize. And the prophecy might have had something to do with it because...'

'It's time to go.' Byron was standing in front of us. I thought he'd been glaring before; now he looked about ready to wring my neck.

'In a minute.'

'The MacQuarrie Chieftain wants to speak to his son.'

I was surprised, I hadn't realised Angus was so high up the food chain. I was also very irritated at the interruption. What prophecy?

'I'd better go.' Angus stood up, his eyes crinkling with bonhomie. He took my hand and pressed it against his lips. 'Until next time, Chieftain Adair.'

A thrill ran through me at his words. Only Lily had ever called me that before; there was something gratifying about hearing someone else repeat the title, especially with Aifric Moncrieffe's son and heir standing beside me.

'Call me Integrity,' I told Angus.

He bowed and I watched him go, enjoying the warmth I felt at knowing that not every Sidhe was against me. I was sure that there had been no guile in Angus's words or expression.

Byron, apparently, had a different opinion. 'You should be careful who you make friends with.'

'Why's that?' I inquired, turning my attention back to him.

'You know most nobles here would be happy to see you gone.'

'Really? Even after I saved all your sorry arses by helping you with the Foinse?'

'Don't be so naïve, Integrity,' he snapped.

'Well, don't you be so antagonistic,' I bit back.

He came closer. 'Me antagonistic? You should take a look in the mirror.' His voice was low. He reached out and took a strand of my hair in his fingers. 'How can you show up, looking like that with your Adair hair, and expect me to believe that you're not deliberately trying to annoy every damn person here? We know what you are, Integrity. There's no need to flaunt it.'

I was taken aback. Someone had clearly got out of the wrong side of bed this morning. It was only hair. Considering the dramatic clothes that everyone else was wearing, I could hardly be accused of being showy.

'My appearance is annoying you? Really? Maybe if I wore a nun's habit, you'd think it was more appropriate.' I pointed at his muscular legs, visible beneath his kilt. 'Although you're displaying a lot more skin than I am. Are your balls as blue as you thought they'd be?'

'Would you like to check and see?'

I felt Bob stir from the folds of my Adair tartan scarf. He was virtually quivering with excitement. Bugger it. Worry surged through me at the prospect of the genie doing something stupid and it was like a bucket of ice water. It didn't just dampen my irritation; it also provided sudden brisk clarity.

'You're jealous,' I breathed. 'That's why you're so annoyed. You don't want me making 'friends ' with anyone apart from you.' I glanced at Tipsania's retreating back. 'What would your fiancée make of that?'

Turmoil flickered across his face. 'It doesn't sound like I'm the only jealous one around here,' he pointed out. 'And she's not my fiancée.'

'Not yet. The only way you'll escape that particular noose is if you win these Games.' The corner of my mouth tugged up in a smile. 'Right?'

He folded his arms. 'I have responsibilities, something you don't seem to understand.' He shrugged. 'And maybe I am jealous. We left a lot of business unfinished when we first met. I seem to recall you were particularly keen to be on top.'

Memories of our assignation in his hotel room in Aberdeen assailed me. 'What can I say? You're not unpleasant on the eye and I've always had a soft spot for blonds.'

'That's it?' he asked, his voice dangerously quiet. 'That's what you like about me?'

'That and your sexy legs.'

Something flared in his eyes. He cursed to himself. 'This is ridiculous.'

'I know,' I agreed. 'I don't even really like you that much.'

Byron grinned suddenly, his expression lightening. 'Ditto. You're far too much like hard work.'

'Yeah, I'm worth it though.'

'I'm starting to think that maybe you are.'

I licked my lips. 'We should probably just have sex and be done with it. Get all this,' I waved a hand in the air, 'tension out of our systems.'

He took a step closer. 'What colour would your eyes turn, I wonder, when I made you scream in ecstasy?'

'You're very sure of yourself.'

His grin widened. 'I have good reason to be.'

'Jerk.'

'Witch.'

We stood there, smiling at each other like idiots. 'It's probably easier if we just stay away from each other.'

'Yeah,' he sighed. 'Probably.'

My body relaxed. 'In another life perhaps, Byron.'

He turned away, his kilt swinging sexily as he walked off.

'Uh Integrity!' Bob screeched in my ear. 'What is wrong with you? That man is sex on legs and he's panting after you like you're on heat!'

'His father tried to kill me.'

'I thought you'd be the last person to apportion blame to children for what their parents have done.'

Bob was making good sense. 'True,' I replied. 'But he's got Tipsania.'

'Isn't she shagging a sweet Wild Man?'

'I can't tell Byron that. And I'm starting to think that the pair of them are being forced into a relationship, whether they like it or not.'

'All the more reason to encourage him to break it off.'

Byron's figure was being swallowed up in the crowds leaving the grandstand. I gazed after him, my eyes savouring every last moment. Just before he disappeared, his head turned and he sought me out. I lifted my hand to wave. Then he was gone.

'I can't,' I said to Bob, ignoring the remaining competitors who were nearby. By their expressions, they seemed to think that I was holding an in-depth conversation with myself. 'He's the one in a relationship. He's the one who needs to make a move.'

I thought of Aifric. Even if Byron were completely innocent of his father's actions, I couldn't imagine him being pleased if I told him the truth, no matter how good the sex was. Thanks, Byron, I did indeed scream in ecstasy – oh and by the way, your father is trying to kill me. Nope. Not gonna work. And at some point he'd work out I'd stolen part of his Gift.

'Pff! You Sidhe are ridiculous,' Bob muttered.

'Yeah.' I couldn't disagree.

I walked off, choosing not to follow everyone else but to look at the field. The dead, blackened heather crunched beneath my feet. No matter what Angus had said, it was still an awesome display of power, suggesting that the Carnegies had absolute control over both life and death. And that life was a fleeting thing, not to be cherished too dearly or it would be snatched away.

'Integrity!'

I turned to see Lexie jogging towards me, her blue hair swinging in the breeze. 'That was brilliant! Did you know the Polwarths were going to do that?'

I waited until she caught up. 'Not a clue,' I admitted.

'Maybe they're one of the decent Clans,' she said. 'They can't all be bad, right?'

I thought of the MacQuarries and smiled. 'No, I guess not.'

'Did you...?' Her voice faltered slightly. She pointed at the dead flowers.

I pushed back my hair. 'Yeah,' I said reluctantly. 'Not the destructive part. I took the growing part though. I didn't mean to. It just ... happened.'

She nodded. 'We all saw the old woman pause.'

I sighed. 'I'm going to have to learn control. I can't just steal from people whenever I see them use their Gift.'

Lexie blinked. 'Why ever not?'

I considered her question. 'Their Gift is not a *thing*,' I said finally. 'It's not a cold, hard object. I'm taking away part of them and leaving them weaker because of it. It just feels ... wrong.'

I could see she was about to start arguing but then something caught my eye. 'Look,' I said suddenly.

'What?'

I bent down, my fingers lightly brushing the ground. 'Here. They tried to obliterate all those flowers but there's one left. One survived. You can try to destroy everything but it's a lot harder than people realise.' I grinned. 'After all, I'm still standing. Maybe the will to survive is greater than the will to destroy.'

Lexie looked at me. 'Tell that to the dodo,' she snorted.

*

By the time we made it to the main tent and caught up with Speck, Brochan and Taylor, drinks had been distributed by tartan-clad servants. Taylor was staring morosely at his glass. 'All that money they put into these Games,' he muttered. 'All that time and effort and they couldn't even get hold of a decent malt for their guests.'

I laughed. He gazed at me balefully. 'I mean it, Tegs. I'm thrilled you managed to get the three votes you needed, but seriously.' He held the glass up. 'It's been months since I had a decent whisky.'

Brochan rolled his eyes and looked away. 'You shouldn't be drinking anything that doesn't belong to us.'

'It came out of the same bottle as everyone else's. I'm not entirely without wit,' Taylor answered benignly.

'Sorry, Taylor. I did try to get you something better beyond the Veil,' I said. 'I found an old dusty bottle of something called Auchen...' My brow furrowed, as I tried to remember. 'Auchen-something. I had to use it to save that Fomori demon.'

Taylor stared at me as if I were mad. 'You used malt whisky to save the life of a Fomori demon? Malt whisky from the Lowlands? That would have been more than three hundred years old? That no-one has drunk in ten generations? You used that to save a demon who tried to kill you?'

I shrugged. 'Yep. Sorry.' Clearly I wasn't.

'What was the name of it?' Brochan asked. There was an odd tone in his voice.

This time I managed to wrap my tongue around the name. 'Auchentoshan.'

'You're sure?'

I nodded. 'Yeah.' Brochan looked troubled. 'What?' He didn't answer. 'Brochan, what is it?'

His gills, visible on his neck, tightened. 'When I was stuck out at sea, I used to try to calm my nerves by drinking.'

'Well,' Speck said, 'you were surrounded by liquid.'

'Leave the jokes to Tegs,' Brochan growled.

I brightened. 'Really?' At the looks on their faces, I returned to the subject at hand. 'Sorry, Brochan. Go on.'

He exhaled. 'The point is that I know a lot about whisky. There were only five Lowland whiskies in production before the Fissure and I can assure you that Auchentoshan, whatever it is, wasn't one of them.'

Lexie shrugged. 'So?'

'So someone's been brewing.'

'The Fomori are probably bored. There can't be much fun to be had across the Veil.'

'No,' Speck said, shaking his head, 'Fomori demons don't drink.'

Lexie stepped backwards. 'What? Never?'

'How do you know that, Speck?' I asked quietly.

'It was one of the many reasons they gave for the Fissure. They didn't want to be near heathens such as ourselves who partook of such evil substances.'

'The evil Fomori demons brought war against Scotland and stole half our country because of the demon drink?'

He look at her, exasperated. 'Hardly. But it was one of their excuses for what happened.'

Lexie blew air out through her pursed lips. ' 'Excuses' is right. Evil substances! Honestly!'

I nibbled my bottom lip. Speck knew his history. All the same... 'It was three hundred years ago, Speck. The Fomori might have changed their attitude towards booze.'

He shrugged. 'Sure, they might have. But put that into context with the message you found on the wall of that house and...'

'And there weren't just people trapped on other side of the Veil immediately after the Fissure. Their descendants are probably still there now.'

'Or their descendants at least.'

I tugged at my scarf, suddenly feeling hot. 'Everyone assumed the original inhabitants were all slaughtered when the Fomori demons invaded.'

'Yeah.'

'I didn't see anyone when I was there, only the demons. If there are still humans, pixies, even Sidhe beyond the Veil, then...' I couldn't finish the sentence.

'Then,' Brochan said grimly, 'they're probably being kept as slaves.'

Lexie's hand grasped at her throat. 'That's awful,' she gasped.

'What do we do about this?' Speck finally asked. 'We can't just leave them there. If they *are* there.'

My gaze flitted towards Aifric Moncrieffe. He caught me watching him and beckoned me over. I sighed. 'In an ideal world, I would tell the Steward and he'd deal with it.'

Brochan followed my gaze. 'Except the current Steward is *him*.' His voice was laced with disgust. 'He's not going to care.'

'He might. Just because he wants to kill me doesn't mean he won't want to know about the Lowlands.'

'You can't trust him, Tegs.'

There was a glimmer of irritation from Aifric that I hadn't immediately jumped at his command. 'I know.'

'And how are you going to explain to him that you visited the Lowlands? If you tell him about Dagda's harp, he'll probably make the Carnegies introduce a new rule to prevent you from using it.'

'I think the fate of thousands of people who might be held in subjugation and slavery is more important than winning these Games, regardless of what I could do with the prize.' I wrinkled my nose. 'And I don't have to tell him the whole truth, do I?'

I walked over to Aifric, weaving in and out of the packed crowds. Most people saw me coming and leapt out of the way – they were probably still afraid I was going to boost all their fine jewels and fripperies. I had half a mind to make notes so that I could stalk them once the Games were over and do just that. It would serve them right. There again, I probably didn't need any notes; Speck, Lexie, Brochan and Taylor had probably already made a comprehensive list all on their own.

'Steward Aifric,' I said when I reached him.

He deliberately took several moments to react, focusing on the conversation beside him. It was a childish manoeuvre to make me understand that if I was going to keep him waiting, he'd do the same to me. I wondered idly if that meant he was dropping the 'friend' act but when he finally turned to me with a beatific smile, it was clear that wasn't going to happen.

'Integrity,' he boomed. 'I'm so pleased that you've made it through and that you'll compete.'

Yeah, yeah. 'Me too.'

He took my hand, drawing me to the side. I felt a shiver of revulsion at the touch of his skin on mine but I could dissemble when I needed to. If I could walk into a gambling den filled with trolls and Bauchans and stroll out with all their hard-earned cash, I could handle Aifric Moncrieffe.

'I must apologise for not speaking up to endorse your bid to compete in the Games,' he said quietly. 'I thought it would look better to the rest of the Chieftains if you had support from others rather than me. After all,' he added, squeezing my fingers, 'everyone knows how highly I regard you.'

The man had no shame. 'Oh,' I said, the very picture of innocence, 'so you knew that Polwarth, Scrymgeour and MacQuarrie would give me their votes?'

'Of course! I'm the Steward, I know everything that goes on.' He lowered his head. 'Between you and me, I did encourage the Bull to add his voice to the others. It was the least I could do.'

Oh, you stupid, stupid man. 'Thank you,' I murmured. 'It's much appreciated.'

'You're welcome.' He smiled at me magnanimously.

'There is one thing I need to talk to you about,' I said, treading carefully.

'Oh yes?'

I bit my lip. 'I recently had cause to pass through the Veil.'

Whatever Aifric had been expecting me to say, it obviously wasn't that. He blinked several times and stepped back. 'You...' He shook his head. 'Why would you do that?'

I thought about what Taylor had said. There was no reason not to live up to expectations. I shrugged. 'Oh, looking for riches that I could sell on the black market.'

His mouth tightened. 'That was ... unwise, my dear. It's a very dangerous place.'

'Oh, so you've been there too?'

'Goodness gracious, of course not. I don't think anyone has visited the Lowlands in generations.' He lowered his voice. 'Did you find anything of value?'

'Nothing to speak of,' I demurred.

'And did you see any Fomori?'

There was something in his eyes which made me pause. It wasn't eagerness exactly, but whatever it was put me on edge. 'No,' I lied. 'I didn't stay long and there was very little to see.' Which was sort of true; it had been very dark.

If I hadn't been watching him so closely, I'd have missed the flash of relief. 'That's probably for the best, my dear. I dread to think what those vile creatures would have done if they'd spotted you.'

'Indeed. Anyway, I did see something which you should know about.' I explained about the message written in blood and the bottle of Auchentoshan whisky, although I didn't say where I'd found it.

'And do you have this whisky now?' he inquired.

'Er, no. I left it behind.' In a manner of speaking.

'I wouldn't worry about it,' Aifric said, patting my shoulder and setting my teeth on edge.

I pressed ahead. 'But it could mean that there are people there. Not just demons but humans and Sidhe and...'

'If that were the case, we'd know about it.' He smiled. 'The youth of today. I was the same at your age. I remember I went to my father and asked to lead an expedition into the Lowlands to see if we could negotiate with the Fomori. They can't be reasoned with, though. And there's no one of our kind there, I can assure you of that.'

'But...'

'Don't worry your pretty little head about it. Concentrate on the Games, my dear. Who knows? You may acquit yourself well enough to place.'

I opened my mouth to argue further but he'd caught someone else's eye and was moving away. He strode off and I stared after him. He may not have given the reaction I wanted but I'd certainly learned something from our little chat.

I twirled a curl of my hair round my little finger. Aifric was right about one thing: I had to concentrate on the Games for now. Once they were over, however, I reckoned I'd be making another visit beyond the Veil. I didn't need his help.

# Chapter Eleven

The five of us stood in the main hall, eyeing the gigantic board displaying the Games' league table. Every Clan was listed there, along with each competitor's name. Not only was I down at the bottom but there was no denying how insignificant Clan Adair was compared to the others.

'Look on the bright side, Tegs,' Lexie told me. 'At least you don't have to compete against people you actually like.'

Someone jostled me sharply from behind. I spun round to see a MacBain competitor giving me a shrug in a vague – and obviously faked - apology. I narrowed my eyes. Whether they had proof or not, they clearly still believed I had stolen their Chieftain's necklace.

'You know,' I said loudly, 'I had a great joke about fighting.' The MacBain guy stiffened. I glanced at Lexie. 'Except all I can remember is that it had a good punchline.'

'Keep that up, Tegs,' she growled, with a toss of her blue hair, 'and I'll be the one punching you.'

I grinned. Brochan and Taylor rolled their eyes. Speck didn't seem in the slightest bit interested. 'This board is running off a simple interface,' he said, oblivious to everything else. 'I could easily hack it and...'

'Let's not do that, Speck,' I interrupted, before someone overheard him and mistook his techy musings for a plan to cheat. 'We're doing this by the book, remember? It's the only way I won't get thrown out.'

'I'm just saying,' he mumbled.

'It won't matter,' I said decisively. 'Once I play Dagda's harp, my name will be at the top of the board. And it'll stay there.'

Brochan rumbled, 'We still don't know if the harp will work. You've not tried it yet.'

'Bob didn't think it was a good idea to test it.'

'I don't trust that genie.'

'It's not as if we have any alternatives. If the harp doesn't work, what am I going to do? Sing?' Brochan's answering look was enough.

'If every competitor gets five minutes to perform and there are one hundred and twenty, not including you, it's going to be an age before this first challenge is over,' Lexie complained. 'Do we have to sit through every single act?'

'I certainly hope not. I was planning to do a little ... digging while everyone else is otherwise occupied. I'll watch the first couple then sidle out.'

Speck pouted. 'But you told us we couldn't nick anything!'

'I'm not going to sneak out to steal. I'm going to spy.'

'Like James Bond?'

'Without the car chases. Or guns. Or explosions.'

Speck brightened. 'Great! I'll be Q. Taylor can be M.'

'Who am I then?' Lexie asked, her hands on her hips. 'And if you say Moneypenny, I swear I'll...'

'Enough.'

Taylor arched an eyebrow. 'Why are you bothering to watch the first few performances, Tegs?'

'Because that's when people will see me. They'll pay attention to me sitting down and won't notice later when I slip out.'

He nodded. 'Right. I understand.' His brow furrowed and he glanced at the others. 'Which Clan is performing first?'

Lexie cocked her head. 'I have no idea.' She shaded her eyes and looked up at the league board. 'Whose name is that at the top? My eyesight isn't what it used to be.'

'I think it starts with an M,' Speck said slowly.

'MacBain?'

'No. Is it Moncrieffe?'

I sighed. 'You lot are very funny. Not.'

They all ignored me, even Brochan. 'So you're saying that Byron Moncrieffe will perform first?'

Taylor made a great show of surprise. 'I suppose he will. But Tegs wouldn't be interested in watching *him*.'

'No. She doesn't go for pretty-boy types. Besides, there's a good chance he's working with his father and trying to kill her.' Lexie grinned.

'Guys...'

'Not to mention,' Speck said, 'that sooner or later he's going to notice that his Gift has been, er, stolen.'

'Only part of his Gift,' I snapped. 'And I didn't mean to do it.'

They threw each other amused looks. 'Don't worry, Tegs,' Lexie said loudly. 'I have a lot of experience with men who are too sexy for their own good.' She winked at Speck and he coughed, his cheeks turning scarlet. 'I'll hold you back if you can't stop yourself from rushing him when he walks out with his gold hair ruffling in the wind and his kilt picking up ever so slightly to show off those muscular thighs.'

'You are hysterical,' I said flatly.

'To be fair to Tegs,' she mused, 'his eyes are a wonderful shade of green.'

'More emerald, I'd say.' Taylor rubbed his fingers together.

Brochan winked. 'And with that tanned skin...'

'Hey,' Byron said from behind me, 'checking up on the competition, are you?'

I froze, my cheeks turning as red as Speck's. I slowly turned, meeting those very same green eyes. Lexie stifled a giggle.

'Hi,' I said stiffly.

Byron frowned, obviously confused. 'Are you ready for the Artistry challenge?' he asked.

'Pretty much,' I muttered.

'Hi, Byron,' Lexie said coyly, hooking her arm through his and smiling up at him.

He scratched his chin. 'Uh, hi.'

'Don't you think Integrity is looking rather wonderful this morning?'

I was going to kill her. Byron's gaze flicked to me, seeming to understand what was going on. 'I think she looks stunning. As always.'

'Her hair is very soft,' Lexie continued. 'She has a new shampoo. Touch it.' She grinned. 'It smells lovely too.'

I cleared my throat. 'I am going to get the harp.'

'Aw, but Tegs, it's only polite to reciprocate and tell Byron how wonderful he's looking this morning too.'

I spun on my heel and walked away. Who needed enemies when you had friends like those? Honestly.

*

Dagda's harp was wrapped in a makeshift case which Taylor had fashioned so there was no need to strap it to my back this time. Bob was pacing up and down in front of it, making a show of keeping guard. Ever since the 'break-in', we'd made sure that at least one of us kept an eye on it at all times.

The genie gave a tired salute. ''Bout time,' he grumbled. 'Deanna Troy will be missing me.' He blew the harp a kiss. 'Bye, darling.' Then he blinked away in a flash of blinding light.

I scooped up the instrument from the corner of the cabin and went to the auditorium where the Artistry challenge was going to be held. I wasn't due to play until the next day but I wasn't taking any chances that the powers-that-be would suddenly change their minds and move me up the roster. And I felt better with the harp in my arm where I could keep my eye on it.

It felt lighter than before, almost as if it were sentient and was aware that, after years of disuse, it was going to be played again - even by fingers as clumsy as mine. I picked my way back along the path, taking care not to trip as I cradled it against my chest.

With the harp in front of me, my vision was slightly obscured and it didn't help that my thoughts were on what had happened back in the main hall. I was almost past the competitors' village before I realised that there were three figures up ahead waiting for me and deliberately blocking my path.

'Well, well, well, look who we have here,' the larger of the three called. 'It's the murderer's offspring.'

I peered round the harp and eyed their tartans: Clans Riddell, Kincaid and Blair. The Clans were working together to bully me. How sweet.

'Is your hair white because your darling papa shocked you so much when he slaughtered a thousand Sidhe in front of you?'

'He didn't kill anyone,' I replied in a calm, clear voice.

'No wonder she's friendly with the MacQuarries,' the Blair Sidhe sneered. 'She's as crazy as they are.'

'You don't belong here,' his Riddell buddy broke in. 'You're not going to win the Games and you're not welcome. You should fuck off back to your own kind.'

The Kincaid idiot got in on the action. 'Yeah. You should be with the dirty Clan-less. The Cruaich is for those of us who belong.'

Did they believe that they were so intimidating that I'd run off into the sunset with my tail between my legs?

'Careful, Pike,' the Riddell Sidhe said in a mock falsetto. 'Piss her off and she might nick your wallet.'

Pike smirked and reached into his pocket and took out his wallet. He flipped it open, took out a penny and threw it at me. Rather than sidestep, I let it hit my cheek. The three men fell about laughing.

'There you go, bitch. That should be enough for you.' Pike looked like he'd just found the meaning of life.

I sighed, laid the harp carefully on the ground and watched them all.

'She's not done yet,' said the Blair bully. 'Give her another penny. See what she does then.'

'I've got a better idea.' Pike raised his eyebrows and leered. 'She's quite pretty. I bet we could show her a good time before she goes.'

The Riddell guy looked repulsively excited. He licked his lips. 'What a great idea.'

There weren't many times when I regretted my pacifist stance but now was one of them. I even considered pulling out Bob's letter opener and waking him up to ask for that wish but I didn't want to give those idiots that kind of compliment. If I couldn't deal with them on my own, I really didn't deserve to be here.

Pike, apparently the ringleader, advanced. I leapt out of his path and performed a perfect landing onto the soft snow next to the path. He smirked as if he were already enjoying the chase. He wasn't particularly canny, though. I'd landed feet away from the fire-cleared path; Pike chose to step across it, not realising that the pyrokinesis which had created the handy walkway had also melted the edges around the path. As the water re-froze it changed from snow to deadly ice. The second his foot landed he slipped, his legs flying out from under him. He landed flat on his back with a heavy thump and a loud groan.

'Bitch,' he muttered, like it was my fault he'd lost his footing.

His friends scuttled over to help him but he pushed them away. This time all three of them advanced on me.

It was handy that there were so many trees around. I leapt upwards and caught hold of a sturdy branch, swung out above their heads and landed behind them. I should have tried out for the Scottish gymnastics team; I would have given those bendy Russian girls a run for their money.

The three boys below me – because they were boys – howled in frustration. I dusted snow off my thighs. 'Give up yet?'

The Blair idiot screwed up his face. The air crackled and I realised with a sinking feeling that he was using his Gift – whatever it was. When a dark cloud appeared between us, twisting and turning before taking the form of a hooded creature holding a scythe, I rolled my eyes. Virtuosity – or Illusion as it was also known – held all manner of possibilities but creating a three-dimensional version of the Grim Reaper smacked of someone who wasn't really trying.

Unfortunately for me, Blair was rather talented and this wasn't an insubstantial vision. Death swung at me and although I scooted away just in time, his scythe caught the edge of my hair, causing several strands to float down. The boys laughed. Pricks.

'I expend a lot of energy avoiding split ends,' I growled, as Death took yet another swipe. 'I don't appreciate a damned Illusion undoing all that work.'

'Tell you what,' Pike said, 'stop fighting us and we might leave your pretty hair alone.'

'Aw,' the Riddell Clanling protested, 'but I like it when they fight.'

Something inside me tightened. I tilted back my head and concentrated on the snow-laden branches above the Grim Reaper's head. It took very little effort to shake them and a heavy pile of snow dropped off, landing on his dark cloak. Like a roadrunner cartoon, his form collapsed into a puddle on the ground while his arm hung on for an extra few seconds, gripping the scythe until it too vanished. That was easier than I expected.

'Get her!' Pike roared.

I'd had enough of this. Using Byron's Gift once more, I focused on the snow pile I'd just created. It swirled upwards, forming a whirling barricade between me and my assailants. I could just make out their flailing arms and hear their shouts of irritation. It wasn't quite what I wanted, though. My brow furrowed and I drew in more snow from the surrounding embankments. It solidified into chunks, combining and coalescing. I lifted up my index finger and spun it round. The snowflakes bound together, forming bricks which I piled higher and higher around the three idiots. Their vision was so obscured that they didn't realise what I was doing until it was too late and they were trapped by my snow tower.

I stepped over and prodded the outer edge. It might look like snow but it was as hard as the ice upon which Pike had slipped. Unless one of them had a match, a lighter or pyrokinesis, they'd be trapped there for some time.

'You bitch!' I heard Pike yell. 'I'm supposed to be backstage getting ready! If I'm late, they won't let me participate.'

He should have thought of that before he tried to attack me. I bent down to pick up the harp and turned my back, ignoring their shouts. I had to go; I didn't want to miss Byron's performance, after all.

\*

When I finally arrived at the auditorium, a sniffy Carnegie official tried to make me leave the harp in a side room with the other Sidhe instruments. I shook my head and pushed past him. Fortunately for him, he didn't try to stop me. I really wasn't in the mood.

I stomped in, still fuming. When I caught sight of the stage and the vast crowd seated in front of it, however, I forgot my annoyance. This was something else.

The stage was huge, with varnished oak underfoot and hundreds of lights trained on its centre. There was a raised dais to one side with a lectern, which was no doubt reserved for the Carnegie officials, and heavy red velvet curtains on either side. There were hundreds of seats in a gentle arc around the stage area. The self-styled important Clans were at the front, with Aifric sitting dead centre.

I avoided looking at him in case I drew his attention. Instead my gaze swooped round. Although the other competitors who wouldn't be performing until the next day like me were visible, the majority of the spectators were other Sidhe proudly displaying their Clan colours. Some had made banners – and not all of their messages were positive. At least there was no confusion over who hated whom and which Clans possessed strong affiliations. I committed as many of them to memory as I could; Clan politics could turn on a dime but it wouldn't hurt to know which Clans were working together right now. Every scrap of information was potentially useful.

I spotted the Polwarth Chieftain, made a show of turning towards him and bowing and noted the murmur as several other Clans took note of what I was doing. By acknowledging him first, I was giving Clan Polwarth superiority over Clan Adair. Not only would the Chieftain appreciate that I wasn't going to forget his support during the opening ceremony, it might make him amenable to further approaches later on. I already had enough enemies; it was time to start making allies. I didn't bow towards the Bull, though – I just winked at him and he glared in return. Ha! Let those nosy spectators make of that what they wanted. Although, in the evil-looks category, the Bull had nothing on Chieftain MacBain.

'It would be wise to avoid antagonising the MacBains,' a voice murmured in my ear.

I turned and recognised Angus MacQuarrie. 'Believe me,' I said honestly, 'I'm not trying to do that.'

'She can be ... touchy,' he told me. 'But she does have many fingers in many pies. It would be good for you if that necklace showed up.'

I wrinkled my nose. 'So you also think I stole it?'

'Actually, no.' He leaned forward. 'But I reckon if you tried hard enough you could get it back. I've heard you have a knack for doing such things.'

I scanned his face, wondering what he was getting at, but his face was innocent. 'I have some skills,' I said slowly.

Angus grinned. 'When you have some free time, my Chieftain would like a word.'

'I'm free now. I will meet with Chieftain MacQuarrie whenever he requires.' I meant it; I owed him a considerable amount for his support. Not to mention what had happened with Lily.

'He's not here,' Angus said. 'He doesn't like the Games much so he's only going to show up when it's absolutely necessary.'

My eyebrows shot up. 'Why doesn't he like the Games?'

Angus shrugged. 'He sees them as yet another opportunity for the more powerful Clans to show off.'

'But surely anyone can win?'

'He reckons they're rigged.'

I wasn't surprised. And if Angus hoped to dismay me, then he was going to be disappointed. I'd lived most of my life as Clan-less and I was used to having to cheat, cajole, steal and manipulate. If anything, the MacQuarrie suspicions warmed my heart. Honour was just a pain in the arse: it was nebulous and, as Aifric kept proving, far too easy to set aside. Honest underhandedness was much more straightforward.

'Well,' I said, 'Chieftain MacQuarrie is welcome to come by our cabin any time. Just knock first.'

Amusement flickered in Angus's face. 'In case you're not decent?'

I thought of Bob's Brunei-borrowed opulence and grinned back. 'Something like that.'

He gave a friendly farewell as I caught sight of my friends. I went to join them, sat next to Brochan and handed him the covered harp. He glowered at me. 'What happened to your cheek?'

Puzzled, I raised my fingers to touch it. They came away wet, with a smudge of blood on their tips. 'Let's just say that people have been throwing money at me.'

The merman looked annoyed but Taylor watched me for a moment before smiling slightly. 'Good for you.'

Pride flickered through me at my old mentor's approval. I smiled at Brochan. 'Don't worry.'

'How can I not be worried? We're stuck here with a bunch of people who are trying to kill you. I can think of other things I'd rather be doing.'

My smile vanished. He'd been in a good mood earlier so what had changed? I looked at Speck and Lexie. Neither of them seemed particularly happy either. In fact, only Taylor appeared to be cheerily buoyant. Something stirred inside me. 'What's happened?' I asked.

'Nothing!' Taylor replied sunnily. I knew that look.

I cursed. 'You've been gambling, haven't you?' I should have known. This was a competition, after all; there were probably bets going on all across the auditorium. 'Goddamnit, Taylor, it's not like we have any money to spare. Where did you get your stake from?'

Lexie looked uncomfortable. 'I gave it to him,' she admitted. 'He told me it was to get something to help you.'

I sighed. Taylor threw up his hands as if to ward me off. 'It is to help you! We make money off this and it'll help all of us.'

'Taylor...'

'Relax, Tegs.'

I ground my teeth in frustration. When that didn't help, I glared at Lexie for lending him money and then at Speck and Brochan for not stopping Taylor from placing any bets. Finally, I crossed my arms and saved my best scowl for Taylor himself.

He looked back at me with puppy-dog eyes. 'Integrity.'

'Don't. Just don't.' It wasn't really his fault because he was a gambling addict but that didn't make me feel any better. It was fortunate for him that the Carnegies chose that moment to start the challenge.

A drumroll sounded and the same lordling strutted onto the large stage. There was nothing on it save a microphone on a stand; if that was all we were getting to support our performances, it was just as well I had the harp. I concentrated on breathing in and out, calming myself, as he began to speak.

'Esteemed ladies and gentlemen. Thank you so much for attending our humble little Games. We are proud to be the organisers of these challenges and, considering the line-up of competitors, there is no doubt that you are in for a thrilling time.'

'Yeah,' Brochan grunted under his breath. 'Amateur musical performances are always thrilling.'

Several people turned round and threw him nasty looks. All five of us returned their looks in kind and they hastily moved their eyes to the front again.

'This place is packed,' Lexie whispered. 'Just think of what we could...'

'No. No stealing.'

She wrinkled her nose. 'That's not what I was going to say.' When she saw my disbelieving look, she smirked mischievously.

The lordling continued. 'Each of the competitors will be granted five minutes to perform. Any and all instruments are allowed, whether living or otherwise.' I swallowed my faint nausea. Dagda's harp might possess magic I couldn't understand but it was definitely not a living being. What kind of instrument was? A nervous giggle escaped me as I imagined someone playing a cow like a set of bagpipes. A few people turned and threw me dirty looks; even the lordling glanced my way in annoyance.

'Performers are also permitted to utilise their Gifts if they see fit,' he boomed. 'But they can only do this during the individual performances and they will be judged by our wholly impartial panel.' He swept an arm out to the side where a spotlight focused on a table where three older Sidhe were seated.

'They're all Carnegie?' Brochan asked.

I squinted. 'Yeah. They're all wearing the Carnegie tartan.'

'Is that good or bad?'

'Difficult to say.' I shrugged. We all knew there was no such thing as an impartial judge. There was also Angus's warning to consider.

Taylor, apparently eager to make amends, leaned across. 'The Carnegies are in a long-standing feud with Clan Jardine and Clan Darroch. They have strong allies with Ochterlony though. That might help us.' He met my eyes. 'Coira Adair, your mother, originally hailed from Clan Ochterlony.'

I grimaced. 'I'm not sure that will help. Let's face it, she wasn't exactly a highly placed Sidhe noble.' It was about the only thing I knew about her. 'Plus, they weren't in a rush to speak up when I was looking for my three votes of support to enter the Games.'

'You need to use every advantage you can. I've heard the word honour bandied around far too much over the past few days. I think they're trying to convince themselves that they're filled with it.'

'The Clans doth protest too much, you mean?'

Taylor nodded. 'Indeed.'

I considered his words. I'd been banking on Dagda's harp to do all my work but if I could add some old-fashioned manipulation into the mix to help my cause, that would be all to the good.

'Thanks.'

'Does that mean I'm forgiven?' Taylor batted his eyelashes.

'Don't push your luck.'

A fanfare sounded and Byron strode out, still wearing his kilt from yesterday. I ignored the looks which Lexie and Taylor sent me and focused on him. With his shoulders back and his head high, he looked every inch the heir to the highest-placed Clan in Scotland. It occurred to me that what I'd once believed was arrogance had more to do with self-belief. It must feel good to have such unshakeable self-confidence. I thought I did a pretty good job myself but I didn't exude that kind of power.

Byron's gaze swept round the auditorium as if he were searching for someone in particular. I couldn't prevent a flash of hope that it might be me but that was a ridiculous notion. The stage lights were too bright so there was no chance he could see this far up.

When his eyes alighted on someone and he bowed and blew a kiss, my heart hardened. The object of his affection stood up and curtsied. Tipsania. Of course. I had no idea what game the two of them were playing but I meant what I said to Byron. It would be safer to keep as well away from them as I could.

A gigantic timer appeared over Byron's head and was lowered so that it was visible from every angle. Five minutes flashed up, followed by a loud gong and his performance began.

He dropped his head. Five seconds went by, then ten. I frowned. What on earth was he doing? I looked at the clock as a full half-minute ticked by, my heart in my mouth. Was this deliberate? I hoped it had nothing to do with me inadvertently nabbing part of his Gift. Just as my stomach squirmed in panic and the crowd started to murmur, there was a faint squeak of wheels from the wings. As if it were propelling itself, a baby grand piano appeared and wheeled its way towards Byron. He smiled but, other than that, remained perfectly still.

The moment the piano halted, the first note sounded, slow and melodic to begin with before speeding up into a pounding, powerful beat. Byron was at least five feet away from it; he was playing the piano through his Gift. The only thing that indicated he was responsible for the sound was the movement of the muscles in his face and body – a twitch of his forehead here and a bunching of his fingers there. As the music rose into the air, swelling in majesty, I forced myself to empty my mind and focus solely on the tune. The last thing I wanted was for my own mind to rip away more magic from him.

I didn't have to try that hard. The tune, whatever it was, was so stirring that it felt like it was consuming me. The piano keys moved, changing from fast to slow and from hard to soft, a velvety rhythm that overtook me completely. My heartbeat seemed to change, mimicking the melody. The auditorium was filled with the sound and I didn't need to look at the rest of the audience to know that they were as rapt as I was. How was it possible for a simple piece of music to be so imbued with emotion? Goosebumps rose on my arms and I felt odd stirrings of patriotism when I heard birls and lilts that were unmistakably Scottish. As Byron manipulated the keys into a crescendo, my blood buzzed and the music fizzed through my veins. And when the last note echoed away, I felt the wound on my cheek sting because I'd been crying without realising it.

The crowd rose to its feet, bellowing approval. I hastily wiped away my tears and joined them.

'That was unbelievable!' Lexie yelled.

Brochan remained seated. 'If you like that sort of thing.' His eyes were suspiciously glassy.

'If I was wearing underpants, I'd be tempted to take them off and throw them at him,' Taylor admitted. 'No wonder you like him, Tegs.'

Byron bowed and turned to the judges. They each pressed a button, lighting up screens that were set into the league table. Nine. Nine. Ten.

'I can't believe he didn't get a perfect score,' Speck muttered. 'I can see why they keep harping on about how dangerous these challenges are. If everyone else is that skilful, then I'm in danger of losing my heart.'

I took a deep breath. 'Speaking of harping on, it doesn't matter how impressive Dagda's harp is,' I said. 'I think I'm pretty much screwed. I can't compete with that.'

Not one of my friends disagreed.

# Chapter Twelve

I stayed for the next few performances. Although none were as impressive as Byron's, they were still very proficient. I was tempted to disturb Bob and get him to listen and see if he thought that Dagda's harp was going to be enough for me not to come last. But there were too many people around and it was probably too late to do anything about it anyway. Even though I was bottom of the list and wouldn't perform until late tomorrow, I wouldn't acquire any musical ability by then, no matter how much I wanted it. I'd just have to keep my fingers crossed that Dagda came through.

When the five Moncrieffe competitors finished and Tipsania glided onto the stage, I decided it was time to do something. Leaving the rest of them to maintain appearances, and after passing the harp to Brochan, I slipped out the door. With most of the Cruaich's visitors in the auditorium, it was the perfect opportunity to see what I could find. There would be less chance of bumping into anyone who wanted to make an example of me, like the trio who had set upon me earlier.

There was no question about who I was most interested in. As Steward, Aifric was beholden to his guests and forced to remain in the auditorium; it wouldn't do for him to publicly snub a Clan by leaving during a performance. What was no doubt a pain in the arse for him was a godsend for me. All I had to do was locate his quarters and I could snoop around to my heart's content.

I had a vague idea where all the rooms and suites were located after my last visit here but the Cruaich castle was still a maze. With twenty-four Clans staying, not including my own, it would be a waste of time for me to skulk down every corridor in the hope of finding flashes of the Moncrieffe tartan so, rather than wander around aimlessly, I strolled into the main hall and looked for someone who would help.

The Sidhe nobles might despise me because of my lineage but the lesser Clanlings were far more amenable. In fact, they often seemed in awe of me. It was one of the many things that made me wonder what my father was really like. Unfortunately, I wasn't sure I'd ever get an answer.

Spotting a scurrying pixie, I barred his way. 'Hello!' I beamed.

The pixie, obviously flustered, gave a brief bow. 'Chieftain Adair.'

I tried not to look too happy that he'd used my real name and title. 'I wonder if you can help me,' I said to get the pixie on side.

'Of course. Would you like some refreshments?'

'No, thank you. I'm hoping for a tour of the castle. Is there anyone who could take me round? It's just that I'm new here and I'm constantly feeling wrong-footed. If I had a better idea of the layout, I'd know what people are talking about when they discuss the Cruaich's history.' I tittered. 'Last time someone asked me to meet them in the library it took me hours to find it!'

The pixie blinked at me. 'Er...'

He was reluctant to point me in the direction of someone with free time. 'Let me guess,' I said drily, 'you've heard the rumours about my thievery skills too.'

He had the grace to look embarrassed. 'I don't believe them, Chieftain. Honest.'

Considering I *was* a thief, he shouldn't have been so quick to dismiss those whispers. Either way, I did have some sympathy for his position. 'But if someone finds out that you showed me around and something went missing...'

He nodded, the flesh under his chin shaking. 'I'm sorry.'

'That's okay. I understand. You're probably very busy and have a lot to do.'

His relief was palpable. I stepped out of his path and let him continue on his errand. The staff weren't going to help – I'd have to find another way to locate Aifric's chambers.

When I heard footsteps behind me, I turned and realised I had a more useful person to target. 'Jamie!'

The Moncrieffe Sidhe's eyes widened when he caught sight of me and I had the feeling that he wished he were somewhere else. I trotted up to him before he could escape. 'I really enjoyed your performance,' I told him.

It was true. He'd chosen to go the more traditional route and played the bagpipes, using a lilting Scottish lament to enthrall the audience. Most bagpipe music just sounded like noise to me but Jamie's dexterity with the instrument had elevated my appreciation. He'd not used his Gift but that wasn't surprising. Like most Sidhe, Jamie only had one Gift and his was psychometry, the ability to touch an object and learn its history. I couldn't see how that would be useful in entertaining a large group of people – though I could use it for something else.

'Thanks,' he mumbled. He tried to move past me.

I sighed audibly. 'I'm sorry that you still feel awkward around me. That wasn't my intention.'

His eyes dropped. 'I know.'

'What we did wasn't anything to be ashamed of.'

He grimaced. 'Try telling that to Byron.'

There was an odd fluttery sensation in my stomach. 'I'm sorry if you got into trouble for consorting with the enemy.'

'It wasn't like that. It's just...'

'What?'

'Nothing.'

I desperately wanted to prod him to tell me more but this wasn't the time. 'Okay.' I bit my bottom lip. 'Look, I was wondering if you could help me out.'

He looked almost as uncomfortable as the pixie had. 'Um...'

'It's won't get you into trouble.' I held up my hands. 'I promise. It's an object I have that I want to know more about.'

Jamie started to relax then a thought seemed to cross his mind and he stiffened. 'It's not a necklace, is it?'

I groaned. 'You think I took Chieftain MacBain's pearl monstrosity? I promise you I didn't, although this is related to her.'

His eyes shifted. 'In what way?'

I told the truth. 'I crossed the Veil. There was something in the Lowlands that I needed.' The colour drained from Jamie's face as I ploughed on. 'I found a ring there. It wasn't what I was looking for but I think it's important. It was on the finger of a corpse which I spotted inside an old house. Written above it was the name Matthew MacBain and the ring has the MacBain crest on it.'

Despite his shock that I'd passed into the Lowlands, I could tell that Jamie was interested. 'Why not give it to the MacBains then?'

I shrugged. 'I tried. I arranged a meeting to do just that but then I was accused of stealing the necklace. I don't want to be accused of stealing the ring too. If you could use your Gift to find out more about it, you'd be able to tell I didn't steal it.' I paused. 'Not from anyone living, anyway.'

'Matthew MacBain.' Jamie shook his head in wonder. 'There are lots of stories about him but no one really believed he'd gone through the Veil.'

'I'm pretty sure he did,' I said quietly. 'And that it didn't go well for him.'

He swallowed. 'Okay. Where's the ring?'

I grinned. 'It just so happens I have it right here.' I glanced around. 'There are a lot of servants around. It would be better if we went somewhere private. I'd hate someone to see what we're doing and for others to find out before Chieftain MacBain does.'

'We could go outside...' Jamie began.

'Or to your room,' I interrupted. 'That way we can be sure of privacy.'

His alarm returned. 'I don't think that would be a good idea.'

My grin widened. 'We don't have to go to your bedroom. In fact you're right. The village is quite a way off. There must be a Moncrieffe sitting room up here in the castle somewhere.'

He eyed me warily. 'I suppose.'

'Brilliant! Let's go then.'

*

I walked quickly, not because I was in a hurry but because I didn't want Jamie to change his mind before we reached the Moncrieffe quarters. Aifric would be installed here at the Cruaich because he was the Steward and I was banking on the fact that he'd keep his Clan close to him. The competitors only formed a small part of the current population; there were plenty of other hangers-on here for the entertainment.

Jamie, moving quickly to match my speed, loped up the stairs to the sixth floor. He turned left and led me into an impressive drawing room with a huge fireplace and artfully arranged furniture. Looking around, you'd never know that the Moncrieffes were struggling for cash.

I was dubious. 'Are you sure this is a good spot? If we're interrupted...'

'It'll be fine. This is the Moncrieffes' own space. It's only used when the Steward has to meet privately with someone. His personal quarters are next door. No one would dare venture in here without an invitation.'

Perfect. I made a show of considering and then agreed. We perched on a sofa, which was as hard and uncomfortable as it looked, and I dug into my pocket and pulled out the ring. Jamie didn't move, he simply stared at it. 'That's certainly the MacBain emblem.'

'I thought so but it's good to have it confirmed. You know your stuff.' I took care not to overdo the compliment but I could tell by his smile that he appreciated it.

He took a deep breath. 'And you really found this in the Lowlands?'

'Yep.'

He didn't try to take it. As the silence grew more awkward, he ran a hand through his hair. 'It's not an exact science,' he admitted. 'My Gift, I mean. Sometimes, especially with older objects, it's hard to control what I see. There's a flood of images and so many memories that it can be difficult to separate things out.'

I suddenly understood what he was referring to. 'You're afraid of what you might see.'

Jamie nodded. 'If Matthew MacBain died violently, if he was wearing this ring while he was in the Lowlands and bad things happened to him...'

'You'll see it all.' His reluctance made sense; useful as his Gift might be, it didn't sound like it offered its user many pleasant experiences. No doubt the unhappy memories were the ones which would stick. Tragedy was often like that.

'Don't worry about it,' I said softly. 'If you don't want to do this, I'll find another way to prove I didn't steal it.'

'No. I'll do it.' He exhaled and reached out, his fingers curling round the ring. He lifted it, taking care not to touch me. Then he closed his eyes, stood up and shuddered.

I wondered if I should support him as he swayed backwards and forwards but I doubted he'd appreciate my help so I withdrew. When Jamie's eyes finally opened, he was pale and shivering.

'I can assure Chieftain MacBain,' he said in a stilted voice, 'that you took this from her uncle's body in the Lowlands.'

I nodded, trying to remain calm. 'What else did you see, Jamie?'

'The demons,' he whispered. 'The Fomori. There are thousands of them.' He paused. 'Hundreds of thousands.'

I swallowed. 'Did you see anyone else?'

He wouldn't meet my eyes. 'I think I should leave everything else for Chieftain MacBain.'

I didn't press him. The horror of what he'd seen was still written across his face. I silently thanked the heavens that my subconscious had decided not to steal this particular Gift. 'I'll leave the ring with you,' I told him quietly. 'Do with it what you will.'

Jamie didn't reply. I raised my hand in gesture of both gratitude and farewell and left him, shoulders drooped and skin clammy, as he absorbed what he'd seen.

I didn't have time to reflect on what Jamie was experiencing, much as I felt guilty about it. I left the drawing room door and jogged to the next door. I knocked once and, when no one answered, twisted the doorknob and peered inside.

These were Aifric's rooms all right. The Moncrieffe tartan was everywhere and if that wasn't enough of a clue, the suit he'd been wearing yesterday was hanging on the side of the huge oak wardrobe. The bed was neatly made and there nothing on either of the side tables next to it. I opened the drawers, using the cuff of my jumper. I doubted that Aifric ever dusted for fingerprints but it paid to be circumspect.

There was a small bottle of pills inside. I picked it up and examined the label, whistling softly. Strong stuff. So the Sidhe Steward was having trouble sleeping - as well he should. I replaced it carefully, closed the drawer and looked around.

I couldn't find much that interested me. There was a heavy chain inside a small glass cabinet, probably a symbol of the Stewardship, and there were carefully ironed clothes in the wardrobe. The rest of the room was spartan in its tidiness and emptiness. I wondered what Aifric was getting out of his position – it certainly wasn't money; his Clan was all but penniless. I'd not heard of him enjoying any romantic dalliances so sex was out of the equation. I thought about the way he comported himself and decided it had be a power thing. What an idiot; real power comes from inner peace and contentment, not or-dering others around. Half the servants in this place could probably have told him that.

There were two other doors. The first one led into a well-ap-pointed bathroom with mod cons which looked out of place in such an old castle. The second door opened into a small study. Yahtzee. There was a large desk, covered with letters and papers. I was bound to find something here.

Sitting down on the cracked leather chair, I looked through the first bundle. There were a lot of petitions from different Clans: the Kincaids wanted to search for the Foinse, which had flown off after I'd released it from the cavern deep in the Scottish mountains; the Jardines were in the middle of a land dispute with the Carnegies and demanded that the borders be re-drawn, while the Chieftain of the Innes Clan was hoping for a loan from the Cruaich coffers so he could go hunting for the mythical white stag. I snorted.

One unsigned letter caught my attention. I had no way of know-ing who it was from but my own name stood out like a beacon. Someone was demanding that I be taken care of - apparently I was a danger to society. It was suggested that I'd hidden my Gift because, like the last one of my father's, it was soul punching. That is, the abil-ity to draw inside an opponent and yank out their life essence. Ap-parently it was how he'd killed so many so quickly. The suggestion in the letter was that any moment now I might slaughter every one of the Sidhe in vengeance for what had been done to my Clan.

Now that was interesting. Why would I want vengeance when it was supposedly my father who'd done the killing that had left me alone in the world? It was another piece of evidence that he was in-nocent and that, somehow, Aifric Moncrieffe was involved in setting up my father and committing genocide.

The knot of anger in my chest expanded. It was an unfamiliar sensation; Taylor had taught me to take each day as it came and to appreciate what I had without worrying about the past or the future. I had elected to avoid the Sidhe wherever possible – unless it was to steal from them, of course. Now, whether my entire Clan were dead or not, it felt like I'd let them down. I was still floundering around in the dark for the truth.

Abandoning the desk, I looked for a safe where Aifric might hide more sensitive materials. I couldn't find it. Unless Aifric was using magic to conceal it, there was no safe here.

Irritated, I stood up. Considering all the effort it had taken to get here, I had very little to show for it. I tilted my head backwards and stretched my neck – and that action that made me spot the one thing that looked out of place.

The study was lit by a small chandelier, much like the other rooms I'd seen in the Cruaich. This one was as finely made as the others, with little crystal shards decorating the frame in a spiral pattern, but something darker was teetering above the glass. I pulled over the chair and, standing on it, I grabbed the edge of what felt like cold metal and brought it down so I could examine it more closely.

When I saw it, my veins ran cold. It was a tiny pewter lion on its hind legs and with its paws in the air as if ready to do battle – in fact, it was exactly the same as the tattoo I'd spotted beneath May's battle scars when I'd fought her when I was beyond the Veil. Whatever I'd been expecting to find, it wasn't this – because here was proof positive that Aifric was working in some way with the Fomori demons.

# Chapter Thirteen

By the time I returned to the auditorium, the performances were finishing for lunch. I looked around for a friendly face. I couldn't see any of my group but I did spot Byron in a cluster of giddy-looking girls. Clearly, he'd not lost his playboy touch. Pushing back my shoulders, I marched over.

'It's her!' one of the girls gasped.

I licked my lips and looked her up and down. She blanched. Dear me. 'Girls, if you could excuse Lord Byron for a moment…'

A dark-haired Sidhe, who was clearly the boldest of the group, stepped forward. 'If he doesn't want to talk to you, he doesn't have to.'

My eyebrows flew up and I glanced at Byron. 'You don't want to talk to me?' I dropped to my knees and clasped my hands. 'But why? It's not fair!' My voice rose with every word until we were attracting quite an audience. 'I want you to talk to meeeeee!'

Byron folded his arms. 'Integrity,' he sighed. 'Is this really necessary?'

'I thought you were my friend.'

'The last thing we are is friends,' he grunted, although his mouth twitched and I didn't imagine the hint of smoky promise that crossed his face. 'Ladies,' he said with a bow, 'perhaps you could give us a few minutes.'

They glared at me but they weren't about to gainsay Byron. They swirled away, voices low and irritated. I held out my hand so Byron could help me up.

He didn't move. 'I think you can manage by yourself.'

I shrugged and stood up. 'True.'

The people who'd been watching my little show returned to their own conversations. I grinned at Byron.

'I was under the impression that you thought we should stay away from each other,' he remarked.

I jabbed a finger at him. 'Hey, you're the one who approached me this morning. Anyway, you looked like you needed rescuing. And I wanted to congratulate you on your performance this morning. It was sensational.'

'Is that another joke?'

'No,' I said honestly.

His eyes scanned my face. 'Then thank you.'

I curtsied. 'My pleasure.'

His expression softened and we looked at each other for a moment in silence. My stomach tightened. Crapadoodle. I had other things to focus on than the hot, zippy feeling in my groin.

'So, Integrity,' Byron said, finally breaking the silence. 'What do you really want?' There was no denying the suggestive lilt to his tone.

I pursed my lips and watched him carefully. Focus, Integrity. Focus. 'Fomori demons.'

He blinked, taken aback. He'd obviously been expecting me to say something else. 'What about them?'

'Have you ever met one?'

'Of course not.'

'Are you sure?'

'I think I'd know if I had,' he answered drily. 'What on earth has come over you?'

I pressed on. 'What do you think of them?'

He stared at me. 'You mean besides the fact that they're blood-thirsty bastards who changed the face of our country forever and ruined what could have been a wonderful place? Well,' he said sarcastically, 'I think they're fabulous.'

He looked puzzled and vaguely irritated. Yes, all these Sidhe were damned good actors but I didn't think he was faking.

'Great!' I said sunnily. 'Thanks!'

I turned to go but he caught my arm. 'What was all that about?'

I caught sight of Jamie out of the corner of my eye. He was hovering in the background, looking nervous. 'Ask your mate,' I said flippantly. Then I wandered off.

Lexie, Speck, Brochan and Taylor were huddled in a cluster by the door, looking worried. I strolled up and looped my arm round Taylor's broad shoulders. 'Everything alright?'

I received four identical guilty looks. Clearly everything was not alright. 'Did you find anything?' Brochan asked gruffly.

I nodded. 'Yeah.' I lowered my voice. 'Aifric is working with the demons.' They stared at me in stunned silence. 'I thought that would grab your interest.'

'When you say demons,' Brochan said slowly, 'you mean...'

'Fomori.'

'That's insane,' Lexie whispered. 'I knew the guy was a vile prick but how could he ally himself with them?'

Taylor shook his head in disbelief. 'You're sure?'

'Yep.' I told them about the little iron lion.

Speck sucked in a breath. 'That's nuts.'

Lexie agreed with him. 'It doesn't make any sense. Why would he do that?'

'Beats me. But I'm guessing it's to do with my dad.'

'We'll find out the truth,' Taylor said, his eyes meeting mine.

'You bet your arse we will.' I paused. 'That's a metaphorical bet, by the way, not a literal one. Now tell me what the problem is.'

Lexie attempted an innocent expression. 'What do you mean?'

'When I walked over you all looked as if the world was ending. What gives?'

Brochan tapped his foot. 'These Sidhe are too good.'

'*Too* good?'

'Musically,' Speck broke in. 'You've got no chance. Some Kincaid performer dropped out and one of the Blairs didn't show up either.

Unless more of them decide they're not good enough and back out, you're screwed.'

'The harp...'

'Play one note and you'll beat everyone? There's no way, Tegs. There was a Darroch woman who made butterflies dance.'

'And that woman with the stupid name who's shagging the Wild Man with the even stupider name sang so beautifully that Brochan gave her a standing ovation.'

I shot him a look. 'Really?'

His eyes dropped. 'She was very proficient.'

'The point is,' Taylor said, 'that you need to be prepared for coming last, harp or no harp.'

'It's just one event,' I reminded him. 'And I have faith in Bob.'

They exchanged looks. 'It might not matter,' Speck said.

I frowned. 'What do you mean?'

He shuffled his feet. 'We were right to wonder about the judges,' he said. 'I cloned one of their phones.'

'And?' I asked warily

'And the Carnegies are under orders to place you last no matter what you do.'

My spine stiffened. 'Orders from whom?'

'Moncrieffe,' Speck mumbled.

A dark hole opened in my chest. 'Byron?'

'Aifric.'

I balled my hands into tight fists. Shite. Despite my conversation with him about how I wanted to win so I could ask for permission to join the Bull's Clan, Aifric wasn't taking any chances. He obviously didn't trust me any more than I trusted him. I gritted my teeth and tried to think. 'This could be a good thing,' I said finally.

'I fail to see how,' Brochan rumbled.

'If he's contacting the Carnegies without disguising his tracks, he's being open about how he feels about me. We can use that.'

'You have a plan?' Lexie asked eagerly.

'No.' I chewed on the inside of my cheek. 'Yes.' I glanced at Speck. 'How did he contact them? Was it a call?'

He shook his head. 'Text.'

I snapped my fingers. 'So you cloned his phone. Text the Carnegies back and say you – he has changed his mind.'

'We can do that,' he answered, 'but then we're showing our hand as much as Aifric is. Right now, he thinks that you believe him. When he discovers otherwise, things could change drastically.' He paused. 'As in more assassination attempts.'

'Or,' Lexie added darkly, 'successes.'

'That's a good point,' I said. I pressed my lips together. 'Okay. Make that a last resort. As far as I know, the Carnegies aren't particularly close to the Moncrieffes. All we have to do is to encourage them to ignore that order.'

'They might not like Aifric Moncrieffe but he's still the Steward. They won't want to piss him off or they'll receive the fallout themselves.'

'Then,' I said, 'we'll have to be bloody careful.' I grinned suddenly. 'I have just the thing.' I looked around the room, my eyes alighting on a table laden with scones and sandwiches. 'Watch this space.'

I strode over to it and leapt up. My heel landed smack bang in a large chocolate cake, sending ganache flying in all directions. 'Oops,' I said to the wide-eyed Sidhe who gaped at me from below. 'Is that a cake or a meringue?' I frowned. 'No, I was right. It's definitely cake.' I winked. 'I guess you have to be a real Scot to get that joke. Am ah wrang?' I asked, deepening my accent.

'Integrity, what on earth are you doing?' Byron strode over, his brow furrowed.

A couple of Sidhe nudged each other. 'Told you she was as mad as the MacQuarries,' one of them said.

My foot slipped, inadvertently sending a gloop of chocolate towards her. It landed on her cheek and she shrieked.

'I'm so sorry,' I mouthed. Then I cleared my throat. It was unnecessary; I already had the attention of the whole room. 'Ladies and gentleman,' I shouted, in my most formal tone. 'For those of you who don't know, my name is Integrity Adair. I'm the only Adair left in the world because my father was a dishonourable bastard.' There was an audible intake of breath. I silently apologised to my Clan – and my father – but I reckoned they'd understand. 'I didn't know him but I still represent Clan Adair and I want to prove to you all that I am honourable. I know there are rumours that I'm a thief, that I stole a necklace from Chieftain MacBain and that the apple doesn't fall far from the tree. But I'm not a murderer and I no longer break the law. Instead, I've been saving lives by working with mountain rescue. In fact, just a couple of weeks ago two Moncrieffe Sidhe survived partly because of me. I am making amends for my past.'

I paused. Although a few people were softening towards me, most of the crowd was still against me. 'I understand that honour is vital to our kind. I have heard the word many times in the past few days; these Games are all about honour. We seek to honour our Clans by participating. Winning is not important compared to being able to look your fellow competitors in the eye and act with the same honour that they show to you. That is why I must speak the truth.'

I took a deep breath. The three Carnegie judges had entered the room and were standing at the back. I met each of their gazes in turn as I continued. 'Recently, there was a Carnegie ship in the dock at Oban. I spoke to one of the sailors on the ship and discovered what was on board. It wasn't deliberate on my part; at the time I had no idea the Games even existed. But I learned information which places me at an unfair advantage and which dishonours Clan Adair. In the interests of fair play, I can do nothing but share this information with every competitor here. We live and die by honour, after all.'

There was an angry murmur from several of the watching competitors. 'What?' someone shouted. 'What did you find out?'

I glanced at Byron. He was looking at me thoughtfully. Right now, however, he wasn't my target audience – those judges were. I focused on them. 'I discovered that a giant spider is being brought here. It can only be for these Games. This is knowledge which I gained unfairly and which I now have to share with you. I need to prove to you that Clan Adair does have honour.' I bowed my head.

Speck, Lexie, Brochan and Taylor began to clap. Some pixies and trolls joined in, along with several humans. Applause is often infectious and soon most of the occupants of the room were acknowledging my 'honour'. I stepped down from the table, wiped the chocolate cake off my shoe and joined my friends.

'Nice work,' Taylor said approvingly.

I kept my expression serious but he'd noted the gleam of satisfaction in my eye. 'It was worth giving up that advantage to get a fair hearing from the judges,' I said. 'And it might make everyone feel a bit less antagonistic towards me. Goodness knows, I mentioned honour often enough.'

'I might have clapped but I don't really understand what's going on,' Lexie whispered.

Brochan leaned over to her. 'Tegs just positioned herself as the most honourable person in the room. She gave away vital information that would have helped her win the challenge. If the harp does what Bob says it will, those judges won't get away with giving her a low score. Integrity has made too big a deal out of being a proud Sidhe who's brimming with uprightness. If they act maliciously, everyone will know it. And because of this little speech, everyone will pay attention.'

Speck smirked. 'Integrity has integrity.'

I grinned. 'Not really. But Integrity is prepared to look as if she has to manipulate the hell out of this lot.'

'Amen,' Taylor murmured. 'Amen.'

                                        *

The following day, my confidence was less obvious. As I was the last competitor to go on the stage, I was alone in the waiting room behind the wings. Alone apart from Bob, of course.

'Uh Integrity,' he said frowning, 'couldn't you have dressed up for the occasion?'

I glanced down at my outfit. 'What do you mean? I'm wearing the Adair tartan.' I twirled round; I'd fashioned a length of it into a skirt which I thought looked rather fetching.

'No,' he tutted. 'Pink is not your colour.'

I glared at him. 'Pink is exactly my colour. It matches my eyes.'

'I hate to break it to you but just because your hair is white does not mean you are an albino. Your eyes are not pink.'

'They're violet,' I said through gritted teeth. 'It's the same colour-family as pink. And this is coming from the genie who was wearing a cocktail dress and a feather boa not too long ago?'

He winked at me. 'And don't you wish you had my style?'

I rolled my eyes and turned to more serious matters. 'Is this going to work?' I asked him, hefting the harp in my arms. 'I've taken you at your word and told the others that I trust you but...'

'But?' he shrieked. 'But? If you trust me, then there is no but!'

'I'm just checking. It's not as if I know how to play a buggering harp.'

Bob puffed up his chest. 'There are strings,' he told me self-importantly. 'You take your finger – any of them will do – and you pluck one string.'

'Which string?'

'C sharp.'

I gazed at him in panic. 'Which one is C sharp?'

He snapped his fingers and disappeared in a flash of light, just as the door opened and a dark figure ushered me forward. Crapadoodle. My stomach was churning and I was certain that the piece of stale bread I'd munched on for breakfast was about to come back up again. That would make an interesting display for the audience, I thought sourly, as I walked down the long corridor.

I shook out my hair and attempted to focus. How hard could this be?

The auditorium was packed. I'd been told that usually most of the audience had dwindled away by this point - after all, there's only so much musical prowess that even the most dedicated listener can take. But my performance in the tent the previous day had reversed the norm. I didn't know whether they wanted me to fail spectacularly or they were on my side because I'd made such a point about the importance of honour. As long as I didn't come last in this challenge, I was still in with a shot of winning the Games. I kept that thought firmly in mind as Angus MacQuarrie strode off the stage and stopped beside me.

'How did you do?' I asked, glad to have something else to focus on.

He grinned. 'Better than I expected. Music isn't really my thing.'

I grimaced. 'It's not mine either.'

He raised his eyebrows. 'And you're playing the harp? Isn't that meant to be the hardest instrument to master?'

'I wouldn't say that I've exactly mastered it,' I said.

The official standing next to us tapped his clipboard and pointed at me. I inhaled sharply. My hands were trembling. I smoothed my palms down my thighs and shuddered. I'd never wanted to be a popstar or an actress when I was a kid; public performances weren't my thing.

'You'll be fine,' Angus said warmly. 'Just picture the audience naked.'

'That's such a cliché,' I muttered. 'Does it work?'

'Are you kidding? With all that flabby flesh?' He leaned closer. 'I know for a fact that the head judge is wearing a leopard-print thong. I saw his bum crack this morning when he bent over to pick up a piece of paper.'

I blinked. The official glowered and grabbed my arm, propelling me onto the stage. The lights were blindingly bright, making it difficult to see anything but the only thing I could think of was which one of the judges was an animal lover. I sent a grateful nod towards Angus; if nothing else, he'd taken my mind off the hundreds of pairs of assessing eyes.

There was a red spot in the middle of the stage. I walked towards it, gently put down the harp and stared at it dubiously. C sharp couldn't be that hard to locate, could it? I thought of *The Sound of Music* and attempted to run through the octave in my head. Maria Von Trapp hadn't mentioned C sharp, though. Or played the damn harp.

The audience quietened. If nothing else, the instrument looked impressive as the stage lights bounced off of it. Looking at it more closely, however, I spotted a little dark spot on its polished surface; it was probably a remnant from the dip the harp and I had enjoyed in the Clyde. As the massive clock above my head began to tick, I leaned over to wipe it away. Unfortunately, I inadvertently brushed one of the strings and a single note rang out. Shite, that wasn't C sharp. Or it probably wasn't: I wasn't musical enough to tell.

Before I could correct my mistake, the audience erupted. I glanced up, baffled. Were they laughing at me already?

'Give me a bloody chance,' I whispered under my breath. I scanned the first row. Every face was contorted in hysterics. Some people were doubled over, clutching their stomachs. So they were all still against me. Bastards.

I stared again at the strings and chose one at random. Whatever. This was only five minutes of my life and I was already making a fool of myself. What did it matter which string I plucked? I twanged it and another perfect note spun out, almost breath-taking in its clarity.

The laughter stopped abruptly. There was a loud gasp, followed by a sob from somewhere to my right. I plucked the same string again. Yeah, yeah. So I couldn't play any kind of tune.

There was another sob and several people cried out. I gritted my teeth; I was probably making their ears bleed, just as Taylor had foretold. I glanced at the few visible faces and saw that most of them were crying. Eh?

I flicked another look at the judges. Two of them had their arms round each other, while the third was wiping away tears with a large spotted handkerchief. I shook my head in confusion and stared at the harp.

'Okay dokey,' I whispered as I realised what was happening. The first note had made everyone laugh; the second one had made them cry. Dagda's harp really was magical. Awesome. Then I shrugged; enough adulation. I ran my hand from one side of the harp to the other. The sound was extraordinary, a chiming thrum that grew in tempo and volume.

I focused on one woman in front of me. Her face twisted from glee to anger to abject misery. By the time the notes faded away, she was clutching her heart with such an expression of delight that I almost fell backwards. It was too much to look at.

I turned my head and checked the clock. It felt like half an hour had gone by but I was barely into my second minute. I was done though; I shrugged, picked up the harp and walked off.

The official who'd been so annoyed with me moments earlier was on his knees, gaping at me. Even Angus, who hadn't left yet, stared at me in awe. A heartbeat later, there was a roar of what sounded like thunder. I frowned. It hadn't looked like a storm was coming when I arrived. Then I realised it wasn't thunder – it was applause.

I peered out from the curtains. The audience were on their feet, not just clapping but stamping and shouting for more. One of the judges called for an encore. I pulled back, dropping the harp as if it had burned me.

'I've never heard anything like that in my life,' Angus breathed. 'So much for not being musical.' He grasped my hand and squeezed it. 'That was incredible.'

'Er, it wasn't really me.'

'Don't be so modest. You were amazing.'

With the clock ticking down the last few seconds, the crowd continued to roar. The judges consulted and I held my breath. When the scores flashed up, it took a moment for them to register.

'A perfect score,' the official gasped. 'Wonderful! Simply wonderful!'

'Um, thanks.' I didn't know where to look. Bob and Dagda had come through, and then some. I gingerly stretched out my hand, my fingers curling round the cool wood. The harp felt exactly the same, apart from the slightest vibration that was invisible to the eye. 'You were fabulous,' I whispered. I didn't think it was my imagination that the vibrations grew momentarily stronger before fading away entirely.

I left Angus and the official gaping after me and quickly covered the harp before picking it up and walking into the bathroom nearby. As soon as I was inside, I locked the door and pressed my forehead against the mirror. If I thought I was shaking before, it was nothing compared to now.

Light flashed and Bob appeared. 'Told you!' he sang out. 'Aren't I wonderful? Don't you want to have my children?' He bounced up, landing on my shoulder and moving back my hair to whisper in my ear. 'Don't you want to make a wish right now out of gratitude for my awesomeness?'

I pulled back. 'I think it's the harp that's awesome, not you.'

'I'm the one who found it for you. And it's not as if you played it particularly well. I told you to choose C sharp, not strum it like a guitar. You're lucky that things didn't go completely tits up. Some of those strings create notes that can cause difficulties for weak-minded people who aren't fabulous genies like me.'

'Why didn't you tell me it was going to have that effect?'

He tutted. 'What did you think would happen? That's what Dagda's harp does. Honestly, Uh Integrity, sometimes I despair of your naivety.'

There was a sharp knock on the door. 'Tegs? Are you in there?'

Bob grinned. 'The others are coming to congratulate me. Let them in. We should get this over with before I start to feel embarrassed.'

I unlocked the door and Lexie flew at me, her small arms wrapping me in a hug. 'I knew you could do it! You were brilliant!'

'Thank you,' Bob said.

'I have to admit,' Brochan rumbled, 'that was pretty amazing.'

'I know, I know. There's no need to go on about it, though,' the genie continued.

'Shut up, Bob,' Speck said. 'Tegs, you are a musical genius.'

'She didn't do anything!' Bob howled. 'Why are you praising her? I'm the one you should be thanking!'

'Actually,' I said, glaring at him, 'I think the harp did all the work.'

'It was you who played it,' Lexie said loyally. 'And you got full marks. That means you're top of the table. Let's head out there and gloat.'

'I'm not sure that's a good idea,' Taylor said, frowning. 'They love you right now but it doesn't take much for adoration to turn into jealousy. You should play things down. It would be better to head

back to the cabin and keep a low profile. Besides, we ought to prepare for the Adventure challenge. I don't think the Hunt will be easy,
even for Tegs.'

I nodded. 'Taylor's right. This lot are fleeting with their loyalties.
Let's get out of here while we can.'

Lexie pouted but agreed. Bob, however, crossed his arms. 'You're
denying me my moment of glory.'

'Bob?'

'Yes?'

'C sharp when you cross the street or you're going to B flat.'

'Is that a threat?' he demanded. 'Are you threatening me, Uh Integrity? Because grammatically it doesn't even make sense. Just because you wish you were as magnificent as me.' He sniffed loudly.
'You were right, Taylor. It didn't take long for some people to become
jealous.'

I ignored him and looked at the others. 'Come on. Time to va-
moose.'

*

The audience were leaving the auditorium. I noticed more than one
Sidhe with mascara streaks running down their cheeks – men as well
as women. Several people congratulated me but I merely inclined
my head in brief acknowledgment and kept moving. Lexie, Speck,
Brochan and Taylor formed a helpful cordon to ward off the more
enthusiastic well-wishers as we squeezed our way through and escaped into the cold air.

We weren't the only people outside. Taylor jerked his chin towards a copse of trees where I spotted Aifric remonstrating with one
of the judges. He hadn't seen us, which was probably just as well.
I wasn't sure I could cope with his saccharine-sweet falseness right
now.

'Integrity!' I turned to see Byron. He caught up, his eyes raking over me. 'That was some performance.'

I dipped into a curtsey. 'Thank you.'

'Was it you or the harp?'

I shrugged. 'Does it matter?'

'I suppose not.' He tilted his head. 'You were very good,' he said quietly.

I tried not to notice the others slipping away to give us some space and gave an awkward shrug. 'It was just one challenge,' I reminded him. 'There are still two more to go.'

'True. But now you're in pole position.'

'Go me.'

A small smile tugged at his mouth. 'Indeed. Go you.' He took a step towards me and his voiced dropped. 'What are you playing at?'

I stepped back. 'What do you mean?'

'There's more going on here than meets the eye. What was that business with the ring and Jamie? He said you found it in the Lowlands, which is frankly ridiculous. Do you have any idea how dangerous it is to go there?'

Taken aback by the sudden turn in the conversation, I glared. 'Do you? Have you ever passed through the Veil?'

'Of course not! I'm not reckless like you.'

'You mean you're boring,' I shot back.

'Boring?'

This time I stood my ground. 'It appears so.'

'I'll show you how boring I am,' he muttered under his breath. He leaned towards me. Before anything could happen, however, there was a loud curse from Aifric. We both turned to watch him stomp back towards the auditorium.

I licked my lips. 'What do you think that was all about, Byron? Why would your father be so angry at the judges?'

The crackle in the air between us changed to something else entirely. 'Are you trying to insinuate something?'

'I'm just saying that it's a bit strange that he's so worked up.'

His eyes narrowed. 'My father has been nothing but generous towards you. He didn't have to be like that, considering all the trouble you've caused.'

'All the trouble *I've* caused?'

'He's on your side, Integrity. Just like me.'

I hoped that Byron wasn't like his father at all. I shook my head. I could stand here and argue till I was blue in the face but Byron wasn't going to listen to a word against his dear daddy. I sighed. 'I have to go.'

He reached for me but I whirled away and ran after the others. I didn't look back.

'What was that about?' Taylor asked with a glint in his eye.

'Not what you'd like it be,' I sighed. 'I'm just burning bridges.'

# Chapter Fourteen

The rest of the day passed slowly. We spent most of the time discussing what might occur during the upcoming Adventure challenge. Considering my role with mountain rescue, I was well-placed to win. The trouble was that the Carnegies – and Aifric – would be very aware of that. When night fell and I curled up in bed to get some sleep, my mind was still whirring over the possibilities. I had to be prepared for every eventuality. If I slept, it wasn't for long.

It was a relief when dawn came. I spent some time applying make-up to hide my bruised eyes and dressed carefully so that I looked my best. I didn't want anyone to think that I wasn't ready for whatever the second challenge would bring; showing weakness of any kind was not an option. In any case, it was worth the effort when I glimpsed the briefest flash of irritation on Aifric's face as I joined the other competitors in the main hall. I also caught the Bull grinning evilly at me. Clearly he was hoping – and expecting – that I'd fail miserably. I resisted the temptation to order him to start cheering my name but it wasn't easy.

'We would like to thank Clan Carnegie for the wonder of the Artistry challenge,' Aifric boomed. 'And we are excited by what the Adventure challenge will bring.'

From my left, Angus nudged me. 'Is that the royal we?' he said in an undertone.

I smirked. 'Now, now,' I whispered back. 'He is our Steward, after all.'

'He shouldn't be.'

I glanced at him, surprised and not entirely sure what he meant. There wasn't time to ask, though, because Aifric was speaking again.

'We trust that there have been no further leaks and that the nature of the Acumen challenge remains under wraps.' He didn't look at me as he said this but several others did. I tried to look innocent.

'We will pass over to the Carnegies to explain how the challenge will work. In the interests of fairness, only the competitors and the organisers shall remain in this hall.' He bowed once and swept out.

The supercilious lordling who seemed to be the MC stepped up. 'Competitors will be blindfolded and transported to the challenge site, then released onto the course in groups. You are permitted to work with others to achieve success but any points garnered will be your own. As I'm sure you are all aware, Adventure asks a lot of all the competitors, both emotionally and physically. Your progress will be tracked sporadically via drones, and the audience will watch from the auditorium so as not to disturb the action. Places will be decided by the order in which you return with your Clan flag in hand.' He smiled coldly. 'Your ultimate goal is simple. Find your flag. You will receive clues at particular points throughout the challenge to help guide you on your way. Hopefully most of you will return in one piece. In this challenge, anything goes.'

I frowned. 'What does that mean?' I asked Angus.

'That competitors can use their Gifts as they see fit,' he murmured. 'And they can interfere with others, as well as help them. In theory, it's the Carnegies' job to make sure that no one gets injured. In practice, the more blood that's spilt, the better.'

Bugger. That didn't sound particularly good, especially as I would now be a target with my name shining out from the top of the league table. Maybe winning the Artistry challenge hadn't been so wise after all.

Most people were dressed for action; even Tipsania had foregone her voluminous skirts for a jumpsuit. I noticed her at the front, clinging to Byron. No matter what was going on between me and him, it irked me that she was cuckolding him behind his back. I reminded myself that it wasn't my problem but it didn't help.

She simpered as a piece of paper was handed to her. I scowled. Tipsania did a good job of playing the role of helpless female; I didn't think she was any more helpless than I was.

The paper was a map and we all received a copy. It wasn't very detailed but there was enough information to indicate where the first clue was located. It seemed that we were to start at the base of a small group of hills and move towards the ocean's edge. On the map the distance didn't appear far; neither did the terrain seem treacherous. Judging by the way the Carnegie MC had spoken, however, those would both be dangerous assumptions.

I studied the map closely, then folded it and tucked it inside my jacket. Another official came over and gave us each a cursory check, looking for forbidden items. He eyed Bob's letter opener and my bottle of water. 'You are only permitted to bring one object with you,' he intoned. 'The water or the,' he paused, 'knife.'

I thought that calling the letter opener a knife was being overly generous but Bob would be pleased. I weighed up my options and decided on the genie. At this time of year, there was bound to be snow I could melt down if I got dehydrated. And Bob would be entertaining, if nothing else.

Angus watched me make my choice. 'Wouldn't a pocket knife be more useful?' he inquired.

A wet sponge would probably be more useful, I thought. I smiled though, aware that Bob would be listening. After the lack of glory yesterday, he could probably do with some ego stroking. 'Oh, this scimitar is more useful than you think,' I said airily.

Angus's eyebrows shot up. 'Scimitar?'

I coughed. 'Yes. What are you taking?'

He pointed. 'Rope. My grandfather used to say that there was nothing more useful. There's a lot that can be done with it.'

It was a sensible choice. 'I'm sure it'll serve you well,' I said sincerely. I glanced round, trying to see what the others were bringing along. There was a worrying number of weapons. I made a note to avoid anyone who was carrying anything of that ilk and began to stretch.

Angus seemed amused. 'Getting ready for a sprint? The Adventure challenge is more of a marathon.'

'I want to make a quick start,' I told him. It was true. In discussion with Taylor the previous day, we decided it was the only way. Go too slowly and others would follow me; go slowly and I'd end up caught up in their tracks and mistakes. To be successful, I had to pull away from the herd. If necessary, I'd choose a circuitous route even if it was longer. The Hunt was going to be difficult enough because we were being sent out in staggered groups. Also, I was used to relying on a team so doing this alone would be tough. But it was not insurmountable; this kind of challenge was far more suited to my skills than music.

Angus nodded. 'Interesting. You don't want to team up with me and work together? We'll both be in the last group, after all.'

I grinned. 'Thanks but I'm probably going to draw considerable fire. You'll do better on your own.' Plus, he'd slow me down.

'Fair enough.'

We fell silent as the first group – the Moncrieffes, Scrymgeours and Kincaids – stepped up. A Carnegie tied black masks around each person's head. Byron turned to me just before the mask hid his eyes and I caught a flash of emerald before they were covered up and he was led away with the others to a waiting vehicle.

'There go the winners,' Angus said, without a trace of rancour. 'I'm surprised they didn't change the order after your showing in Artistry.'

I shrugged. 'I'm surprised you're not more bothered about your place. You got a decent score too.'

'Not decent enough. No one expects me to win and I know I'm not going to.'

'So why take part?'

'You know the answer to that already.' He raised his voice. 'Honour, darling. It's all about honour.'

I was really starting to hate that word.

Enjoyable as Angus's company was, it wasn't easy waiting around before we were called to go. With twenty minutes between each group setting off, I regretted not staying behind in the cabin so I could snooze. The fact that everyone was called up in groups of three also worried me. When the MacQuarries were called along with Angus, and I was the only person left standing, those worries were confirmed: the Carnegies were making up for their failure to keep me at the bottom of the league table the day before. Whether I wanted to team up with others or not, they were making the choice for me. I tried to keep my expression blank; I wouldn't let them see how much their decision to separate me from everyone else rankled.

By the time I was motioned forward, my veins were buzzing with the need to get started. Let them do what they wanted, I decided. I submitted to the blindfold, although the official who tied it made the bindings uncomfortably tight. Roughly, he led me outside. I heard an engine running and I was pushed unceremoniously into a vehicle. If I hadn't known better, I would have thought I was being kidnapped.

I concentrated as the car moved off, listening to the sounds and trying to note the twists and turns but the journey was too long and, without my sight, I was soon lost. I estimated that well over an hour passed by the time we came to a halt.

The same rough hands hauled me out. I felt the crunch of snow beneath my feet and I shivered.

'Count to twenty,' a gruff voice said. 'Then remove the mask.'

I wrapped my arms around my body and started to count. A bitterly cold wind assailed the exposed parts of my skin. I listened hard as the car drove away, gears squealing, then there was nothing but me and the elements. That was odd: I'd expected to hear some noise from the other competitors.

The moment I reached twenty, I tugged at the blindfold. With the brilliant white of the landscape, it was difficult at first to adjust my vision. When I finally looked around, my heart sank. Bugger those Sidhe.

It was clear that I was in a bad situation. There was no sign of the three hills which I'd seen on the map and neither were there any tracks from previous competitors or drones. The only signs of life were the tracks from the car which had just left. Uneasiness trickled through me as I scanned the barren landscape, searching around in case this ended up being an ambush rather than a competition. It appeared, however, that I was completely alone.

'Bob!' I hissed. He didn't answer. I drew out the letter opener and shook it. 'Bob!'

There was the familiar flash of light and he appeared, blinking and yawning. 'What is it?'

'Haven't you been paying attention? The second challenge has started. I need you alert in case I have to make a wish.'

He shook himself. 'Are you going to make a wish?'

'Not yet.'

'Well then,' he huffed. 'I'm going back to my beauty sleep.' He looked me up and down. 'Something you should consider too.'

'Bob, this isn't the time. Pay attention. Where are we exactly?'

'Unless you say the magic words, Uh Integrity, I'm not going to tell you.'

I counted to ten in my head. 'Really? Because if you take a look around, you'll see that we're smack bang in the middle of a frozen wasteland. Just me and you. If I die of hypothermia, how long do you think you'll lie here before someone picks you up? One year? Five? Maybe,' I said with an evil grin, 'it'll be decades.'

'Uh Integrity,' Bob said petulantly, 'I don't know why you feel the need to torment me. I have done nothing but help you. Without me, you would be nothing.'

'An ugly nothing.'

He nodded. 'Exactly. Although if you'd take my beauty tips we could sort out the ugly part.'

'Thanks,' I said.

He peered at me. 'Are you being sarcastic?'

'I wouldn't dream of it.' I took out the map and unfolded it. 'We are supposed to be here, Bob.' I jabbed at the spot on the map. 'But it doesn't seem like we are.'

'We're not,' he said cheerfully. 'Can I go now?'

I cursed. 'They took me to the wrong damn place. Why would they do that?'

'They don't want you to win, dummy. Or, like you said, they want you to die of hypothermia.' He grinned. 'It's lucky I'm around or you'd never know anything.'

His words made sense. If I came last in this challenge, the Sidhe wouldn't have to worry about me. And if their reasoning was even more sinister, they might be looking for a way to get rid of me permanently. If I walked off in the wrong direction, I could easily freeze to death. The Carnegies would make a great show of wringing their hands at my loss, Aifric would be satisfied – and I would be a block of ice. So much for honour; I supposed honour only counted when people were watching.

I had to choose the right direction. I squinted into the weak morning sun. No doubt I wasn't too far away from the main event – we couldn't have travelled that far. And if I ended up as a frozen corpse on the other side of the country, questions might be asked.

'There are some bumps over there,' I mused. 'Do they look like hills to you?'

Bob had taken out a nail file and was giving himself a manicure. 'Hmm?'

'Bob!' I snapped my fingers. 'Pay attention. Do those look like hills?'

He glanced over. 'Yeah. They're not the hills you want, though.'

I frowned. 'How do you know?'

He shrugged. 'I just do. I know many things, Uh Integrity because I am a...'

'A magnificent being with power and knowledge of which I can only dream of. As you have already said many times, Bob. If those aren't the hills I need, then where are they?' He didn't answer, absorbed in shaping the perfect rounded tip. 'Bob. You're a magnificent genie.'

'I know.' He still didn't look up.

'Can you use that magnificence and tell me which direction to go in?'

He sighed as if a heavy burden had been placed on his shoulders. 'This isn't a wish?'

'No. But if I die here...'

'Then someone will find your body and I'll be transported back to the Cruaich.'

I gritted my teeth. 'What I was going to say was that if I die here, then I'll never get the chance to make that wish that I promised you. I still have two to go, remember?'

He paused then tossed the tiny nail file to one side. 'Very well. Wait here.' He wagged his finger at me. 'And no stealing my teleportation.'

'It's not a conscious thing!' I protested. 'I don't know how to stop myself from stealing people's Gifts.'

He pursed his lips. 'Walk over there and turn around.'

Maybe a bit of distance between us would work, although it hadn't with that old Carnegie flower-growing woman. I emptied my mind of thoughts of teleportation and Bob and fixated on the ground. The snow was different here to up in the mountains near Oban; it seemed coarser and more crystalline. I knelt down and traced my name on the surface with my gloved finger.

'Vanity is a terrible sin,' Bob said in my ear.

I jumped about half a metre. 'Did you have to creep up on me like that? And why haven't you left yet?'

He looked at me smugly. 'I left, I saw, I came back. And all so that you can conquer.' He jumped off my shoulder and landed in the snow, sending up a spray of it towards my face.

'*Et tu Brute*,' I grunted.

'Don't you want to know where to go?' he asked.

'Yes.'

'Then say it.'

'Say what?'

He tutted. 'Pretty please with a side order of chocolate-dipped cherries and Princess Leia in a gold bikini dropping them into my mouth.'

'I'm not saying that.'

'I thought you liked science fiction.'

'I do, but that is stupid. Just tell me which direction to go in. We're wasting time.'

'Okay. I'll tell you where to go if you put on a gold bikini and wear it back at the cabin when we return. You have to put your hair into giant ear muffs as well.'

'She didn't have that hair style when she wore the gold bikini.'

Bob shrugged. 'Those are my terms. And don't get any ideas about why I'm asking for this. It's not because I've got the hots for you, it's because I enjoy ritual humiliation.'

I crossed my arms. 'At least you're honest.'

He smiled at me. 'Promise.'

I could not believe I was doing this. 'Fine,' I snapped.

He held his hand up to his ear. 'I didn't hear that exactly. What will you do?'

I pictured Bob strung up on a tree and being attacked by a million midges. 'I promise to wear a gold bikini.'

'And the hair?'

'And I will put my hair in giant ear muffs.'

He grinned. 'Thank you!' He flew up and hugged me. Considering his arms didn't go round my neck, it was more like having a small, damp snowball thrown at me.

'Bob,' I said. 'Which way?'

He peeled himself off. 'North!' He pointed.

I peered ahead. I couldn't see anything. 'You're sure?'

'Uh Integrity...'

'Fine, fine. I'm going.' And with that, I started jogging. I had to make up for lost time.

\*

The wanker who had left me was smarter than I'd given him credit for. After twenty minutes of maintaining a good pace, I realised that I'd been travelling up a light slope. Thanks to a trick of perception, when I reached the top the hills I was aiming for were suddenly visible. Without Bob's help I'd probably have set off in the opposite direction – and doing that might have killed me. I'd have to be on my guard; it wouldn't take long for them to realise that their ploy hadn't worked. Until I caught up with some of the other stragglers, I was alone – and therefore at risk. So much for simply climbing up an ice wall or two before triumphantly collecting my flag and emerging victorious. At this rate, I'd be grateful to emerge alive.

I picked up speed, moving faster now that I had a bead on where to go. Even with my decent footgear I slipped a few times, but such minor mishaps only made me more determined. I ran around this sort of place for a living so a wet, bruised arse wasn't going to slow me down.

Just an hour or two after I was supposed to be at the starting point, I finally arrived there. The hills were smack bang in front of me and there were footprints. Most were going in the same direction although a few competitors had decided to take less direct routes. That was what I'd planned to do as well, but I was so far behind that I had little choice but to opt for the shortest possible distance.

'Yay!' Bob shouted, perched once more on my shoulder. 'We made it! Now we can go back and you can wear that bikini!'

'No,' I said patiently. 'Now the challenge is really on.'

He blew a raspberry. 'You're not going to win. You might as well quit now.'

'Adairs don't quit.'

'Uh Integrity, how many Adairs do you know?'

'I know me. Now hang on.' And with that I took off.

Anyone who's ever run on a beach – or through snow – knows how hard it is. What the organisers hadn't counted on was that the feet that had gone before me had done a great job of stamping out a path. I knew that I was moving faster than the others. It didn't mean I'd catch them up but it did mean I had a chance.

I hit the tree line before noon, just as the first buzz of a drone sounded overhead. It hovered above me, as if even the machine couldn't quite believe what it was seeing. I tipped back my head and addressed it.

'You thought you could delay me by dropping me in the wrong place,' I said. 'Or maybe even kill me. But here I am anyway.' I grinned and stuck out my tongue. 'You can't keep a good Sidhe down.'

Unfortunately, because I was still moving and not looking where I was going, I slipped again and landed flat on my back. I eyed the drone while it continued to watch me. As soon as it gave up and took off, I pushed myself to my feet and continued.

The Carnegies had picked a pretty spot for their Hunt. Even in winter, with the branches of the evergreens bowing with snow, and crisp cool air that was less gusty now I was out of the open, it was a stunning vista. I called up a mental image of the map. I didn't think the first clue would be too far away now.

My vision cleared and I frowned at the path: something was wrong with those tracks. No sooner had the thought entered my head than a shape barrelled out of the trees with an inarticulate war whoop.

I leapt out of the way and the shape flew past me, halting a few feet away and spinning round. 'Who are you?' I yelled.

'You know exactly who I am, you bitch!'

I regarded the pretty blonde carefully. I'd seen her face before but I couldn't place her. 'Um,' I demurred. 'You're...'

'Kirsty Kincaid,' she snarled.

'Oh.' I nodded wisely, as if I should have already known. 'Hi, Kirsty. What can I do for you?' It was a daft question; it was clear she was here to stop me in some way. The Kincaids had been in the first group that set off and she should have been miles away from here by now.

'You stole the Foinse. Where is it?'

Oh for goodness' sake. 'I didn't take the damn Foinse. It flew away.'

'So where is it then?'

I threw up my hands. 'How should I know?'

Kirsty glared. For some reason, she seemed to believe me but she wasn't done yet. 'You forced my cousin out of the competition.'

'Pike?' I snorted. 'That was his fault. As you probably already know.'

She glared at me but she didn't mention Pike again. 'You killed my Chieftain.'

I kept my arms by my sides and my tone calm. 'No, I didn't, I tried to save him. He fell.' It was true. On our return journey from the Foinse, he'd unbalanced himself whilst crossing a precarious rope bridge. I'd done what I could to save him; if it hadn't been for Aifric, I'd probably have been successful.

Something like panic crossed her face. 'Liar.' There was little conviction behind the word.

'No. I'm not.'

She flung herself at me, her hands curved into claws and her nails raking my face. I winced and pulled away. 'I'm kind of busy here, Kirsty. Maybe we could have this conversation some other time.'

'Fuck you!' She attacked me again, grabbing hold of my hair and yanking it hard. Buggering shite. Give me a guy any day over this; women fought dirty. 'Tell me why!' she shrieked. 'Why did you do it?'

I prised away her fingers and held them at arm's length. She tried to swipe me with her other hand but I dodged. 'I didn't do it,' I said patiently.

She glared at me. 'I'll get the truth.'

I half snorted. I'd given her the truth, whether she realised it or not. Although, it would admittedly be lovely if you could just desire the truth and then receive it in turn. It would certainly make my life a lot easier with tracking down what had actually happened to my Clan and what Aifric was up to.

She freed herself from my grip and stepped back, her eyes wide. 'Why did you kill William Kincaid?'

My skin tensed in goose bumps. They felt unnatural. 'I didn't kill him,' I repeated. 'And what exactly are you trying to do to me?'

'You're a witch!'

I shrugged. It was hardly the worst insult in the world. 'Kirsty...'

'Did you kill him?' she demanded.

Good grief. My skin prickled again. 'No.'

Her nose wrinkled. 'It doesn't make any sense,' she whispered. 'Why isn't it working? What are you doing? Why isn't it working?'

The penny finally dropped. 'You're a Truth Seeker.' And I'd half-wished for that kind of ability. Dread spun through me then, before I could stop it, I felt her Gift. It was as if something in my blood called out to hers. Nausea, worse than before, flooded through me. I gasped and stumbled. 'Get away from here.'

She shook her head in confusion. 'What...? I feel strange.'

'Kirsty,' I said though gritted teeth. 'Run!' I turned and started running away from her, hoping that the distance between us would work but it was too late; I could feel her power pumping through my veins. She gave a soft moan and there was a thud. I looked round. She'd already collapsed and was lying unmoving in the snow. 'Shite.'

The drone returned at that moment, its buzzing filling the sky. I was well aware of how this looked: Kirsty Kincaid was unconscious and I was standing next to her. I cursed loudly. The Carnegie MC might have said that anything went as far as the challenge was concerned but my popularity would hardly increase if the people watching back at the Cruaich thought I'd done her in. Maybe I had.

I edged closer and knelt down to check her pulse. It was still strong. As long as she could get to safety, she'd be fine. 'You need to get someone here!' I yelled up to the drone. 'She needs medical attention!'

'Uh Integrity,' Bob said, muffled within the folds of my scarf, 'they're not going to help her.'

'You don't know that,' I snapped.

'It's the name of the game. You come out here, you take the consequences.'

'How do you know?'

'Because I'm a magnific...'

'Shut up.' I eyed Kirsty's prone form. Damn it, Bob was probably right. If I wanted to win I had to leave her behind, but if I left her behind she'd freeze to death. Apparently it was the price you had to pay for daring to compete. I sighed in irritation, then scooped her up in my arms and threw her over my shoulder in a fireman's lift. Bob scuttled to my opposite shoulder. 'What are you doing?' he asked.

I threw a rude gesture towards the drone. It didn't react but continued to hover above us, transmitting every image. Bloody thing.

'She'll die if I don't do something. There's no point taking her back to the starting point because there's no one there. I'll just have to bring her with us.' To the people watching, it probably looked like I was talking to myself. Screw them.

'She'll slow you down,' Bob said.

'No shit.'

'She attacked you.'

'She scraped my face and pulled my hair,' I returned. 'I think I'll live. Besides, she obviously thought she was justified.'

'Are you making excuses for her?'

I shrugged. 'It's my fault she's unconscious.'

'You'll come in last if you do this,' Bob warned.

I rather thought that Kirsty would come in last but I took his point. 'I won't be last if I'm smart,' I said.

'What's that supposed to mean?'

I smirked and twisted to my left, plunging into the trees and leaving the footsteps and the path behind.

'Uh Integrity!' Bob shrieked. 'What are you doing?'

'It was a long shot to think I'd catch up with the others,' I said. 'The map only leads to the first clue. There's nothing that says I can't skip it and find the flags instead.'

'How will you find the flags without directions?'

'Lady Luck, Bob.'

'You're a freaking idiot,' he muttered.

I grinned, shifting Kirsty's weight to make her easier to carry. 'I know.'

# Chapter Fifteen

There was more method to my madness than Bob realised. I'd planned all along to avoid the trail left by the others; I was just doing it earlier than expected. I never trusted solely to luck - I wasn't that stupid - but Bob didn't need to know that. It would be fun to see his expression when he realised my shortcut was working.

I'd noticed that Kirsty doubled back before she threw herself at me. She'd already been to at least one other clue before apparently deciding she couldn't win so she might as well go after me instead. I fumbled as I walked, eventually finding the folded paper in her coat pocket. I scanned it carefully: it was the third clue. I wriggled in delight before adjusting my direction. Despite Kirsty's weight, her attack was proving to be a boon. Now I knew exactly where to go.

With the time I'd lost from being dropped in the wrong place, as well as my slower pace now I was carrying Kirsty, this new route was exactly what I needed. I could avoid what looked like a giant loop designed to irritate the competitors. Nipping through the woods would take me to the end point faster than wending my way through all the marked clues and, because of the tree cover, the drone couldn't follow me.

I picked my way through the trees, moving north-east to where the end point should be. From time to time, Kirsty stirred, mumbled something under her breath and then collapsed again. If I needed proof that my inadvertent theft of Sidhe Gifts could cause problems, this was it – although I was pretty excited at the thought of trying out Truth Seeking on Aifric. It could get me the answers to all my questions – and then some.

Despite the cold air, sweat was pooling uncomfortably between the tight fabric of my bra and my breasts, but even with this mild discomfort and my worry about Kirsty the challenge so far wasn't unpleasant. Occasionally there was a chirp from a passing bird or a scuttle from something in the undergrowth. The thick pine trees gave off a heady scent unlike the sharp freshness that I was used to at higher altitudes with mountain rescue. As someone who'd spent most of her life among urban dwellers, I was rapidly beginning to appreciate more rural surroundings. That didn't mean that I wouldn't enjoy sitting in a pub with a hot toddy and a roaring fire though. A skilled masseuse would be equally welcome because my back was aching from lugging around Kirsty. Unfortunately I doubted I'd find one around here.

I'd been on the move for a good two hours when I spotted the first tracks. My heart leapt in my chest because they weren't from any Sidhe competitors. These tracks were far too small – and whatever had made them was three-legged.

I propped Kirsty against a nearby tree and checked her over. There was a faint bloom to her cheeks but she'd not yet come around; I really hoped I'd not done her any permanent damage. Reassured that she wasn't in any immediate danger, I went back to the tracks and knelt down to examine them.

They were definitely the same as the ones I'd seen up on the mountain when I was with the rescue team but I wasn't any closer to working out what had made them. Some kind of winter creature? If I knew, I might have been able to work out whether they led deeper into the forest or would take me back out.

I hissed to Bob. 'Hey! Take a look at this.' There was a faint snore, obviously faked. 'Bob, stop being annoying. I need your help.'

He snorted. 'Well, blow me down with a peacock feather,' he muttered. 'You walk off into the creepy woods and then you need my help. *Big* surprise.' His head popped out from under my scarf. 'What is it?'

'What made these tracks?'

He looked down. 'How the hell should I know? Probably some kind of bird.'

'Bob,' I sighed. 'How many birds do you know with three legs?' There wasn't any answer. 'Bob?'

'What? I'm waiting for the punchline.'

'That's not a joke, it's a real question. You're a magnificent being who knows everything, right?'

'I never said I knew *everything*. I just know most things, that's all.'

I reminded myself that patience was a virtue. 'So do you know what made those tracks?'

'Nope.'

I considered them for a moment. 'Wait here,' I said decisively. 'Keep an eye on Kirsty.'

'What? Where are you going?'

'I'm going to follow the tracks.'

'Uh Integrity! You can't do that!'

'Bob, sweetie, I can do whatever I want to. Besides, I won't be long.' I pinched him between my thumb and forefinger and dropped him on Kirsty's head. She didn't even twitch. Then, enjoying the freedom to run, I took off.

I followed the tracks for five minutes, curiosity fighting against the desire to keep going in the challenge. I didn't want to expend too much energy on this but maybe the tracks would lead somewhere helpful.

Whatever had made the trail was on its own; there were no other tracks to indicate a family of three-legged creatures. In the end I gave up and went back. My three-legged friend wasn't going to show itself and I couldn't count on it to lead me anywhere useful. I probably only had an hour or two left of daylight and I couldn't afford to waste it on foolish errands, tempting as they were.

When I reached Bob and Kirsty again, he was poking her cheek with a stick and she was swatting at him with her hand as if he were a fly. She hadn't opened her eyes yet but she was definitely coming around.

'Kirsty?'

'Mmph?'

I gestured to Bob to get out of the way. He stuck out his tongue but did as I requested. Kirsty opened one eye, fixing it on me. It took a moment or two for recognition to set in and, as soon as it did, her expression hardened. 'You.'

'Me,' I said cheerfully. 'Good to see you're awake again.' I peered at her. 'How do you feel?'

'Okay, I guess,' she said grudgingly, pushing herself away from the tree. 'Where the hell are we?'

I grinned.

She opened her other eye and looked around. As she glanced from tree to tree, I saw awareness set in as she realised how isolated we were. 'We're in the forest.'

'That's why there are trees. What did the little tree say to the big tree?' Kirsty blinked at me as if I were mad. 'Leaf me alone!'

She got to her feet and began to back away.

'It was a joke,' I tried to explain. 'Not an order.'

'What are you going to do to me?'

I frowned. 'Er ... nothing.'

'If you hurt me, people will find out about it!'

I put my hands on my hips. 'Kirsty,' I sighed. 'You've been unconscious for hours. If I wanted to hurt you, don't you think I'd have already done so?' I ignored the fact that I had hurt her by stealing her Gift but Bob raised his eyebrows. He wasn't going to forget it.

Kirsty rubbed her forehead and continued to back away. 'Something's wrong,' she whispered. 'I don't feel right. What have you done to me?'

My insides tightened. 'Besides carry you here so you didn't die of hypothermia? Nothing,' I said, crossing my fingers. 'You're the one who tried to attack me, remember?' Then, because my first attempt at a joke had fallen so flat and I needed to get her to relax so we could get going again, I said, 'What did the lipstick say to the mascara when it tried to pick a fight?' I paused. 'Let's make-up!'

Unfortunately my words seemed to have the opposite effect and Kirsty completely freaked. She spun round, narrowing avoiding smacking into Bob. Luckily she was so panicked that she didn't see him. Then she started running, streaking through the trees with admirable speed considering she'd only just woken up.

'She's smarter than I gave her credit for,' Bob said as we watched her. 'Your jokes make me want to run away screaming too.'

'She's not screaming,' I pointed out.

There was a sudden high-pitched shriek. 'She is now,' Bob said.

'Shite.' I took off after her. The forests of Scotland, even in Sidhe country, rarely contained dangerous creatures but I'd already come across one set of strange tracks. It was possible there was something else out there. I pelted forward, ready to rescue Kirsty once again.

However, it wasn't a dangerous sharp-toothed, three-legged monster that had Kirsty in its clutches: it was Byron and Tipsania.

'She's trying to kill me!' Kirsty howled. 'Help me!' She clutched at Byron, wrapping her arms round him in a way that made even Tipsania raise her eyebrows.

I came to a stop as Byron looked over Kirsty's head. He didn't seem surprised to see me. 'I might have known you'd catch up,' he grinned.

My stomach did an odd twist as Tipsania rolled her eyes. 'Honestly. Integrity is obviously trying to hurt her competition and take us out one by one. *Look* at the Kincaid girl,' she snapped.

'Help me!' Kirsty moaned.

Exasperation overtook me. 'Oh for goodness' sake, I'm not trying to hurt you! I *helped* you. Use your damned Gift to find out.'

Kirsty twisted round, her back firmly against Byron's chest. She took a deep breath as she tried to compose herself. She really was terrified.

'It's alright, Kirsty,' Byron murmured, with a questioning glance at me.

'Are you going to hurt me?' she demanded.

I tilted up my chin. 'No.'

Kirsty's legs seemed to give way; if Byron hadn't been holding her, she'd have sunk down to the ground. 'It's gone,' she whispered.

Byron frowned. 'What's gone?'

A trickle of dread ran down my spine.

'The girl is hysterical. Leave her be,' Tipsania interrupted.

'My Gift,' Kirsty whispered. 'It's completely vanished. I can't feel it any more.' She raised her eyes to mine. 'What did you do to me?'

'She couldn't have done anything,' Byron said. 'Your Gift won't have gone anywhere.' Something dark crossed his face. 'It'll just be the stress or something.'

Or something indeed. Had I really taken it all from her? I bit down hard on the inside of my cheek.

'It's gone,' Kirsty repeated. 'It's really gone.' And then she smiled.

I did a double-take. She was happy?

'I can't believe it,' she said, shaking her head in awed disbelief.

Byron's expression turned grimmer. 'What happened?' he asked me. 'Why are you two together?'

I drew in a breath. 'She was waiting in the trees for me. She tried to attack me then she, er, collapsed.' It was sort of what had happened, I'd just omitted a few significant details.

'I wanted answers,' Kirsty mumbled. She was still beaming from ear to ear.

'Are you sure your Gift has disappeared?' I asked cautiously.

She nodded. 'I think so.' She pulled away from Byron and twirled round in the snow. 'This is fantastic!'

'You don't seem upset.'

Kirsty continued to dance. 'Do you have any idea how tiring it is to know when people are lying?' she said in between spins. 'It's a shitty Gift.'

Tipsania folded her arms. 'Whatever do you mean?'

'When my mother told me she didn't have a favourite child, I knew she was lying. When my fiancé told me he loved me, I knew he was lying. Ignorance is bliss.' Kirsty looked at Byron. 'Do you remember the Christmas ball? When you told me I looked pretty?' Her mouth flattened. 'I knew you were lying.'

Byron winced. 'I'm sorry.'

'It's not your fault. You were just trying to be nice. And I *was* wearing a rather garish form of pink.' I frowned. Garish pink was the best kind.

Kirsty didn't pay any attention to me as she gazed meaningfully at Byron. 'That's the trouble with my Gift. I can tell when someone's lying but I don't know the reason behind the lie. And sometimes people don't tell the truth because the truth hurts. People lie for all sorts of reasons. It's not necessarily a bad thing.'

I pondered over Kirsty's words. I could see what she meant. If she was going to be so thrilled at losing her Gift, I wasn't going to feel any guilt about using it.

Kirsty turned to Tipsania. 'Lie to me,' she begged. 'Say anything you like as long as it's untrue.' Tipsania looked at her like she was insane.

'Go ahead, Tipsy,' Byron murmured.

She sighed dramatically. 'I have blue skin.'

Something deep within my veins buzzed. Lie. Duh. As I tried to absorb what I'd experienced, Kirsty gave a peal of laughter. 'Brilliant! I felt nothing!' She reached over and hugged Tipsania who stiffened, her arms remaining rigid by her sides. Kirsty tossed her hair. 'I'm out of here, losers!' She turned on her heel and marched away, a bounce to her step.

'Er ... Kirsty?' I called. 'Where are you going?'

'There were only two reasons I had to compete,' she replied over her shoulder. 'One was to try and win so I could ask the Chieftains to put money into research for ways to stop our Gifts. But I was too far behind so it wasn't going to happen. And it doesn't matter because I don't need to win any more to stop my Gift.'

Byron looked puzzled. 'What was the second reason?'

'To attack me for killing William Kincaid,' I muttered.

'But you didn't kill him. His death was an accident,' he said

I threw up my arms. 'I know!' Kirsty's shape disappeared among the trees. 'I should go after her. She's just spent half the day in a coma. She has no idea where she is or where she's going.'

'She'll be fine,' Tipsania said dismissively. 'There's a clue point about a half a mile away. All she has to do is wait there and someone will pick her up.'

I gave a sidelong glance. 'Really? Or will the Carnegies just leave her to freeze to death?'

'They wouldn't do that.'

I wouldn't bet on it. I reckoned that they were bloodthirsty enough to do just that – and not only to me. Kirsty wasn't important enough in Sidhe hierarchy to merit a rescue. Judging by the expression on Byron's face, he thought the same. I shook my head. 'I suppose you guys are out in front?'

'Of course.'

That was something; by taking a risk, I'd found the leaders. In fact, because I was in the last group to depart I was in now in first place. I could take time out to make sure Kirsty was alright.

'Great. Good to see you both. It's, um, nice that you're working together.'

Tipsania's eyes narrowed. 'What does that mean?'

'Exactly what I said.' I grinned. 'Toodle pip.'

I started to jog after Kirsty, following her tracks. There was the crunch of footsteps behind me, then Byron was by my shoulder. 'What are you doing?'

He shrugged. 'Coming with you. Kirsty's more likely to listen to me than to you.'

That was true. 'But I'm in the lead,' I pointed out, while striding forward once more. 'Sort of anyway. You need the extra time to get ahead of me. Don't you want to win?'

'There'll be time enough to beat you.'

No chance. Rather than rise to the bait, I reminded him we weren't alone. 'Can you beat Tipsania?'

'I can catch up to Tipsy later. I am working with her, after all.' He sent me a sly glance.

'Why?' I asked.

'Why am I working with her? Let's just say our desires currently converge.'

What did that mean? I decided I wasn't going to give him the satisfaction of asking.

'You know,' he commented, 'your cheeks are almost as pink as the colour of your tartan. It's rather adorable.' Adorable? What was I? A puppy? He continued in the same tone of voice. 'Did you have anything to do with Kirsty losing her Gift?'

The easiest way to reply to a question you don't want to answer is to ask another question. 'How could I have done that?' I asked flatly. 'I don't even have a Gift of my own.'

He scanned my face. 'I'm starting to think that's not true. The Bull seems to think you have one.'

My mouth pursed. The Bull was meant to be keeping quiet about that. He'd probably found some irritating way to work around the command I'd placed on him. He and I would have words later. 'I wouldn't tell the Bull what toothpaste I use,' I replied, 'let alone my supposedly secret Gift.'

'You can trust me, Integrity.'

There was another buzz in my veins and instinctively I knew he was telling the truth. Thank you, Kirsty. 'Okay then. You're right, I do have a Gift.'

Byron smirked. 'I knew it.'

I leaned in towards him and licked my lips. 'I'm very, very gifted,' I breathed.

Something flared in his eyes. 'Go on.'

'I have lots of presence.'

He stared at me. 'Very funny.'

Lie. I pulled back and shrugged. 'I thought so,' I said aloud. Perhaps it was time to give Byron a test while Kirsty's Truth Seeking still swirled in my veins. I switched tactics to throw him off balance. 'Why is your father trying to kill me?'

'What?' he blinked, obviously taken aback. 'He's not. He likes you. Why on earth would you think that?'

Truth again. I was surprised by how happy that knowledge made me and I beamed at him. 'For that reaction,' I said airily, 'I'm not even going to tell you the punchline.'

He frowned. 'That was another joke? Do you ever take anything seriously?'

Only people trying to kill me. I pointed at Kirsty's tracks. 'I take Sidhe girls running off into the woods in the middle of winter seriously. Come on. We need to find her.'

Byron was watching me. Despite my new Truth Seeking powers, I had no idea what he was thinking. 'Fine,' he replied eventually. Then he grinned. 'This is a competition. Why not make it more interesting? First one to find her has to pay a forfeit.'

Eh?

'What's the matter?' he prodded. 'Are you afraid I'll beat you?'

I snorted. 'As if.' I tilted my head. 'We're on. On a count of three.'

'Three,' he purred.

'Two,' I added. Then, before he could say another word, I took off. I heard him curse behind me. I laughed and ran for all I was worth.

'Uh Integrity,' Bob said in my ear, making me jerk and stumble. Unfortunately that was all Byron needed to overtake me. 'Were you flirting with that man?'

'Piss off, Bob,' I hissed, picking myself and sprinting after Byron.

'You need to have hot steamy sex with him and get him out of your system,' the genie continued blithely. 'He is the son of your mortal enemy after all.'

I ignored him in the hope that he'd get the message and shut up. Byron was pulling away from me so I dug down inside myself to find an extra spurt of energy. He might have athletic prowess – which was evident in every curve of every muscle - but so did I. And I was used to this sort of terrain.

Bob sighed heavily in my ear. 'This will end in tears.'

Yeah, yeah. I curved round a large pine and kept my attention on Byron's back. There was less than a metre separating us. Unfortunately, I also caught glimpses of Kirsty up ahead too; we'd be on her in in a matter of seconds. Come on, Tegs, I muttered. You can do this.

It was hard not to keep the exultant smile off my face when I drew level with Byron. He was breathing heavily, the thin air and thick snow combining to make exertion difficult for him. I was coping better - plus I had a clear path to Kirsty while he had several trees to wend round.

'I guess you're going to lose again,' I said.

He grimaced. 'Watch your shoelace. You're going to trip.'

I looked down at my feet just in time to see my lace unravelling. It caught under my foot and I went flying, receiving a mouthful of snow as I crashed to the ground. Byron laughed just as Kirsty turned to see what the commotion was about. I lifted my head in time to see him reach her. He threw me a wink. Crapadoodle.

'I can look after myself,' she said, as I dusted myself off and joined them.

'We're in the middle of nowhere,' he pointed out. 'Just let us take you to the last checkpoint. There's a road there which will lead you to the nearest town. Let us put you on it and then we'll know you won't get lost and freeze to death.'

'Why?' she asked suspiciously. 'You'll lose time. This is still a race.'

'It's the honourable thing to do,' I said, wondering why I was bothering.

Kirsty gazed at me then shrugged. 'It's your competition to lose,' she said finally. 'And this is a free country. Do what you want.' She began walking once more. Byron and I exchanged glances.

'I won,' he said with an easy grin.

'You cheated.'

A lock of bronze hair fell across his forehead. 'How?'

'You made my shoelace come undone with your damned Gift.'

'And?'

I sighed. 'Whatever. You can get your prize later. Let's not lose Kirsty again.'

We caught her up quickly enough and trudged along beside her. For a while all that could be heard were our combined breaths. I could tell from the way that Byron kept glancing at Kirsty that he had something to say. She knew it too.

'Will you stop doing that?' she said eventually. 'If you've got something to say, say it.'

'When you lost your Gift,' he said, 'how did you feel?'

I could feel my spine stiffening.

'I passed out. How do you think I felt?'

'Did it hurt?'

'No, not exactly. But I could feel it leaving me, like it was ripped away. At the time I didn't know what it was and I blacked out before

I could think about it.' She considered her next words while I tried not to look guilty. I had a horrible feeling I knew where Byron was going with this and I really wished he wouldn't but I had to listen. I needed to know exactly what damage I'd done. 'Have you ever had chewing gum stuck to your clothes? Or your skin?'

'I guess,' he said doubtfully.

Kirsty shrugged. 'Well, it was a bit like having chewing gum peeled away. Uncomfortable but not exactly painful.'

Byron pressed on. 'And you have no idea what triggered it?'

'Not a clue.' She shot me a look. 'You were there. Did you feel anything?'

I couldn't meet her eyes. 'No,' I murmured, hating myself for the lie.

'Did you see anything?' Byron asked me.

I shook my head. 'Nope.'

Kirsty eyed him, before asking the obvious question. 'Why?'

He sighed. 'I've felt it too.'

Her eyes went round. 'You've lost your Gift?'

'I've got two,' he said. 'And no, they're both still there but one of them is sort of ... less than it was.'

'When? When did it happen?'

'I don't know,' he admitted. 'I didn't feel anything was wrong until the Artistry challenge. As soon as I tried to use it, I knew it was less than what it was.'

I swallowed. So the pause before he'd started playing wasn't deliberate. I felt like a complete shit. I hadn't meant to take his Gift, I hadn't meant to take Kirsty's either, but there was no denying that I had.

Kirsty absorbed this information, a worried expression on her face. 'Have others had this happen too?'

Byron shook his head. 'I don't know. I didn't tell anyone about it because I wasn't sure if I'd imagined it.' He laughed shortly. 'And I didn't want anyone to think less of me.'

'But if it's happened to the two of us maybe it's happened to others.'

He gave a grim nod. 'Exactly. Perhaps they're not aware of it yet or they think they're the only ones and are too ashamed to talk about it.'

'Do you think it's some kind of disease?' Kirsty asked in a small voice.

'Frankly, I have no idea – but it could have serious implications. Imagine if every Sidhe lost their Gift. Where would we be then?'

I licked my lips. 'Would it be so bad? Kirsty seems happy enough.'

'I hated my Gift,' she said. 'Most of the others love theirs.'

A muscle jerked in Byron's jaw. 'I'll have to tell my father about this,' he finally said. 'We can't just ignore it.' He glanced at me. 'I don't suppose you have any theories?'

'I know very little about how Gifts work,' I mumbled. Until I found a way to control what I was doing, I'd have to be very, very careful. 'Look!' I said suddenly, spotting a break in the trees up ahead and relieved to be able to change the subject. 'There's the road!'

We emerged onto its flat expanse. After being surrounded by trees and nature for so long, it was strange to have this reminder of civilisation. I felt like I'd been out here for days, not hours.

Kirsty looked up and down the road. 'My sense of direction is all messed up. Which way was that last clue again?'

Byron pointed to the left. 'Back that way. And with those Baugans waiting with the traps, you don't want to go that way.'

I raised my eyebrows. No wonder I'd managed to catch up. I'd obviously managed to skip one of the more dangerous parts of this challenge. My shortcut was proving more advantageous than I'd realised.

Byron pulled out a perfectly folded map from his pocket and smoothed it out. It was almost identical to Kirsty's apart from one extra mark: the finishing line. I beamed in delight.

'There's only one more place to go and that'll be where the Clan flags are,' he said, jabbing his thumb at a spot that seemed to be back in the centre of the forest. 'I reckon if you continue on down the road to your right, you'll come to Crianlarich. It's a hop, skip and a jump to the Cruaich border from there.'

Kirsty grinned. 'Perfect. Thank you for your help.' She turned to me. 'And,' she added grudgingly, 'thanks for yours too.'

I bowed. 'No problem.'

'It took you ages to show up, you know,' she said. 'I thought I'd missed you.'

I wrinkled my nose. 'Let's just say that I didn't have the easiest start to my Hunt.'

'It didn't take you long to catch up though, did it?' Byron remarked. 'Did you skip all the clues?'

'Er...'

Kirsty's brow furrowed and she delved into her pocket. When her hand came out empty, an odd light came into her eyes. 'You took my map.' I didn't bother denying it. She flicked back her hair. 'Well, thank you anyway. I'm sorry I attacked you.'

I'd stolen her Gift and she was apologising to me; I couldn't have felt more awkward. 'No problem. Look after yourself and don't leave the road.'

'No worries,' she grinned. 'Have fun, you two.' There was a flicker of mischief in her eyes.

'What was that last comment about?' I asked Byron as she walked away.

He leaned towards me and dropped his voice. 'I think she senses the sexual tension between us.'

I gave him a shove. 'As if.'

'You owe me, Integrity. I won the bet.' A smile tugged at his mouth. 'I'd hate to think you're a sore loser.'

'Not in the slightest.' Besides, anything that kept the conversation away from missing Gifts could only be a good thing. 'I suppose you want me to hang around here so you can beat me to the finish line?'

He snorted. 'Hardly. I can beat you without you doing that.'

'So,' I said, crossing my arms, 'what do you want then?'

His smile grew. 'A kiss.'

It took a moment for the word to sink in. When it did, I stepped back. 'You want what?'

'You heard me.'

I flung an arm out towards the trees. 'Tipsania is out there! Your fiancée!'

'She's not my fiancée.' He was telling the truth.

'Not yet.'

'I've told you many times that my relationship with Tipsy is complicated.'

I thought of Candy. 'I'll bet it is but I'm not the kind of woman who interferes in relationships. Even complicated ones. You need to ask for something else.'

'No.' He watched me carefully. 'I won the bet and that is what I want.'

'This isn't going to make things better between us, Byron,' I said.

'It might.' He took a step closer. 'Even Kirsty can sense the tension between us so maybe it'll act like a valve and release some of that ... pressure.' He shrugged nonchalantly. 'And I can't remember much from Aberdeen. Did we kiss then? Because you're probably really bad at it and then I can walk away and concentrate on the Games instead of on you.'

My mouth dropped open. 'Wanker! I'm a great kisser.' The kiss we'd shared in Aberdeen was seared into my memory. Had he really forgotten it? His phrasing hadn't been direct enough for me to use Kirsty's Gift to ascertain the truth – or lie.

His eyes danced with both promise and challenge. 'Prove it then.'

I muttered a frustrated curse. 'This is ridiculous.'

Byron didn't say anything. I sighed. 'Fine,' I said, snapping. 'One kiss.' I leaned over but he pulled away.

'No peck on the cheek,' he warned. 'I'm asking for a real, passionate, proper kiss.'

'You want a snog,' I said flatly, 'like a horny teenager.'

He ran his tongue across his top lip. 'I suppose I do.' He bent his head and whispered, 'And I am horny.' Another truth. Shite.

'I hate that word,' I said, dissembling.

'Horny?' He smiled. 'Would you prefer randy?'

I made a face.

'Lustful?' he inquired.

'More like prurient.'

He shook his head. 'No. Try infatuated.'

For a moment I forgot to breathe. 'Then maybe I will kiss you really badly to rid you of that,' I said.

His eyes held mine. 'Go on then.'

I could think of many reasons why I should just turn on my heel and run away but a bet was a bet. I wasn't Taylor's ward for nothing. I stepped up to Byron and stood on my tiptoes. I could smell his raw masculinity – an indefinable scent which suggested power and sex and a whole lot of other things that I didn't want to think about. Emerald eyes glittered at me.

'What are you waiting for?' he breathed.

I had no idea. Perhaps I was simply savouring the moment. A snappy comeback was on my lips but I ignored it and pressed my mouth against his.

Byron didn't react immediately and I grinned. He was creating his own mini-challenge. Let's see how long he could resist. I coiled my body against his, running my fingers lightly around his waist. When that didn't work, I ran them in the opposite direction. I was rewarded with a sharp intake of breath.

My tongue flicked against his and I deepened the kiss. Byron muttered something and yielded, grabbing my waist and hoisting me up, forcing my hands to leave their teasing dance and reach round his neck. He pushed forward, so my back was pressed against a tree. The trunk was rough but I barely noticed.

Cupping my face and moving in for the kill, Byron's teeth nipped at my bottom lip, sending an explosive burst of pleasure rippling through me. Every semblance of common sense fled and I gave myself up to the heady sensation of his taste, his body and his ardour, which more than matched my own.

It was only a distant buzzing which managed to break through my consciousness. 'Byron?' I murmured, as my insides squirmed. 'Stop.'

His fingers brushed my skin, searing in a way I'd not thought possible. 'Mm?'

'Drone.' I couldn't even form proper sentences. The buzzing got louder and I pushed him away. 'There's a drone coming.'

His breath was ragged as mine. We stared at each other as the buzzing got louder and the drone appeared, hovering above us.

'They should have banned those things. It's not like they've been used before at the Games.'

'It's a brave new world.'

He eyed me. 'Yes,' he said, 'I suppose it is.'

'Byron!' a voice called.

We turned. The four other Moncrieffe competitors – Jamie included – appeared round the corner. The spell was well and truly broken.

'Your Clan like working together,' I said in an undertone.

'Tactics,' he muttered, raising a hand in greeting.

'Where's Tipsy?' Jamie asked.

'Ahead.'

I ignored the suspicious glances they sent me. Jamie frowned. 'How did you get here, Integrity?'

I shrugged and grinned. 'Tactics.' I wiggled my fingers at them. 'See ya!' Then I took off, pelting back into the woods. There was still a challenge to win.

# Chapter Sixteen

There were shouts from behind me but it didn't take long for me to pull away from the group of irritated Moncrieffes. Byron wasn't close enough to pull any tricks like untying my shoelaces with his telekinesis Gift – and somehow I didn't think he'd try that again. In this world, where the word honour was bandied about as if it was as common as oxygen, I thought he probably had some. Apart from when it came to Tipsania.

'Uh Integrity,' Bob said, emerging from his hiding place once more, 'that was some kiss. I'm still blushing.'

'Does voyeurism come as part and parcel of being a genie?' I asked, avoiding a low-lying branch.

He ignored my question. He was probably upset that his prediction about everything ending in tears hadn't come to pass – not yet, anyway. 'You knew I was there,' he sang out. 'You were trying to titillate me, weren't you?'

'Sure, Bob,' I muttered sarcastically. 'That entire episode was purely for your benefit.'

'I knew it!' he crowed. 'You can't fool me!'

Whatever. I kept running. Judging by Byron's last clue, there wasn't far to go. If I concentrated and avoided going off track, I'd still catch Tipsania in no time. It helped that I had the tracks to guide me. Adrenaline fired through me; I couldn't wait to see the look on Aifric's and those damned Carnegies' faces when I got back into first position despite all their efforts to stop me. Or kill me.

Now that I was on my own, I reached the point where we'd left Tipsania very quickly. Her small footprints diverged off to the east and I called up another mental image of Byron's map. Good old Tipsy still seemed to be heading in the right direction. All I had to do was catch her up.

I continued with my fast pace, ripping through the undergrowth in a way that would have impressed even Travis. The trees were getting denser but I was spry enough to dodge through them without slowing down. No problem – or it wouldn't have been if the sky hadn't already started to darken. By the time I reached Tipsy, I could barely see a thing.

No wonder I'd caught up with her so quickly; she was on the edge of a frozen loch and was eyeing it with trepidation. I wasn't in a hurry to test the thickness of that ice either. Climbing up an icy expanse was one thing; falling through ice into frigid water was something else entirely.

As I approached, she turned and tossed her head disdainfully when she recognised me. 'Hi Tipsania!' I called out cheerily.

She looked away. 'Where's Byron?' she asked. 'Or have you stabbed him in the back so you can get in front?'

The guilty memory of our kiss surfaced briefly before I pushed it down again. 'Oh, I'm sure he's on his way, along with the rest of his Moncrieffe crew.'

Something flashed in her eyes. 'The rest of his Clan have caught up?'

I nodded. 'Yep. They seem to like working as a team.' And then, because I couldn't help myself, 'Unlike you.'

Tipsania sneered at me. 'What would you know about it?'

'Nothing apparently.'

'You think you're pretty amazing, don't you? Swanning around like you're better than the rest of us. You've got no idea what it's like to be part of a Clan and to have responsibilities.'

'No,' I said softly, 'I don't. Maybe that's because you wouldn't let me.'

'Just because my father took you in as a charity case, doesn't mean you were ever a Scrymgeour,' she spat. She threw me a glare that Medusa herself would have been proud of. 'Screw you, Integrity.' With that, she edged away from me onto the ice.

I watched her. She'd barely taken three steps when there was an ominous creaking sound. In one lithe movement she sprang back. In a reflex action, I grabbed her arm to steady her. She snatched away and glowered. 'Don't touch me!'

'Are you afraid you'll catch something?' I inquired. 'It'll be like things between us have come full circle then.' I paused. 'Scurvy.'

She gave me a blank look. 'Eh?'

I grinned. 'Never mind.'

'I'm going around,' Tipsania announced. She started walking off. 'Don't you dare follow me!'

'I don't have to follow you,' I called after her. 'I was in the last group to set off – that means I'm already three hours ahead of you.'

She didn't answer; she didn't even look back. I shrugged. If Tipsania was going left round the frozen loch, then I'd go right. I didn't want to be anywhere near her.

Before long Tipsania had disappeared. I was tempted to run round the loch but it was fairly large and there was an odd prickling sensation running down my spine that suggested this challenge couldn't be that easy. Conserving energy seemed sensible. It had been a clear day, so it should have been a clear night but I couldn't see the stars or moon. That didn't make any sense. Even the air around me tasted artificial. No doubt the Carnegies had more up their sleeve than simply making the competitors run around the countryside for a bit.

When there was a sudden whooshing noise and a row of flags at the far end of the loch was illuminated by several dozen flickering fires, I knew I was right. The finishing line was right behind them.

I slowed down and eyed the flags warily. This was a common trick used by museums and art galleries around the world: beam lights onto your most valuable object and draw moths to it like a flame. It worked for the general public during visiting hours and, in theory, worked for sticky fingers like mine. But I wasn't an inexperienced thief and I knew that whatever was most brightly lit was usually an elaborate fake or a ploy to keep would-be thieves away from more profitable items. The Carnegie organisers weren't stupid, they just lacked originality.

As I considered what to do next, pounding feet drew up alongside me and quickly passed. It was Jamie, with another Moncrieffe Sidhe behind him. That meant Byron and the other two Moncrieffes had elected to go the same way as Tipsania. No one would be reckless enough to try the ice.

That thought brought me to a halt. As the Moncrieffes pulled further away, I gazed at the frozen loch and stepped to its edge. The surface was glassy and smooth.

'Mirror, mirror on the wall...' I murmured, then I turned and walked back the way I'd come.

The other competitors were closer than I'd realised and more and more appeared from the dark shadows of the woods. As each Sidhe passed me, I received an array of glares and frowns, most of them suspicious and calculating. They scanned me through the gloom, checking to see whether I had hidden my flag and was strolling past them because I wanted to make a show of being in the lead. I gave them all a happy, innocent smile. Nothing to see here, move along.

Of course, the congregation of competitors meant that the drones arrived too. The noise they made was incredible; so much for the peace and quiet I'd been enjoying earlier. Now it was dark, they were using bright lights to illuminate the area and continue filming. It made it easier for me to see others – and for them to see me.

By the time I reached the spot where Tipsania and I had spoken, I'd counted thirty-three other competitors. It stood to reason that the same number had passed out of sight on the other side of the loch. That was good: I wanted as many as possible to zoom on ahead.

It wouldn't help my cause if my new plan was broadcast. The fact that so many of the later groups had caught up did niggle, however; they must have followed the tracks made by the first Sidhe on the course, just as I had done. It was February; nobody would be surprised that there was snow on the ground. Either the Carnegies were hoping for a thrilling photo finish for the spectators back at the Cruaich or they had something else to throw at us to separate everyone out. Considering there had been little action so far, I reckoned it would be the latter. Oh goody.

It didn't take long before the first figure – no doubt Tipsania – was silhouetted in front of the distant fires. I squinted to watch. When she reached a flag and tried unsuccessfully to pick it up, I knew I was right. More figures joined her, each one with the same result. Those flags weren't any more real than the Carnegies concept of honour. It was a clever illusion – just not clever enough.

'Integrity!'

I turned at the sound of the familiar voice. Angus MacQuarrie. Perfect. I grinned and beckoned him over.

'What are you doing?' he asked, as he jogged up. 'The flags are over there.'

'No, they're not.'

'Eh?'

'Watch.' I pointed across the frozen lake as the frustrated yells from the competitors reached our ears.

'But the map said...'

'We're in the right place but the flags are in a slightly different position.' I grinned. 'Imagine looking into a mirror.'

He was still confused. 'I don't get it.'

'The flags you can see are an illusion. It's a mirror image of them.'

Angus's expression cleared. 'Oh,' he said, finally getting it. 'You mean they're in the loch.' His troubled look returned. 'Under the ice? But...'

'I know,' I nodded. 'It's dangerous but it makes perfect sense. It is supposed to be a challenge and,' I lifted my head towards one of the drones, 'the audience will be hoping for some action.'

Angus swallowed. 'Why would the flags be under the ice here? Why not at the other end?'

'Because when you look in the mirror,' I said serenely, 'everything is reversed.'

He licked his lips. 'You didn't have to tell me about this.'

I patted him on the shoulder. 'Yes, I did. I'm going to need your help.'

He frowned and I jerked my head towards the rope he was carrying. Suddenly a smile spread across his face. 'You can't beat a length of rope.'

We shared a look of mutual understanding. 'Indeed.'

A few other competitors appeared, pausing to stare at us and look dubiously at the ice before shrugging and picking up speed to head round the loch.

'How can we break the ice?' Angus asked.

Tipsania had almost managed that. 'I don't think it's as solid as it looks. If we walk onto it, our weight will probably do the trick.'

He grimaced. 'That's what I'm afraid of.'

We waited until most of the other competitors had gone past. Angus even gestured to three of his fellow MacQuarries to go on ahead. When I shot him a questioning look, he shrugged. 'It'll look odd if all of us hang around here.'

He had a point. Most of the challengers were still near the flags, trying to puzzle out what was going on. It wouldn't take them too long to work it out. The longer we could give ourselves, the better.

Now that darkness had fallen, I felt extraordinarily shivery – and with our impending dip in the loch's frigid waters that would probably get worse. Byron's other Gift was pyrokinesis and it was tempting to enrol him in this breakaway escapade but I couldn't get hold of him without drawing the attention of dozens of others. He was probably at the other end of the loch with the cluster of Sidhe.

Angus uncoiled the rope and looped one end round the nearest tree. It wasn't long enough for both of us; we'd have to do this one by one.

He held it out to me and raised his eyebrows. 'Ladies first.'

'You're giving me the advantage if you let me go first,' I warned. 'Once I get my flag, I'm going to the finish point.'

'Second place is better than anyone expects of me,' he said. 'And I'd like to see the look on those Moncrieffe faces when you win the whole freaking Games.' He dropped his voice. 'It's not all selfless though. If your theory is wrong and there's nothing under the ice, you'll get a freezing cold dunk while I stay toasty and warm.'

I smiled. 'I'm not wrong.'

He gestured at the ice with mock gallantry. 'Go on, then.'

I tied the rope securely round my waist - I really did not want to find myself trapped beneath the surface - then took a deep breath and edged out. The ice groaned and it felt very flimsy under my feet. Although I needed it to break so I could fall into the water below, a part of me still hoped that wouldn't happen. I took another step and another. The ice complained more loudly.

I'd gone about ten feet when something caught my eye beneath the frozen surface. The water was dark but I was sure I'd seen a flag. I squeezed my eyes shut, jumped and landed back on the ice. There was a loud cracking sound and tiny fissures appeared. They weren't enough; I needed more if I was going to manage my swim. I leapt again, this time smashing down as hard as I could. A few seconds after I landed, the ice cracked loudly. I barely had time to hold my breath before I fell in.

The shock of the water was unlike anything I'd ever felt before. I had scant seconds to do what was necessary before I'd have to pull myself out. While the loch might not have the dank, viscous oiliness of the Lowlands Clyde, I knew that the water here was far more dangerous. I dived under the surface but I couldn't see a thing. Great. The Carnegies had lit fires to illuminate the fake flags but not used lights to help locate the real ones.

I fumbled for my pocket, my fingers already seizing up with cold, and managed to pull out Bob's letter opener and rub it against my sleeve. As per usual, he appeared in a brilliant flash of light. It was a risky move – it would have been visible to almost everyone on the shore – but I didn't have much choice.

Unfortunately, the flash provided by Bob's appearance was too brief and too bright to help me see. He floated in front of my face in an old-fashioned Victorian one-piece bathing suit with maroon stripes covering him from his neck to his knees. He waved.

My lungs were starting to hurt. I tried to move my hands to indicate that I needed light but he just waved back. Gritting my teeth, I lunged to shake some sense into him. He pulled away at the last minute, his swimming costume transforming into a mermaid's tail to help him move.

My head hurt and I knew I didn't have long. There was a tug on the rope; Angus was getting worried. Screw Bob, I could do this without him. I began to kick, reckoning that my flag would probably be in the most inaccessible spot. Estimating that I'd already been underwater for at least thirty seconds, I moved as fast as I could.

I trailed my hand downwards, feeling different poles that stuck upright from the bed of the loch. There were too many and this was too much of a crapshoot. I'd have to go back to the surface.

And then the Carnegies did something incredibly stupid.

Whoever was warm and safe in the Cruaich and responsible for the drones' actions was obviously concerned that I'd discovered the flags' location before anyone else. From underneath the layer of ice, I heard the buzzing as the drones converged over my head. They were not only noisy, they were also bright. With their lights beaming onto the ice, I suddenly had enough light to see. And there, less than five feet away, was the flag emblazoned with the Adair tartan.

Bob gave me a thumbs up but I ignored him, kicked out towards it and curled my hands on the sodden material. I tugged but it wouldn't come free. Shite. I tugged harder. Come on, come on. I was almost out of breath; I had to get the bloody thing now.

I tried and tried but I didn't have the strength. I pulled back and concentrated. As bad as I felt for stealing part of Byron's Gift, it was proving useful. With a bit of focus, the flag finally came free. I closed my eyes in relief and took off.

With the drones now lighting the way, I could see almost all the Clan flags and make out the hole that I'd created in the ice. Thankfully it wasn't cold enough for the water there to re-freeze. I swam like I'd never swum before, reached the gap and pushed my head upwards.

'Ice, ice, baby!' Bob yelled. He was bobbing on the surface. He had foregone the mermaid look in favour of spiky hair and large sunglasses.

'There are drones everywhere,' I hissed. 'They mustn't see you.'

He stuck out his tongue but unfortunately it landed on a chunk of ice and got stuck. He flapped his arms and I rolled my eyes. He managed to peel away his tongue before flipping back his hair like he was some kind of Bond babe emerging from tropical waters. 'That's okay, Uh Integrity. I'm ready for my close-up.'

There were shouts from the shore as the Sidhe competitors ran towards us from all directions, finally realising what had been right in front of their faces all along. Angus waved to me frantically. 'Integrity! You've been in too long!'

I waved back to him. There was one more thing I had to do. I took another deep breath and plunged down again. Fortunately, the drones stayed where they were and I knew the location of all the flags. The MacQuarrie ones were nearby. I wrapped my hand round the nearest one and it came free almost immediately. Surprise, surprise. What were the odds that the only flag that had difficulty in parting itself from the waters was the Adair one?

I pushed back to the surface as more Sidhe came onto the ice. Some were less careful than others and fell in because they'd chosen spots where it was particularly thin.

'Get back!' I shouted. 'The flags are here. Take the shortest route or you'll freeze to death.'

Most of them ignored me. I didn't have time to worry about them – I had to get out. I grimaced. 'Bob, go and tell them to stop being idiots.'

'I thought you didn't want anyone to see me.'

'Better they see you than that they end up drowning or dying of hypothermia,' I grunted, starting to swim for shore.

'If you make a wish, I could...'

'Bob, just warn them. Please?'

'Pretty please?' he asked. 'Pretty please with...'

I swam as fast as I could before I had to deal with any other silly demands.

'Where are you going, Uh Integrity?'

'I have to get out now or I'll freeze to death.'

Bob didn't say any more. I heaved a sigh of relief as Angus pulled on the rope and helped me out. Considering how much of the ice had now broken as a result of the enthusiastic competitors, his assistance was welcome.

As I fell onto the bank, I rolled onto my back, panting. Angus grabbed me and yanked me upwards, wrapping himself around my body. 'You're freezing,' he muttered. 'I'll help you warm you up before I go in for my flag.'

I'd never felt cold like this. 'No need,' I said, teeth chattering. 'I've got yours too.' I held up both flags.

'Integrity Adair,' Angus murmured. 'You are amazing.'

I looked over Angus's shoulder, beyond grateful for the heat of his body, as Bob yelled something at a bunch of stunned Sidhe. A few feet away, glowering at me, was Byron. He turned on his heel and faced the ice, using pyrokinesis to melt as much of it as possible and help those who were stranded under the surface.

'We need to get out of here, Angus,' I said. 'Everyone else has caught up.'

'Then,' he grinned, 'let's go and win this thing.'

# Chapter Seventeen

We knew where the finish line was, directly behind the row of illusory flags. Bob continued squawking, even though those who had plunged into the freezing loch were now being helped by Byron's efforts. Angus and I silently agreed to compete against each other. He took off around the left side of the water's edge and I went right.

Chaos reigned. The drones were buzzing manically as energy and adrenaline overtook everyone. Some ran past me, heading towards the side where I'd started my swim; others were splashing in the water, gasping for breath. I estimated there was probably less than a mile to the end of the race. Now that everything was lit up, I could see Angus pulling ahead of me on the opposite bank. I put my head down, blotted out everything else and ran – and that was almost my undoing.

As soon as I passed the far end of the loch itself, a shadow fell across my path. I should have been alerted by the drone following my progress closely from overhead but stupidly I assumed it was there because I was about to win. Instead I almost crashed into the hairy giant who was blocking my way, only just managing to pull myself up in time.

He leered at me with a slack-jawed grin. I saw Angus in an attack stance on the other side of the loch, facing his own giant; there were glowing balls of an eerie green colour in the palms of Angus's hands, suggesting that his Gift was of the more violent sort.

'Let me past,' I grunted to the giant in front of me, 'and I won't hurt you too badly.'

He guffawed and a line of spittle dangled from his chin. Physiologically, giants have large brains but they aren't known for their intelligence. He would be under strict orders to do whatever was necessary to bar my path and his single track mind would be focused on that and that alone. Nothing I could say would help me. I thought about the competitors behind me and hoped that none of them would hurt him. The Carnegies shouldn't have inveigled him into this. It simply wasn't fair.

The giant threw back his head and let out such a massive roar that I could swear the ground shook. Then he lunged forward with a massive swipe that caught me on the side of my head and I went flying backwards. Shite, shite and shite again.

Gasping for air, I struggled to my feet. The giant cracked his knuckles in anticipation. There was a howl of pain and I glanced over to see one of Angus's green orbs smack into the other giant's chest. He fell backwards and Angus wasted no time in swerving round him and running off. It didn't look like I was going to win this challenge after all.

My distraction served my opponent well and he took full advantage of the opportunity, punching out again and this time catching me full on the chest. Yet again I was almost unable to breathe. I wheezed and spluttered but managed to stay on my feet. Just.

I looked to my left. I could avoid my opponent by going towards the loch. I might even get lucky and the ice would hold my weight but somehow I doubted it - and there was no way that I was going to brave those waters again. To my right, the banks were steep and covered with ice and snow. I was agile but I knew my limits. If I tried to leap up there, I'd slide back down again and that would lead me to my doom.

The giant grinned vacantly. His left flank was completely open and I could have attacked him there and made my move. I was aware of distant footsteps behind me; it wouldn't be long before I was overtaken by more than just Angus. I gritted my teeth and ran forward full pelt.

At the very last minute, as the giant's huge arms swirled in my direction, I ducked and threw my body into a rolling dive. I skidded through the gap in his legs, closing my eyes to avoid the unsavoury temptation to peek under his heavy kilt. While the giant heaved in frustration and tried to turn, I was already on my feet.

'Run!' Angus yelled.

I faltered. Angus had stopped right in front of the flags. Why hadn't he already passed the finish line? What was he waiting for?

I picked up speed, skidding to a halt next to him. 'What are you doing?' I shrieked. 'You could have won by now!'

One corner of his mouth curved up in a disarming smile. 'I'm under orders from my Chieftain,' he said. 'He's been called away on business so he can't meet with you like he planned. Between you and me, he's thrilled to have the excuse to avoid the rest of the Games but he's disappointed not to be able to do this himself. I think that he'll appreciate my timing though.' His smile grew. 'Clan MacQuarrie is prepared to pledge allegiance to Clan Adair and we will prove our loyalty in any way necessary.'

I stared at him. 'There is no Clan Adair. There's only me.'

Angus's smile grew. 'The Kincaids might be the only Gifted with foresight,' he said, 'but my allegiance to you is about more than what happened with Lily. We haven't forgotten the prophecy.' I frowned. There was that prophecy palaver again. What did he mean? Before I could ask, he glanced towards the sky and noted the drone above us. He knelt down and for a bizarre moment I thought he was about to propose. 'On behalf of Clan MacQuarrie,' he intoned, 'I swear fealty.'

It was a bold, public move that made no sense. My mind spun. Was it really to do with the mysterious prophecy? I didn't believe in mumbo-jumbo like that any more than I thought I'd one day perform my own comedy routine on stage. I continued to gape at him, like a guppy on its slowest setting.

'You should get a move on,' Angus said. 'Tipsania and Byron have just reached the giants.'

I finally found my voice. 'Get up,' I muttered.

He did as I bade. 'My lady.'

I pointed at the finish line, glittering ahead of us less than twenty feet away. 'Go.'

He frowned. 'No.'

'You won this fair and square, Angus,' I said firmly. 'If these Games are supposed to be about honour then you need to show everyone that you've come first.'

'You need the win,' he argued.

'I'm already in the lead. Coming second won't change that. Besides, the staggered start might still work in my favour.' I grinned. 'I might still beat you even if I wander in after you.'

'But...'

'You swore fealty to me,' I reminded him. 'You should do as I say.'

He gazed at me then gave me an easy grin and a sloppy salute. 'As you command.' He took off and jogged to the finishing line. As soon as he passed it, there was an explosion of fireworks that lit up the night sky with multi-coloured flowers and sparkles. I waited for as long as I dared. I really did think he deserved first place.

When I finally heard footsteps pounding behind me, I ran after Angus. Byron was hot on my heels and Tipsania came right after him. Both of them were soaking wet. I couldn't help noticing how Byron's clothes clung to his body so that every muscle and bulge was clearly delineated. When I caught his look and glanced down, I realised I was in the same state.

Campbell Carnegie appeared from nowhere. 'Angus MacQuarrie wins the Adventure challenge!' He grabbed Angus's hand and held it aloft.

'You let him win,' Byron said in my ear. 'Why?'

'It was the right thing to do,' I murmured.

'You bitch! You did that deliberately so I would come fourth!' Tipsania shrieked.

I flicked her a puzzled look. 'Eh?'

'That's not even a word! You have the manners of an oik!'

Thoroughly confused, I looked at Byron. 'I managed to get past the giant on my side easily enough because Angus had already used up most of its energy. You didn't fight your giant so...'

Oh. 'So Tipsania had to do it.'

'You're goddamn right I did!' she yelled.

I glanced past her. The giant was flat on his back, although his chest was still rising and falling. Streams of competitors were racing past him to reach the finishing line and get a decent placing. I shrugged. 'Is he okay?'

'Who cares?' Tipsania flounced.

The Carnegie MC, obviously upset that the attention wasn't on him, cleared his throat. 'In second place, we have Byron Moncrieffe.'

Our heads snapped towards him. Byron frowned. 'Integrity Adair was second,' he said evenly.

'Unfortunately,' Carnegie purred with an evil smirk, 'Integrity Adair has had marks deducted for dishonourable behaviour.'

'What? What did I do?'

Carnegie's thin nose twitched. He was really enjoying this. 'You brought a genie with you. This is meant to be a solo event.'

Anger spurted up through me. I should have known.

'That's not fair,' Byron said, aware that I was about to say something that I would regret.

Carnegie inclined his head deferentially. 'The decision has been taken.'

Tipsania crossed her arms. 'I think it's fair. These Games are based on honour, after all.'

Angus looked at me helplessly as I cursed under my breath. 'The genie didn't help me win,' I said. 'And besides, at the beginning of the Hunt I was left in the wrong place. I wasn't dropped at the start line like everyone else.'

'Rubbish,' Carnegie blustered. My veins buzzed as the lie tripped out of his mouth. So, the slimy master of ceremonies was in on the plot.

'It's true,' I said calmly. Byron's interruption had given me the breathing space I required. They wanted me to get worked up; acting sensibly and appearing unperturbed was the only way I had a chance.

Cheers sounded from behind as, one by one, the other competitors crossed the line. I didn't look at them; my attention was wholly on Carnegie.

'Not only that,' I added, 'but I made what I was bringing very clear. I didn't try to hide it. You can check the footage from the waiting room. I was asked whether I wanted to bring a bottle of water or this.' I pulled out the letter opener and shrugged. 'I chose this.'

Carnegie's eyes narrowed. I might not have been open about the fact that Bob lived inside the blade but I hadn't concealed what I was taking into the challenge. That had to count for something.

'There you have it,' Byron said, sounding bored. 'Integrity comes second.'

'Byron!' Tipsania complained. He didn't look at her.

Carnegie sniffed. 'I shall take this information to the judges to consider. Final places will be announced tomorrow.' He pulled back his shoulders and marched off.

'Were you really dropped off in the wrong place?' Byron asked.

I opened my mouth to answer but Angus walked over looking troubled. 'You should never have let me win, Integrity,' he said miserably.

'It's done now. Let's get back to the Cruaich.' My clothes were still dripping wet and I could feel a deep chill settling in my bones. 'I really need a hot bath.'

*

'It's absolutely ridiculous,' Brochan blustered the next day when the final decision was handed down. 'Ten points deducted! That means you're placed fifth on the league table when you should be first!'

'I suppose we should be grateful I've not been thrown out of the competition,' I said. No doubt Byron's intervention had something to do with that. I'd have to thank him later. 'At least they took the mitigating circumstances that Bob didn't help me win into consideration.'

'Pffft!' Lexie said. 'And after all that trouble I went to with the drones.'

I raised my eyebrows. 'You mean when they lit up the ice for me?'

She nodded. 'We knew something was up when you weren't filmed starting like everyone else. I got to know the control room guys well enough to point out that the drones shouldn't miss any of the action when you went under the loch.'

'Thank you,' I said fervently. 'Without that intervention I'm not sure I would have made it out of there.'

The pixie blushed slightly. 'You're welcome. It wasn't much of a hardship, they're a fun bunch of guys. Even if they are Sidhe.'

Speck scowled. 'Let's focus on the matter in hand. Integrity can still win the Games.' He glanced at me. 'I've been through all the permutations. It helped a lot that Angus MacQuarrie won that last challenge. He did too poorly in Artistry to win overall so we don't have to worry about him. All you have to do is beat Byron Moncrieffe and Tipsania Scrymgeour and you'll come out on top.'

A mental image of the last time I was on top of Byron floated into my mind. I coughed. 'That's great.'

'What happened out there?' Taylor asked. 'There was a lot the drones didn't capture.'

I took a breath and ran through the details, including Kirsty but omitting what happened in the forest with Byron. Taylor rubbed his chin thoughtfully. 'So you took her entire Gift? She doesn't have it any more?'

'Nope.'

Speck brightened. 'Maybe that's the way to stop the Gifts you steal from running out. Take away every last trace from their original owner.'

I didn't like the thought of that. 'She could have died,' I pointed out. 'For a while I thought she was going to.'

'But you can still tell when someone's lying?'

I nodded. 'It's like my blood hums or something and I just … know.'

Speck whistled. 'Cool. Lie detectors can be beaten but Truth Seeking as a Sidhe Gift? Just think about the applications it could have.'

'Mm,' I murmured non-committally.

'For now, I'm more interested in this prophecy business,' Taylor said.

I grimaced. 'I was hoping you'd know something about it.'

He shook his head. 'I've never heard of such a thing.'

'I'll have to talk to Angus about it,' I mused. 'I still can't believe he swore fealty like that.'

Speck deepened his voice. 'Clan Adair. The return of the Sidhe.'

'I always preferred *The Empire Strikes Back.*' We shared a grin.

'As nerdy as that might be, you'll have to watch for the Sidhe striking back,' Brochan said. 'They'll be trying even harder now to make sure you don't win.'

I sighed. Buzzkill. 'I know but we can't worry about that now.' I nibbled my bottom lip. 'I've got a promise I need to keep.'

He gazed at me quizzically but I didn't elaborate. Instead I shooed them all out of the cabin before calling on Bob. The genie emerged in his usual flash of blinding light. He had a deliberately casual expression on his face and a shiny gold medal round his neck. I ignored both.

'Well,' I said, 'I promised you a gold bikini.'

Bob frowned and leaned in. 'What colour?'

'Gold,' I replied flatly.

He cupped his hand to his ear. 'Pardon?'

'If you don't want me to...'

'No, I do! I do! I just wanted to highlight what a pretty colour gold is. It's the colour for winners, you know, Uh Integrity.' He held up his medal.

'So I hear. Can we get this over with before the others get bored and come back?' Bob grinned and pointed to the medal. I sighed. 'What?'

'Medal. Gold.'

'I see that.'

He beamed. 'You know why I'm wearing it?'

'Why don't you just tell me?'

'Because, Uh Integrity, I am a winner.' He leaned forward and enunciated carefully. 'Winner.'

I clearly wasn't going to get anywhere until I played along. 'What have you won, Bob?'

He pouted. 'Isn't it obvious? I have won the hearts and minds of the Sidhe. After all, I rescued them from certain death.'

'You told the stupid ones to stop taking the long way across the frozen loch,' I said. 'And, I might add, at my behest.'

'But,' he said dramatically, 'now everyone knows who I am. Forget Robert the Bruce. I am Bob the Brave!'

I wondered how bad things would get if I told him that no one had been interested in his name. 'Yes,' I said, 'you did very well.' I paused. 'Who gave you the medal?'

He puffed out his chest. 'I gave it to myself. It's a shame you didn't come to the medal ceremony. It was quite something.'

'I'm sorry I missed it,' I said drily.

'You bet you are!' He continued to admire the medal.

'Bob?'

'Call me Sir Bob. You're my friend, after all.'

I counted to ten in my head. 'Sir Bob. A promise is a promise and...'

'And you promised me gold bikinis and ear-muff hair.'

'Gold bikini singular. But yes.' I gazed at him meaningfully. 'I don't of course own a gold bikini...'

'That's not a problem, Uh Integrity. Let Sir Bob perform his magic for you.' He magicked up a tape measure from nowhere and held it up, squinting. 'Say the magic word,' he intoned.

Heavens above. 'Please.'

Bob tsked. 'Don't be silly. Abracadabra.' I rolled my eyes. 'Uh Integrity...' He wagged his finger.

'Fine. Abracadabra.'

Bob grinned and snapped his fingers. A half second later I was bloody freezing all over again. I gazed down at my body. A gold bikini might have suited Carrie Fisher but I had milk-white skin. It was just as well no one else could see me.

There was a knock from outside and Bob shouted out. 'Come in!'

The door opened before I could yelp a word of warning. Byron's face went stiff when he caught sight of me. I could be embarrassed or I could brazen this out. No choice, really.

'Hi honey!' I said cheerily. 'Pool party?'

He glanced past me into the cabin's plush interior, which Bob hadn't bothered to return to its spartan chill. 'No wonder you didn't want to move. The genie did all this?'

I nodded. 'Yep.'

From one of the red velvet cushions, Bob waved enthusiastically. 'Hi Byron!' he gushed. 'It's great to finally meet you! Uh Integrity wouldn't let me show myself before but now that the whole world knows my name, there's no point in staying hidden.'

Byron ran a hand through his bronzed hair. 'What *is* your name?'

Bob was suddenly crestfallen. 'You don't know? It must be because the sight of Uh Integrity in that bikini has surprised you into forgetting.'

Byron flicked a look at me. 'Nothing Integrity does surprises me these days,' he said. He kept his eyes firmly on my face. I was tempted to do a little jiggle, perhaps even a belly dance, but it probably wasn't a good time. I cleared my throat.

'It's Bob the Brave!' the genie interjected before I could speak. 'That's spelt B – O...'

Byron held up his hand. 'I got it. Thanks.' He paused, taking Bob's measure. 'You did a wonderful thing by helping everyone out of the loch and directing them away from the water.'

Bob folded his arms and smiled smugly. 'I know.'

Byron stared at him for another moment. Finally he spoke again. 'Do you think you could give us a moment or two so I can speak privately to Integrity?'

'Your wish is my command!' Bob swept a bow and vanished in a blinding flash of light before I could warn Byron to cover his eyes. He winced, blinking rapidly to clear his vision.

'I didn't make a wish,' he said.

'I know,' I reassured him. 'Bob knows too.'

'Because using a genie and making wishes is incredibly dangerous, Integrity. Tempting as it may be, you would do better to get rid of the genie before something bad happens.'

Something bad like someone trying to kill me? I gave a tight smile. 'I'm not an idiot.' I tossed back my hair. At least I'd not yet put it up into those silly coils. 'Is that why you're here? To warn me about the risks that Bob poses?' I grinned. 'Why did the genie cross the road?'

He sighed. 'Please don't.'

'Fine. If you're not here for my keen wit, what are you here for?'

He met my eyes. 'I'm sorry about what happened.' Our kiss. It hadn't taken him long to regret that little dalliance. 'It wasn't fair for those points to be deducted,' he continued, surprising me yet again. 'There are wards in place to prevent competitors from seeking outside help of a magical nature. I checked the list and genie magic is included. The Carnegies already knew you hadn't cheated.'

I blinked. 'Oh. Um, thanks.'

A tiny furrow marred his perfect brow. I dropped my gaze from his vivid eyes and focused on the little scar on his cheekbone. I needed something to distract me.

'You don't seem that bothered,' he said.

'It's the sort of behaviour I've come to expect from the Sidhe.'

'We're not all bad.'

I shrugged. 'Perhaps not. You're not all honourable either, no matter how much you protest otherwise.'

'I've spoken to my father. He's going to do whatever he can to impress on the Carnegies that they need to deal with you fairly.'

'Is he now?' I murmured.

'He's the Steward, Integrity,' Byron said. 'The Carnegies will listen to him. So will the other Clans.'

'That's what I'm afraid of,' I said under my breath.

'Pardon?'

'Nothing.' I felt like a sullen teenager. This was stupid.

'I should go,' Byron said. His eyes travelled down my body for the first time. 'You're obviously ... busy.'

'I'm only wearing this because I promised Bob. I really was dropped in the wrong place at the start. I probably wouldn't have made it to the start line without his help.'

He gave me a long, considering look. 'I'll speak to Carnegie again. He really shouldn't have let that...'

I held up my hand. 'Don't bother.' The supercilious MC would only snigger behind Byron's back at his naivety.

Hurt flashed in his eyes. 'Suit yourself.'

'I didn't mean it like that.'

'It's fine, Integrity. Good luck with the final challenge. I'm told that the points accrued mean that either I, you or Tipsania is going to win.' He stuck out his hand for me to shake. I took it and a shiver ran down my spine. He leaned closer. 'I should probably go. Seeing you in that get-up makes it difficult not to pounce. Princess Leia has always been a bit of a fantasy of mine.'

And then, before I could respond, he turned and left.

Light flashed and Bob reappeared with a whoop. 'I told you that bikini was a great idea!' he crowed.

I tutted. 'Were you listening?'

'I was. And I can tell you that he might be a handsome bastard but he's gone down in my estimation. Get rid of me! Honestly!'

I tried to smile.

'Uh Integrity,' Bob said, suddenly serious, 'you need to tell him the truth about his father.'

'And that I stole part of his Gift,' I sighed. 'Yeah, I know.' I slumped onto the edge of the nearest bed.

'What are you doing?' he screeched. 'Hair, girl! Hair! Come on! You still owe me!'

Shite.

# Chapter Eighteen

Byron wasn't the only person to come knocking. After managing to persuade Bob to allow me to change back to my regular clothing, and Lexie, Speck, Brochan and Taylor had returned from scoping out potential future targets for thievery, someone else appeared on the doorstep.

It was Speck who answered. He didn't say anything, he simply stepped back and gestured her in. The stone-faced MacBain Chieftain strolled in, her back ramrod straight as it always seemed to be. She swept her gaze around the cabin and sniffed. 'So this is what you're putting the genie to use for? Soft furnishings.'

I bit back a sarcastic response and pasted on my best smile. 'Chieftain MacBain. We are honoured by your visit.'

She sniffed again. I wondered if she had caught a cold. 'I won't stay long,' she said. 'I received the ring.'

'Good. And, for the record, I didn't steal your necklace.'

'If you say so. I'm prepared to overlook the entire incident if you tell me where the Foinse is. It's vital that we recover it.'

'I don't know where the damn Foinse is. How many times do I need to bloody well repeat myself?'

She gave me a long, cold stare. 'Very well,' she said finally. 'In the absence of the source of all magic, I will request that you pass the genie to me once your three wishes are completed.'

Of everything I'd expected her to say, that wasn't even close to the top of the list. 'Er ... what?'

She threw me a long-suffering look. 'Do you need me to say that again?'

'What on earth do you need Bob for?' Lexie broke in. 'You can't trust the wishes, you know.'

She didn't take her eyes from me. 'What I do with him is my business. Do we have a deal?'

I frowned. My skin was still itching from the heavy gold material of the bikini and I was certain I was breaking out in a rash. 'He's not a thing to be passed around from person to person. He's a being in his own right.'

'Got that right,' Brochan rumbled.

Chieftain MacBain gazed at me as if I were moon-touched. 'He's a genie,' she said flatly. 'His purpose is to serve.'

'No,' I answered. 'It's not. If he wants to go with you, he's welcome to do so. It's his decision though. He's not my slave.'

Her face didn't so much as twitch but I could feel the coldness emanating from her. 'Very well. Convey to him my ... request.'

'Okay.' I pointed to the door. 'You can go now.'

She didn't move. 'There is one other thing.' Her fingers plucked at her long gloves. 'I have a lot of power. There are things I can do for you. Your friends might be useful but they don't understand the Sidhe. I'm not a mad MacQuarrie, you know. I can help you.'

She'd certainly changed her tune but I had no idea where she was going with this. 'Go on.'

She looked away. 'Bring me my uncle's remains.' I didn't say anything. 'Matthew MacBain,' she snapped. 'If he's beyond the Veil then I'm asking you to fetch his bones and bring them to me. I'll pay you in return.'

I sensed desperation. She might come across as cold-hearted but I'd bet that he meant quite a lot to her. 'I don't need money,' I said. Taylor sucked in a breath but managed to stay quiet.

'I don't think that's true,' she said. 'Name your price.' I made a show of considering and she sighed in irritation. 'Spit it out, girl!'

I tilted my chin. 'My name is Integrity Adair. And I passed girlhood some time ago.'

Angry turmoil spread across Chieftain MacBain's face. 'I apologise,' she said stiffly. I didn't think those were words that she said often. She must want Matthew MacBain's body very badly. 'What would it take for you to bring him to me?'

'A favour,' I said. 'Of the manner and time of my choosing.'

Her jaw tightened. 'You ask a lot. I'll give you a hundred thousand pounds instead.'

Behind me, Taylor bounced from foot to foot; it was a miracle that he'd not already taken over negotiations. 'No deal. One favour. It's my final offer.'

She stared at me for a long moment. 'Very well. Bring me my uncle's bones and I will grant you a single favour.'

She was telling the truth. For all her imperious nature, perhaps Chieftain MacBain was one of the more honourable nobles. That was good to know.

We exchanged a stiff handshake and she departed.

Lexie whistled. 'Things are looking up, Tegs. Keep this up and you'll be the most popular girl – sorry, woman – on the block.'

'Maybe she'd prefer lady,' Taylor interjected, obviously miffed that I'd turned down the money.

'Nah,' Speck grinned. 'Dame.'

'Harridan.' Lexie suggested.

Speck's grin grew. 'Hag.'

'Witch,' said Taylor.

They all glanced at Brochan. He shrugged. 'Damsel.'

Lexie winked. 'Chick.'

'Shut up!' a tiny voice yelled. 'Shut up, shut up, shut up! Don't be mean to Uh Integrity!'

We all paused, taken aback. Bob flew towards me, grabbing hold of my index finger and wrapping his body round it in an odd version of a hug. 'Thank you, Uh Integrity. For what you said to that Sidhe about me. No one's ever been that nice to me before.'

I patted him awkwardly with my other hand. 'No problem.'

He withdrew, hovered in the air and pulled out a massive hand-kerchief. He blew his nose loudly and looked at me. 'Will you wear a Deanna Troy costume for me this time?'

*

Nervous about what the final challenge might involve, I went for a walk after dinner. I saw few other competitors; no doubt most of them were exhausted after the Adventure challenge. There were, however, numerous clusters of Sidhe in the Cruaich grounds and I spotted more than one wad of money changing hands. The bets were apparently on.

I hadn't gone far past the village where the other competitors were staying when the familiar lumbering figure of the Bull came in-to view. He saw me coming from the bottom of the path and tried to head in the opposite direction. For such a large guy, he was very nimble but that didn't help him. I had his true name and he had to do what I asked.

'Wait!'

He froze where he was and I caught him up. 'What do you want?' he snarled.

'Oh, there are so many things.' I gave my prettiest smile. 'I just don't know where to begin.'

The hatred in his eyes deepened. 'Why are you even here? The Steward told me that you wanted to join my Clan, that you'd ask for that as your prize if you won.' He spoke with venom but there was no denying his fear. To be fair, I couldn't blame him. If I joined the Scrymgeours, he'd be expecting me to use his true name to make him obey my every whim.

'I wouldn't worry about that,' I dismissed. 'Do you really think I'd want to go back to being near you and the Scrymgeours? I'm a glutton for punishment but that's taking things too far.' I stepped towards him and dropped my voice. 'That's between you and me though, Cul-Chain. No gossiping about my intentions to anyone else.'

Relief was etched into his face although all he did was grunt.

'Do you know what Tipsania will ask for if she wins?' I asked, more out of curiosity than anything else.

The Bull refused to meet my eyes. 'No.'

Interesting. 'Are you pushing her into a relationship with Byron Moncrieffe?' I inquired.

'None of your goddamned business.'

I tutted. 'Answer the question.' I pushed myself up onto my tip-toes and chucked him under his heavy chin. 'Cul-Chain.'

He snarled but couldn't avoid doing what I'd requested. 'The Scrymgeours are doing well financially but we're still regarded as a lesser Clan because we don't have the history or the status of some of the others.' His bitterness was apparent. 'This will be a good match – for the Moncrieffes and for us.'

'So you cooked it up with Aifric and you're both pushing Byron and Tipsania into marriage.'

'They understand their responsibilities. And you should address Aifric as the Steward.'

I waved a hand. 'Yeah, yeah.'

He glared at me. 'Is that what you wanted? Can I go now?'

'Not just yet,' I replied silkily. 'Tell me what plans are in place to ensure I don't win the third challenge.'

His face contorted. 'I...'

'Tell me.'

He let out another snarl of frustration. 'The challenge will take place out on the main field. It's been cordoned off all day while preparations are made. There won't be an audience. People are being told they can't watch so that the competitors aren't distracted.'

'No drones either?'

He shook his head. Veins were bulging alarmingly at the side of his neck. He needed to go for a medical check-up. 'Then what will happen?'

'I don't know.'

He was telling the truth. No doubt the Carnegies were keeping the details of how they'd get rid of me to themselves. It made sense. So did banning everyone from watching the challenge; no witnesses, no come back. All I had to do was change that.

'You're going to demand that people are allowed to watch,' I ordered the Bull.

'I can demand all I like. Didn't you hear me say that I'm not considered important enough to be taken seriously?'

'All the same,' I said. 'That's what you will do.'

His sausage-like fingers bunched into hard fists but he jerked out a nod. It didn't change the overpowering hatred simmering within him. I'd have to be very careful how I treated him; I didn't need the Bull manoeuvring behind my back and trying to kill me again.

'Thanks!' I spun off.

My next target would be considerably harder to manipulate. I ran through various possibilities in my head but unfortunately there was only one way I could see this going.

I found Aifric seated in the bar area. A large group of hangers-on were clustered around, fawning over him. Was that why he did all this? Because he enjoyed having his ego massaged? I could work with that.

I strolled up, wasting no time in playing games. I could have waited for him to call me over but I wasn't feeling patient. Instead, I joined the group and smiled prettily. 'Steward, you are looking wonderful this evening,' I cooed. 'That shirt fits you like a glove. I can see where Byron gets his good looks from.'

There were titters from around me but I ignored them. Aifric pinned his eyes on me. 'Why, thank you, Integrity. It's very kind of you to say that.' He half-turned as if to ignore me.

I giggled. 'I wonder if I might ask you for some help,' I said girlishly. 'I'm so new here and I understand how important it is to act with honour. I've been trying to emulate the other Sidhe but obviously I'm still getting it wrong. Otherwise I wouldn't have had those points deducted in the last challenge.' Aifric glanced at me. Excellent. I'd hooked him. Now it was time to reel him in. 'I have some information which might put me at a slight advantage in the next challenge. I don't want to lose more points so maybe I could ask for your advice. Then I'll know whether I should share that information or not.'

A muscle jerked in his cheek. He scanned my face, clearly desperate to know what information I had gleaned. He didn't want me to have any kind of advantage, whether there were plans in place to do away with me or not. 'What is it?' he asked. 'I am more than happy to guide you in the right direction.'

I simpered and forced a blush. 'Oh, you're too kind – but it would be better if we could talk in private.' I looked pointedly at the other Sidhe.

'Of course, of course!' he boomed. 'Shall we step outside?' He slid off his stool and offered me his arm. I stared at it; I really didn't want to touch him. When his smile began to waver, however, I hastily placed my hand above his wrist. 'You're such a gentleman,' I gushed. 'I'm not used to this kind of treatment.'

He patted my hand. It took everything I had not to recoil in disgust. 'You're not amongst the Clan-less any more, my dear.'

We walked out and found a quiet spot not too far away from the tent's entrance. 'Now, he said benignly, 'what have you learnt?'

I dropped my pretence. 'The Bull is going to ask that the audience be allowed to watch every thrilling moment of the Acumen challenge.' My eyes were hard and my tone was harder.

Aifric stepped back, clearly confused by my shift in tone and canny enough to be wary. 'My dear, that's simply not possible. The noise they make will be off-putting and you will require your full concentration to succeed.'

I faked a smile. 'I can work under those conditions. When the Bull puts forward his case, you will agree.'

Aifric's expression turned to stone. 'I will not.'

'I have his true name.'

He stared at me as if he couldn't believe what I was saying. 'You can't have. Why would he give you that?'

I shrugged. 'He was under duress. The means aren't important. The point is that you will know I'm speaking the truth when he asks for the audience to be present, regardless of what else you might have ordered.'

'The Carnegies are the organisers. I will not interfere with...'

'Bullshit. You've already interfered, probably on numerous occasions.' I swept a bow. 'And yet I'm still here.'

Aifric inhaled. The mask which seemed to be permanently in place finally slipped and his features took on an ugly twist. 'I knew you weren't the innocent little maid you pretended to be.'

'Oh, I think you're the one doing all the pretending.' I stepped forward and tilted up my head. Anyone watching us from a distance would think I was merely being coquettish. 'When the Bull makes his request, you will back him up.'

'No, I won't. You might have him wrapped around your little finger but you can't tell me what to do, little girl.'

'You want Byron and Tipsania to be together. Am I right?' He glowered at me. 'Well,' I said, inspecting my fingernails, 'I can use the

Bull's true name to make him order his daughter to keep away from Byron. Where will your financial machinations be then?'

'You want my son for yourself,' he spat.

Well, yes, that was true but that wasn't why I was doing this; I wasn't in the business of manipulating romance or feelings. It wouldn't hurt my cause if that's where Aifric thought my motivation came from, though. 'People in love do crazy things,' I said. 'Bring the audience back.'

'What reassurance do I have that you won't split up my son and Tipsania anyway?'

'You have my word.'

'You're a dirty Clan-less bitch. I wouldn't trust anything that came out of your mouth.'

'And now we have it,' I said softly. 'The truth will out in the end.' I dropped my voice to a whisper. 'Always.'

He raised his hands as if he were about to hit me and I waggled my finger at him. 'People are watching, Steward. Do what I say or suffer the consequences.' I sounded like a comic book villain. Maybe I should get a cape.

His gaze shifted to something behind me. The Bull was lumbering towards the tent, his shoulders drooping. I smiled. 'Time's up.' I patted Aifric on the shoulder, pivoted and followed the Bull in.

'Do it now,' I hissed to him. 'In front of everyone.'

The Bull growled under his breath but he walked to the centre of the room and cleared his throat. I glanced behind me. Aifric, looking sour, had also entered.

'I've been thinking,' the Bull rumbled, as the crowd gradually fell silent. 'It's not right that we can't watch the Acumen challenge. There's always been an audience in the past. I move that we let the people in to see the action.'

There were several murmurs of agreement and a few scattered claps but several of the higher-placed Carnegies cast anxious looks at

Aifric. The good old Steward was very, very unhappy but he wasn't about to let this lot see his distress. He pasted on a beatific smile and strode forward.

'What a good idea! I agree wholeheartedly. We should let people watch. The Games are entertainment, after all.' He slapped the Bull's back and resolutely refused to look in my direction. 'What say you, Clan Carnegie?'

There was a brief, awkward silence. The Carnegie Chieftain, a thin wiry man, pushed his way forward. 'We can do that.' He paused. 'If the Steward demands it.'

Aifric laughed heartily. 'Oh, I'm not demanding anything. The Games are yours to run. It's merely a suggestion.'

'Then that is what we shall do,' Chieftain Carnegie said. 'As always, Steward, you are very wise.'

The weak applause started again but soon changed into something louder and more enthusiastic. I didn't know or care whether it was forced or genuine; I'd got what I wanted. With people watching my every move, I'd be as safe as I could be. It would be blatant dishonour for the Carnegies – or anyone else – to harm me.

I turned on my heel and walked out again, passing closely by Aifric. He didn't say a word but I could feel his anger. I'd have enjoyed letting him believe that I'd fallen for his lies for a while longer but, let's face it, the truth was going to come out at some point.

The chill night air was pleasant and briskly reinvigorated both my body and my mind. I didn't pay much attention to where I was going; I was too busy working out what Aifric's next move might be.

I was lost in thought, my head down and my attention elsewhere, when a cold voice emerged from the darkness. 'Look who it is. The girl who's too good to fight.'

I looked up, seeking the voice's owner, and made out two shapes at the top of the hill. Tipsania and Byron. A flash of bitter jealousy zipped through me. For two people who were apparently faking their relationship, they spent a lot of time together. Did she know he'd kissed me? Or that he'd been alone with me a couple of hours ago when I was almost naked?

'Having a little moonlit dalliance, are you?' I called out, an edge to my tone. It annoyed me that I was annoyed; I could deal calmly with Aifric Moncrieffe who was trying to destroy me but, when it came to his son, my emotions overtook my rationality and sense.

'We're discussing strategy,' Tipsania returned coolly. 'If one of us beats you tomorrow, you're going to lose. That's what happens when you're too afraid to fight. If you'd beaten that giant and passed Angus MacQuarrie, you'd be in a better position.'

I marched up to her. 'I'm not afraid to fight,' I said, getting in her face. 'I'm just too good for it. I don't have to throw my fists around to win these Games. When I'm standing on that dais and getting that prize, you'll see exactly what I mean.'

'Never going to happen,' she sniffed. 'Tell her, By.'

'Tipsy...'

She threw up her arms. 'Now you're on her side? Why am I surprised?' Her shoulders slumped. 'This is important. We can't let her win. You know that.'

There was such an air of dejection about her that I felt a ripple of sympathy. 'You know, Tipsania,' I said softly, 'if you don't win the Games, you could just ask your father to give you what you want. He does love you. I'm sure he'll do whatever he can to keep you happy.'

'And what would you know about it?' she snapped. 'Besides, it's not up to him.' She gestured at Byron in frustration. He looked away and she hissed at me, 'Just because you don't care what others think of you doesn't mean the rest of us can afford to be like that.' She picked up her skirts and walked off.

I sighed, sat down on the wall and watched her go. Byron sat next to me. 'You know, she's not as bad as she pretends.'

'She was a real bitch to me when we were kids.'

'I know. But kids can be mean.'

'She's not particularly nice now,' I pointed out.

He sighed. 'She has her reasons. You two hate each other for what happened when you were kids but don't you think her father should be the one to take the blame?'

Everyone seemed to blame their parents for their woes and my father, Gale Adair, received far more censure than the others when he probably deserved it least. I exhaled. 'The sins of our fathers should not be ours to bear.'

Byron's hand touched mine lightly. 'What your father did had nothing to do with you.'

I straightened and pulled away. 'My father didn't do anything, no matter what anyone else says. I wasn't talking about him.' I was talking about you, I added silently.

He didn't answer, simply squeezed my hand and then let it drop. I was painfully aware of his proximity.

'You're going to marry her, aren't you?' I said. 'If you don't win the Games.'

For a long moment, he didn't say anything, then he spoke heavily. 'The Scrymgeours have a lot of money. The Moncrieffes don't.' He sighed again. 'What are you going to ask for?'

I pressed my lips together. 'The Adair lands,' I said. 'They were confiscated after what my father did but I'm still here. The Adairs aren't dead and buried just yet.'

'That's noble of you.'

'Is it?'

'You could ask for money.'

I laughed softly. 'I might be a thief but I know there's more to life than gold.' Byron grimaced.

'There's always another way to get what you need. Your father could resign the Stewardship,' I said. 'Concentrate on building up your Clan again.'

'He's too big hearted for that.'

I almost fell off the wall. Big hearted? Aifric Moncrieffe?

Byron sighed. 'I've suggested it to him several times, but he takes his responsibilities as Steward too seriously. He won't relinquish that position just for personal benefit.'

Because personal financial benefit didn't come close to whatever other benefits he received from being Steward. When it came to his father, Byron was blind.

I took a deep breath. 'He tried to kill me.'

'Who?'

'Your father.'

'Don't be ridiculous, Integrity.'

I sought his eyes. 'It's true,' I said simply. 'Lily MacQuarrie died from drinking poison that was intended for me.'

'Integrity, I understand you think we might have a future together but attacking my father isn't going to achieve that. Besides, you said William Kincaid tried to poison you.'

I pushed off from the wall and backed away. 'I lied. And this isn't about you and me, it's about your father. You can't trust him, Byron.'

'He is a good man. He has a lot of honour.'

Fucking honour. 'Smoke and mirrors. He's an evil bastard and you need to open your eyes to the fact.'

'Now hold on a minute...' he said, obviously upset.

'Stop shouting!' came a shaky, high-pitched voice from the darkness on the other side of the hill. 'You're scaring the snowdrops!'

We both fell silent as Morna Carnegie appeared, taking small unsteady steps towards us. 'This is a very important time for the flowers,' she admonished. 'It's touch and go and they're very sensitive.'

I stared at her but Byron gave a tight smile. 'I apologise,' he said.

She sniffed. 'I don't need you to apologise. I just need you to keep the noise down.' She looked at me. 'You're the Adair girl.'

Bloody Carnegies. 'Integrity,' I said coldly.

'Pfft! No need to get the hump. When you get to my age, every-one is either a girl or a boy.' Her pupils dilated. 'I knew your father, you know. He had respect for his environment.' She cocked her head. 'Don't believe everything you hear about him.'

I drew in a breath. 'Do you mean...'

Before I could finish my sentence, she jerked back. 'It was you,' she whispered suddenly. 'You took it. I can see it in you.'

Oh shite.

'Took what, Morna?' Byron asked.

'My Gift. You stole my Gift.'

I shook my head. 'No, no, no, I didn't.' My voice faltered. I squeezed my eyes shut and sighed. 'I didn't mean to. And I didn't take all of it.'

'You have no control!' she snapped. 'You can't just go around stealing others' magical powers!'

'Integrity,' Byron said slowly, 'what is she talking about?'

'I don't know.' I looked at him. He backed away as comprehension sank in.

'Kirsty,' he said. 'It *was* you who did that to her.'

'It wasn't deliberate! I didn't mean to, it just kind of happened.'

Even in the darkness, I could see his face grow pale. 'You took my Gift too, didn't you? Not all of it but you took some. Ripped it from me. That was why it felt so strange in the Artistry challenge. Are you really that desperate to win?'

'It wasn't like that!' I protested, feeling the situation and my control slipping away. I was desperate for Byron not to think badly of me.

He gave me a long, cold stare. 'You really are a bitch.'

'Byron...'

He shook his head and stepped away. 'Stay away from me, In-tegrity. I don't want you anywhere near me.'

'Wait, Byron.'

It was too late. He'd already whirled away and was striding back down the hill. My shoulders sank.

Morna Carnegie was still looking at me. 'The truth will out, Integrity Adair,' she said. 'It always does.'

Her words were so similar to those that I'd snapped at Aifric that I froze and stared at her. She smiled then squeaked, 'Excuse me.' She reached inside her coat and pulled out a ball of brown fur. 'I told you to stop doing that,' she said sternly. I blinked. The fur quivered in her hands and she sighed. 'Fine. But don't go far.'

Morna bent down and released the ball. It wasted no time in scampering off, leaving behind a three-legged trail. My mouth dropped open. 'Is that...?'

'A haggis,' she said dismissively. 'Bloody things keep running off.'

'Haggis? But...?'

Morna snapped her fingers in front of my face. 'Focus on what's important, girl! People your age get distracted too easily. No wonder you keep making such a mess of things.' Before I could protest, she held up her hand. 'Not everyone is against you,' she said. 'No matter what their fool Clan Chieftains are doing. Come and see me once all this is over. I can help you with your Gift.'

'Gift?' I scoffed. 'Some Gift. Is stealing your magic a fucking Gift?'

She touched my arm. 'The boy will come around.' She watched me then said, almost to herself. 'Maybe the prophecy is true.'

My eyes narrowed. 'What prophecy? I keep hearing it mentioned but I don't know what it is.'

'You don't know?' She paused. 'Then perhaps we should keep it that way. Knowledge is not always a good thing. You might kill yourself trying to fulfil it and then where would we be?'

In the ground most likely. The old woman was right though. I didn't have time for mumbo-jumbo like this.

'Come and find me,' she repeated. Then she walked away.

Left alone on top of the hillside with nothing more than the haggis's trail beside me, I felt more alone than ever. Morna could make all the overtures she wanted; whether I had my friends with me or not, Byron's censure meant that the bottom had been ripped out of my world.

# Chapter Nineteen

When day finally dawned on the morning of the last challenge, I wasn't feeling any better. No matter what Lexie, Speck, Brochan, Taylor or Bob said, I just muttered dull responses. I was supposed to win this challenge for my father and my Clan, and to take the first step towards righting all the wrongs that had been done them, but I couldn't muster the energy to care right now.

Taylor's concern was palpable. 'This challenge is as much about brain work and intelligence, Tegs. You need to snap out of this funk.'

'Yeah!' Bob agreed. He jumped onto my shoulder and started dancing. 'No funk! Let's get funky!'

I ignored him. 'We need to go,' I said. 'I don't want to be late.'

Lexie looked miserable. 'Tegs...'

'I'll be fine,' I told her. I lifted my head and looked at them. 'I will do this. I've not come this far to fail at the final hurdle.'

'That's my girl,' Taylor boomed but he still looked worried. My blues were dampening everyone else's spirits. I took several deep breaths and focused.

'Sorry,' I said. I shook my head. 'I'm letting everything get to me.'

'Tell us a joke.'

I tried to think but even my cheesiest lines had deserted me. 'I'm all out of them.'

Speck brightened. 'Things aren't all bad then.'

Everyone grinned and their warm camaraderie did its usual job. The tight knot inside me loosened and I smiled slightly. As they beamed at me like idiots, I started to relax and I couldn't stop myself from grinning back. Brochan slapped me on the back in a gesture of solidarity. Unfortunately, he didn't know his own strength and I went flying into Speck, who tried to dodge out of the way but ended up tangled in his own feet and crashed against Lexie. The pair of them went down in a mass of writhing limbs.

'Speck, darling,' came Lexie's muffled voice, 'I know you're hot for me but perhaps we should wait until we have some privacy. And until I've shaved my legs.'

The warlock extricated himself awkwardly, pulling back and glaring. She got to her feet, curtseyed and gave him a saucy wink.

Bob and I started to giggle. I clamped my hand over my mouth to try and stop myself. Speck continued to glare but his eyes flickered with amusement – and what I thought might be a tinge of longing.

I straightened up. I was going to win these damned Games and I'd worry later about what happened next. There would be time enough for apologies and recriminations once I had the prize in my hands. If could get back the Adair lands, I'd be making headway towards returning my Clan to where they deserved to be.

*

The remaining competitors congregated at a tent by the entrance to the main field, where we'd been a few days earlier for the opening ceremony. As we entered, we were patted down; we were not permitted to bring in anything for this challenge. I was searched more thoroughly than the others but I submitted without complaint; if they didn't find anything on me now, they couldn't plant anything on me later.

As I looked round, it seemed that the numbers were considerably depleted. Whether it was because of injuries sustained in the Adventure challenge or because some contestants knew that they'd never win, I estimated that we were now down around seventy in total - almost half the original number.

Just like last time, Byron and Tipsania hovered at the front. One of the Scrymgeours was patting Tipsania's brow with a small towel, like she was some kind of prize fighter. I rolled my eyes. Ridiculous.

'We've lost a lot of people,' Angus murmured by my side.

I nodded. 'But there are still too many more.'

'I wouldn't worry about it. You're the only Chieftain competing so it stands to reason that you'll beat everyone else. Besides, I caught a whisper that the number of competitors is about to dwindle even more.'

I frowned but he merely smiled and pointed to the front. Byron was studiously avoiding looking in my direction; his focus was fixed on the Carnegie official who'd just appeared from the tunnel.

'Clan competitors!' the official called.

It was difficult to hear him over the hubbub and he wasn't throwing his voice. Byron held up a hand and everyone fell silent. I bit down the temptation to start chattering loudly to Angus, not because I wanted to annoy Byron but because the naughty child inside me would do almost anything to get his attention. What was wrong with me? I wasn't a lovesick teenager; hell, I'd never been like this even when I *was* a teenager. I hated myself - but I still wished he'd look at me.

'To make the final round as fair and interesting as possible,' the Carnegie official intoned, 'we are going to weed out the chaff. Only the leading competitor from each Clan will be allowed to compete in the Acumen challenge.'

My brow furrowed. 'Did he really just call almost fifty Sidhe nobles chaff?' I murmured to Angus. 'That's brave.'

There were a lot of grumbles and hissed complaints. A lot of people were extremely annoyed and I didn't blame them. If these Games were all about the honour of competing against your peers, a lot of Sidhe had effectively been tossed into disrepute.

The Carnegie official was oblivious. 'Unless you are the sole Clan representative, you must leave the area,' he said, without a trace of emotion.

I shook my head. They just didn't get it. They harped on and on about honour and how important it was, and in the next breath they made it clear that unless you were in with a chance of winning, you might as well not participate. I was surprised that they didn't chuck out everyone apart from me, Tipsania and Byron but perhaps that would be step too far even for this lot.

The discarded competitors filed out. When Jamie passed me, he raised his eyebrows and said, 'Good luck.'

That was nice of him. Obviously, Byron hadn't shared his insights about me with the rest of his Clan. Unfortunately Jamie's friendly overtures were followed by one of the Scrymgeour competitors hissing something about wanting to see my entrails pulled out.

When the tent was empty, and there were only twenty-five of us left, the Carnegie Sidhe spoke again. 'There are only three competitors whose accrued points put them in a position to win. If the rest of you want to drop out, go ahead. This is a short challenge and it won't be long before we have our winner.' No one moved. He shrugged as if we were all idiots and continued. 'You will each take a number from this bag. The number you take corresponds to your assigned door. When the klaxon sounds, you will go through it. Your goal is to find the red button and push it.' He stared at us. 'Simple, really.'

'I doubt that,' Angus whispered. 'We know there's going to be one giant spider to contend with at least.'

And then some. I took my place in the queue, eventually pulling out a small plastic disk with the number thirteen etched onto it. Unlucky for some. We arranged ourselves in numerical order and I was none too pleased to see that Tipsania had drawn number fourteen. As we filed out onto the field, she trod on my heel. 'Oops,' she simpered. 'Sorry.'

I turned to look at her. 'Why are you doing this?' I asked her. 'Why are you being a bully?'

She snarled, 'Your very existence is an affront to all that the Sidhe stand for.' Her words dripped with vile condescension but, for the first time, I saw something behind her eyes that suggested she lacked conviction. Or maybe I was just softening towards her.

We heard the roar of the crowd long before we saw them. The grandstand was filled to capacity. There were a lot of makeshift placards proclaiming support for the competitors and I was shocked to see a few Sidhe from other Clans holding signs up for me. That was unexpected – and probably dangerous for them. Maybe people liked to show that they'd backed the winner; my odds, which had been three hundred to one before the Artistry challenge, now placed me as favourite. I wasn't sure whether to be pleased that my efforts were being acknowledged or to worry about the target that was now placed on my back.

I took my place in front of my assigned door. The field was almost covered with walls of smoky black glass – the ones that I'd seen stacked in the pallets aboard the Carnegie ship. I had visions of a crazy arena inside where we'd be forced to fight each other to the death like some bloody, warped Battle Royale. I clenched my hands. If that was the case then I was pretty much screwed.

The countdown started and Campbell Carnegie's dulcet tones came over the loudspeaker. I bounced up and down on the balls of my feet. If I had to make a run for it then I would.

Five.

Four.

Three.

Two.

One.

The klaxon screamed and a heartbeat later all the doors swung open, revealing nothing but darkness within. Without looking at anyone, I stepped in. I was going to win these Games and I wanted all those Sidhe who'd spat on my father's grave to see me do it.

I ran forward – but not into an arena. The narrow corridor lined with more of the dark glass showed that this was some kind of maze. Heart pounding with anticipation, I took the first turning to the left. The key to successfully negotiating mazes was to be consistent. Left, left and left again. When I hit the first dead end, I spun back round, almost colliding with a wide-eyed Blair Sidhe who backed away from me. I ignored him and pushed past.

After about five minutes I started to realise what an immense structure this maze was. The consistent turning and reaching dead ends then spinning back around again was more tiring than I thought it could be. Rather than continue at a pace I couldn't maintain, I slowed slightly. I'd need some energy for whatever was yet to come. I'd all but blocked out the crowd. I just concentrated on going forward, left, back, left, forward once more.

Then I came to a stop. At the far end of the latest turn, there wasn't just an empty corridor. A body lay prone on the floor and, next to it, a table with two flagons and a set of identical glasses. When I got closer and saw that the body belonged to Angus, my stomach tightened in fear. I bent down to check his pulse, nausea rising in my stomach. If he'd died for the sake of this stupid challenge... I let out a sigh of relief; he was still breathing. He was out for the count and out of the running, but he was okay. There was a glass not far from his hand. I grabbed it and sniffed but whatever was inside was odourless.

I stood up. I didn't have time to worry about him, I had to concentrate on myself.

I examined the table. Both flagons contained clear, identical-looking liquid. I sniffed each one but neither of them smelled of anything. Behind the table was another door. Apparently I had to drink from a flagon: choose the right one and the door would open; choose wrongly and I'd end up fast asleep like Angus.

Written on parchment next to the flagons was a riddle.

*My left is in dress and trousers and suit*
*No key however will unlock my loot.*
*My right is in feline, bold and proud*
*Only a fop would wear this shroud.*

I read through it several times. Shroud had obvious implications – was that choice of words a red herring? I frowned, trying to work out what it meant.

'Dress, trousers, suit,' I muttered to myself. 'Material? Cloth? Zip?' My brain felt cloudy: the harder I thought, the more elusive the answer seemed to be.

The word 'fop' stood out, not just because it was old-fashioned but it wasn't the sort of word a Sidhe would use. Could fop stand for something else? I squeezed my eyes shut and tried to think. All I associated with the word 'fop' was a dandy like the Carnegie MC. A dandy feline.

'Dandelion,' I whispered. I opened my eyes and stared at the flagon on the right. It had to contain essence of dandelion which was entirely harmless. And the flagon on the left was... I grinned. Hemlock. That was the one to avoid.

Without wasting any more time, I grabbed the right flagon and poured myself a shot, muttered, 'Bottom's up,' and downed it in one.

It tasted earthy and fragrant. I held my breath in case I'd made a mistake but the door in front of me opened and the crowd outside roared, either in approval or dismay. I couldn't help throwing my arms in the air in delight.

'Sorry, Angus,' I whispered. Then I moved round the table just as another competitor ran up behind me.

I twisted my head to watch Tipsania. She didn't even look at Angus and neither did she read the riddle – she simply poured from the same flagon that I had. She couldn't have seen what I'd done because she'd been too far behind. I gritted my teeth. No – she already knew which one to choose. I rolled my eyes and ran on. Honour. It was a waste of breath to say the word around here.

The one thing in my favour was that the maze was too complicated for anyone to memorise. All I had to do was move faster to give myself more time at any stations like the last one and I could still do this. I ran even faster, still only turning left. Although the audience weren't visible, they could obviously see what was going on. As I sprinted ahead, I could hear more and more people yelling my name. That was good; it meant I was doing well.

I hit another dead end and spun round, dirt flying up around my ankles. When I turned the next corner, I saw a long, long corridor stretching in front of me.

I stopped, warily. The corridor had to be a hundred feet long. I glanced from side to side. With my blurry reflection bouncing back at me from various angles, and with my white hair falling down my back, I looked a ghost. An avenging ghost, I amended.

It would be wise to be careful here. I yanked off a button from the top of my shirt and threw it forward. Immediately there was a whine and, from above the high walls of the maze, a sharp blade scythed downwards, slicing through the air and what would have been my soft flesh if I hadn't erred on the side of caution.

Feeling like a character in a computer game, I prepared to run again. The difference between me and Lara Croft, though, was that I didn't have an automatic save or infinite lives. Things were about to get hairy.

I watched the spot where the blade had come down, etching it into my memory, then burst forward. Three seconds before I got there, I threw myself into a roll, ducking under the great blade as it made another heavy swipe. I felt the air rush past my head. Damn, that was close. As soon as I was sure the danger had passed, I picked myself up and carried on running. I half-expected a giant boulder à la Indiana Jones to roll after me. Thankfully, that didn't happen.

At the end of the corridor I was greeted by a smooth wall. My stomach lurched. Had I braved that damned scythe only to find myself at another dead end? Of all the shitty things to do... I cursed loudly. As I did, my breath clouded up the glass, revealing something underneath.

I paused, then breathed out some more. Indistinct words began to form on the glass; I breathed several times and read them quickly before they disappeared again.

*Solitary life maketh me 24, my Clan maketh me 20. But add one more and beware for one extra maketh me unclean.*

I smirked: this was easier than the last riddle. It helped, of course, that I'd broken similar codes in the past while breaking in to one or two homes owned by Sidhe who thought they were being clever by creating puzzles to remind themselves of their security passwords. I ran through the options in my head, checking and re-checking. The twenty-fourth letter in the alphabet was X. Put two Xs together and you got the old Roman numerals for twenty. Add one more and we were in Taylor territory with his girly magazines and dodgy porn websites – XXX.

I said it aloud but nothing happened. Pursing my lips, I breathed out to mist the glass again. I drew an X shape with the tip of my index finger, right across the entire riddle; there was a creak and the wall slid open, revealing the next section. Yahtzee.

I pelted round the corner. My palms were clammy and I could feel sweat beading my forehead. I was close now; I could feel it - and when I saw what was right in front of me, I knew I'd been right. It was an open space with a small dais and smack-bang on top of it, in all its shining glory, was the red button.

Unfortunately there was another figure standing in the gap on the opposite side. Byron, panting slightly, stared at me while I stared at him. Distant sounds of skirmishes and cries could be heard from other parts of the maze. For us, however, time seemed to stop. He wasn't ignoring me now: his emerald eyes glittered, challenge reflected in them. It was a mere six or seven strides to the finish – and victory. I could do this.

'It's me or you,' he said.

I lifted an eyebrow. 'It's always me or you,' I replied softly.

Something flashed across his expression, regret perhaps or something else. His muscles tightened as he prepared. From outside the maze, the audience was chanting. I couldn't hear my name being yelled any more. They were all on Team Byron.

'You have a lot of supporters.'

He tilted his head. 'I'm one of the good guys.' His implication was clear. Enough already.

I leapt forward at precisely the same moment as Byron, my hands outstretched towards the giant button. I was almost there when there was a faint rattle and a shadow appeared across Byron's determined face. Debbie's massive jaws lunged down, inches away from his head.

Byron realised the danger at the same time that I did. He jerked his thumb to the right and, doing as he bade, I flung myself against the smoky mirrored wall. Debbie hissed, the hairs on her gigantic legs quivering.

'There's your spider,' Byron grunted. 'Pretty little thing.'

She rose up on her hind legs, then sent a jet of silk towards me. It encircled my arm, pinning me back. 'Little?' I snarled, as I extricated myself, using my free hand to rip away the sticky strands. 'Compared to what?'

Byron bunched his muscles and dived for the floor, rolling until he was behind Debbie's massive frame. 'Your ego,' he said.

I scowled in annoyance while Debbie lumbered round to face him, the sound of his voice leading her away from me. I glanced at the button. It was really close; I could probably reach out from here. Instead I turned back to Debbie.

'Go for her belly,' Byron suggested, breathing heavily as he dodged her snapping jaws.

'I don't want to hurt her.' I took a step back and considered. 'It's not her fault she's here.'

'You need to get your priorities in order.'

I thought of the red button behind me. The man had a point. 'Hey,' I said softly. I reached out and prodded Debbie's arse. Her body tightened and she swung towards me. 'Remember me? We've met before. I'm not a bad person.'

Her eyes glittered with hatred; clearly Debbie didn't have much of a memory for faces. I touched my forehead, using my index finger to wipe away a drop of sweat. It dangled on the tip. 'Sorry about this, Debbie,' I apologised, then I flicked my finger, arcing the droplet upwards. It splashed onto Debbie above her gaping mouth. She let out a strange howl and leapt upwards, disappearing out of sight.

Byron gaped. 'What the hell?'

'Giant spiders don't like salt,' I informed him. I smiled. 'Now it really is just you and me.'

I jumped up, somersaulting backwards until I was right behind the dais and the button. He stared at me expressionlessly as I made my move.

There was a loud rattle. The salt of my sweat had only been a temporary setback for Debbie. She appeared above Byron's head once more but this time the look in her many eyes was rage. Her mouth opened again and she snapped.

I didn't think. I veered off course, missing the dais completely and crashing into Byron. He staggered.

'What the fuck!' he yelled.

Debbie hissed, annoyed that she'd temporarily lost her prey again. She flicked a hesitant leg at me but I dodged it easily. She was scared that I might bombard her with more salty sweat and she was keeping her distance but Byron was still in her sights. I scrambled to my feet as she reared up and snapped towards him again. This time, as I pushed him out of the way once more, he fell backwards, his arms reaching out behind his body to brace himself for impact. Quite by accident, his elbow hit the button and a loud gong sounded, along with a burst of fireworks. Shite.

Byron blinked, stunned, while Debbie pulled back and scuttled away, the sound throwing her off balance. I curved round him and slammed down my own hand to register my position in second place. The gong boomed again but there were no fireworks this time. The winner had already been announced – and it wasn't me.

# Chapter Twenty

I received a warm, tight group hug in commiseration. Several well-dressed Sidhe tutted loudly at the blatant show of friendly contact but we ignored them.

'You came so close,' Lexie sniffed. 'It's not fair.'

'It is what it is. In the end, Byron was better.' I was being overly generous but for some reason I didn't want my friends to think badly of him.

Brochan growled, 'A Sidhe would never be better than you.'

I gave him a watery grin. 'I'm a Sidhe.'

'You know what I mean.'

'If you'd just...' Speck started.

'Speck, leave it,' Lexie said. 'Tegs doesn't need to know the per-mutations of what might have happened if she'd let Debbie go for Byron.'

'Sorry,' he mumbled.

I squeezed his arm. 'You can tell me later.'

Taylor smiled. 'It's not all bad. I just won sixty-five thousand pounds.' His eyes gleamed. 'Gambling's not such a terrible thing after all.'

I gaped at him. 'But I lost.'

His smile grew. 'I didn't bet on you.'

Lexie punched him. 'You gambled away my money on Byron Moncrieffe instead of Tegs? You prick!'

'I won though! Byron won! I was right to do it.'

'So much for honour amongst thieves,' she grumbled.

I tried not to laugh. It might have been overwrought hysteria or it might have been genuine amusement - at this stage it was difficult to tell.

The lights in the auditorium dimmed and we took our seats. As befitted the runner-up, I was directed to the front. I could see Lexie and Taylor beaming as they were moved to the front of the audience with Speck and Brochan right behind. They weren't skulking in the back row now and that was satisfying. We hadn't achieved what we'd set out to but I'd reap the rewards from these Games for some time to come. I had sacrificed my chance of winning to save Byron from Debbie's arachnid stomach. I promised myself that I wouldn't be a sore loser. I was better than that.

I smoothed down the new improved Clan Adair tartan and reminded myself to maintain a proud posture. And I *was* proud. I might be a Clan of one – with some bloody decent friends behind me – but I'd beaten the others against all the odds. I was worthy. I had no idea how I would win back my father's lands but there was always tomorrow. I would always be optimistic. What else was there?

The league board had been moved onto the stage for the prize giving. My name glittered near the top, with Byron's right above it and a single point separating the pair of us. Byron strode up and took the winner's seat next to me; it was several inches higher than mine. I couldn't help noticing that he took considerable pains not to touch me but I tried not to let it bother me.

'Congratulations,' I said.

He didn't look at me; I ignored the sharp stab in my chest and shifted away slightly. I'd respect his wishes, much as I wanted to grab him and yell that nothing that happened had been my fault. Looking at the faces in the watching crowd, many of whom were far friendlier towards me than they had been when these Games had started, it occurred to me that I'd gained many allies. But I'd lost some too. I sighed inwardly; I couldn't blame Byron for how he felt but it didn't stop the hurt from searing through me.

There was a dramatic drum roll, then the Carnegie MC marched out. He was wearing a bizarre cape that flowed out behind him, as if he were some kind of tartan-clad vampire. He took his spot at the front, nodded to the pixie who handed him a microphone, and started to speak.

'Ladies and gentlemen!' he boomed. 'I am sure you will agree that the 2016 Games have been the best ever!' There was a loud cheer from the stands. I noticed that the loudest cheers came from the Carnegie onlookers. 'We have never had such a close-run race or such a nail-biting finish.'

'Or so many clichés,' I muttered. I felt Byron glance at me and fell silent again.

'We would like to welcome our third runner-up to the dais to receive his medal. Clan MacQuarrie will be very proud of their son this evening. Never before have they placed so highly.'

There was a loud round of applause as Angus stood up and walked over. He was smiling broadly but when he walked it looked as if he was still hurting. He bowed his head as the small iron medal was placed round his neck. He made a show of kissing it and held it up to the crowd. Then he looked in my direction and winked.

'Our second runner up is Tipsania Scrymgeour!' Carnegie declared.

Tipsania got to her feet far more stiffly than Angus and walked up to Carnegie. She'd gone all out with her outfit: it was a glittering dress which I could swear was made out of diamonds. There was nothing like flaunting your wealth in front of the great and the good. Now the Games were over, I wondered if she'd notice if I helped myself to a few of those sparkly jewels. It would be minor compensation for what I'd gone through, if nothing else.

Tipsania's medal was bronze. Although she held it up in a similar manner to Angus, her lip curled slightly as she touched it and I grinned. I guessed she wasn't used to such ordinary metals.

'Our first runner up is...' the MC paused, not for dramatic effect but because he felt disgusted by my name on his lips. My smile grew. He still had to say it. 'Integrity Adair.'

The noise from the crowd was remarkably pleasing. Not every-one clapped and many had glowering expressions and folded arms. But I'd won over enough people that there weren't tumbleweeds blowing across the stage. That was enough for me.

I strolled to the front and made a sweeping bow. I wouldn't let anyone see that I was disappointed at not winning. I turned round and Carnegie gazed sourly at me as I bowed my head. He managed to drop the medal round my neck without brushing my skin. I won-dered if he'd practised that move beforehand.

The drum roll started up once more and lights danced across the stage, finally stopping in a circle round Byron. Rather than looking happy, he looked uncomfortable.

'And the winner of the 2016 Sidhe Highland Games is Byron Moncrieffe!'

Naturally the applause for Byron was the loudest and it seemed as if the very walls of the auditorium rocked. There was a large group of girls – and older women – who screamed his name and flashed considerable cleavage. I shot a sidelong look at Tipsania but she was staring ahead, not looking at the supposed love of her life. I couldn't work out why she wasn't happier. She hadn't won, and she'd still have to navigate the minefield of dealing with her relationship with a Wild Man, but Byron was about to release both of them from their awkward charade. That could only be a good thing, right?

Byron strode forward, his discomfort unable to disguise his con-fident, sexy, swagger. There were more girlish screams but he didn't pause to acknowledge the crowd. He simply walked up to the Carnegie MC and shook his hand. He wasn't even smiling.

'Byron Moncrieffe,' Carnegie purred, thrusting the microphone in his direction. 'How do you feel?'

'Fabulous.'

He didn't look as if he felt fabulous. His mouth was pressed in a grim line. My skin buzzed with Kirsty Kincaid's stolen Gift as

I recognised the lie. Going by Byron's expression, I wouldn't have been surprised if he punched Carnegie rather than shaking his hand. Maybe it was supposed to be Sidhe stoicism in the face of victory, another one of those damned honour ideals which had about as much substance as an eyelash in a hurricane.

Carnegie picked up the winner's gold medal and it caught the light, glittering and twinkling as it spun. I felt a moment of bitter regret that I quickly quashed. Byron deserved this moment, much as it galled me to admit it; when it really counted, he'd been better than me.

He bowed his head, permitting Carnegie to drop the medal over his head. Byron's hand briefly touched the metal disk then he turned to face his adoring public. The roar of cheers was extraordinary.

After what felt like minutes, the MC gestured to the audience to be silent. Even then it took some time for everyone to settle down.

'As we all know,' he intoned dramatically, 'the winner of the Games is permitted to ask for any prize. If it is within the power of the Chieftains to grant it, then grant it they shall.' He gave a small smile. 'In fact, there has only been one occasion in the Games' five-hundred-year history when the requested prize was not given – and that was for a unicorn's horn.'

There was an appreciative titter from the crowd. I glanced at Tipsania. Her shoulders were slumped; maybe her dalliance with Candy was nothing more than a way to pass the time. Perhaps she really did want Byron after all.

'Byron Moncrieffe,' Campbell continued. 'What do you request?'

Byron's emerald eyes momentarily caught mine. It was a fleeting look, so swift I wasn't even sure if it had happened. He swallowed once, his Adam's apple bobbing in his throat. I looked away, searching for my friends. The others were watching Byron but Taylor was looking at me. He gave me a bright smile and a thumbs up. I smiled back.

'I would like,' Byron said, 'for the Adair lands to be returned to their Clan daughter.' My head whipped round and my jaw dropped open. He looked at me. 'Integrity Adair.'

I stared at him, shock holding me rigid. His expression didn't flicker.

Carnegie was a different matter, however. He could have caught a swarm of dragonflies with his mouth. 'Are you sure that's what you want?'

'Yes.'

'But...'

Byron turned to him. 'It's my prize to claim,' he said evenly, 'and I have made my request.'

Campbell turned to the Chieftains. In theory I should be with them but I was glad that I wasn't. I didn't need to be beside them to know what some of them were saying; the sparks of anger in their eyes were enough.

Returning my lands was something which would cost the other Clans nothing in in terms of money. There were more than few muttered whispers indicating that they were calculating the risks but, with so many eyes watching, they couldn't deny Byron. He knew it, I knew it and everyone else knew it too.

When Aifric got to his feet, he didn't glance at his son as he addressed the crowd stiffly. 'The Chieftains grant Byron Moncrieffe this prize,' he said. He bowed once as everyone roared in approval.

I turned to Byron but he resolutely avoided my gaze. He folded his arms across his chest and nodded at Carnegie.

'In that case,' the MC boomed, 'I declare these Games over!'

The audience rose to their feet. Everyone was yelling and clapping but Byron was already striding back off the stage. I stood up hastily, pushed back my chair and ran after him.

I spun past Carnegie, who hissed something under his breath. I didn't pay any attention to him, he wasn't important.

'Byron!' I called. He kept walking, not even turning his head to acknowledge me. I caught up with him and grabbed his arm. I could feel his muscles under my fingers.

'You got what you wanted, Integrity,' he said, without looking at me. 'Be happy.'

'But...' I gasped, shaking my head in confusion, 'but why?'

A muscle worked in his jaw. 'Because it was the right thing to do.' He wrenched his arm away from me.

'Your Clan. The money you need...'

His head turned and his eyes met mine for a second. 'There's always another way.' His mouth tugged up at the corner. 'Right?'

I licked my lips. 'Right.' His words didn't alter my disbelief. 'Uh, thank you. Thank you so much.'

He looked as if he wanted to say something else.

'Byron!' Aifric was standing at the end of the corridor. I shivered involuntarily. 'This doesn't concern you, Miss Adair,' he said. 'I would like to talk to my son.'

Irritation flooded me; he had the knack of showing up at the worst possible moments. Why couldn't Byron see the truth about his father?

'Go, Integrity,' Byron muttered.

I gritted my teeth then nodded. 'Fine. I'll leave you in peace.' I flicked a look at Aifric. 'There's just one thing though, Steward.'

He glanced at me. 'Yes?'

'It's Chieftain Adair.'

And then I smiled.

# About the Author

After teaching English literature in the UK, Japan and Malaysia, Helen Harper left behind the world of education following the worldwide success of her Blood Destiny series of books. She is a professional member of the Alliance of Independent Authors and writes full time, thanking her lucky stars every day that's she lucky enough to do so!

Helen has always been a book lover, devouring science fiction and fantasy tales when she was a child growing up in Scotland.

She currently lives in Devon in the UK with far too many cats – not to mention the dragons, fairies, demons, wizards and vampires that seem to keep appearing from nowhere.

CPSIA information can be obtained
at www.ICGtesting.com
Printed in the USA
FSHW010501270320
68529FS